A LIFE SAVING BULLET

Krista Beggan

Publisher Page
an imprint of Headline Books
Terra Alta, WV

A Life Saving Bullet

by Krista Beggan

copyright ©2025 Krista Beggan

To order additional copies of this book or for book publishing information, or to contact the author:

Headline Books, Inc.
P.O. Box 52
Terra Alta, WV 26764
www.HeadlineBooks.com
mybook@headlinebooks.com

Publisher Page is an imprint of Headline Books

ISBN 13: 9781958914601

Library of Congress Control Number: 2024950189

PRINTED IN THE UNITED STATES OF AMERICA

PART 1

If I had known,
now or then,
I would have stopped
to start again.

1

"Can I help you?"

Cade leaned both elbows on the checkout counter and smirked. "Hi, Agnes. Miss me?"

Agnes rolled her eyes behind thick-rimmed glasses attached to a gold chain, the action aging her in reverse. Cade didn't know how old she was, but his best guess was in her sixties. "Not particularly."

"I'm offended."

"You'll get over it."

"Yes, but will I get over *you*? That is the question."

"No, Mr. Foster. I believe the question was, can I help you? And you still have yet to answer it."

"I think we both know there's no help for me." Cade thought he detected a hint of a smile tug at the corners of her mouth. "Is he here?"

"Yes, but he might be surprised to see you so soon."

Cade stifled a laugh at the prospect of his handler being surprised by anyone or anything. "What can I say?" He flashed Agnes another smile. "I couldn't stay away."

Agnes shook her head as she clicked the mouse to the right of her computer. Her frizzy gray hair wafted around her like smoke as she glanced right, then left, making sure they were alone in a bookstore that hadn't sold a bestseller since 1995. Then she straightened in her chair and looked up at him with fingers poised over the keyboard. One eyebrow rose in silent challenge, but Cade only winked at her and dutifully looked over her shoulder to a camera mounted on the far wall.

He had never seen the results of his retinal scan, but he could imagine what Agnes would see:

Name: Cade Foster.
Age: 28.
Service Term: Seven years.
Education: High School Diploma.
Previous Occupations: Mechanic.
Defining marks: Tattoo, left chest.
Injuries/Scars: Bullet wounds (left shoulder, right thigh), dislocated shoulder, three concussions, broken wrist.
Experience: Field officer. Integral in covert operations: Vapor, Sandpiper, Majesty, Falling Leaves, and Turtledove.
Team: Beckett Easton III, deceased.

"You know the way," Agnes said once she'd confirmed his identity.

She glanced over her shoulder in the general direction of the back offices, but Cade hesitated, all his bravado fading as he looked past the aisles to the back of the store. Yes, he knew the way forward.

He could only hope his handler agreed.

Agnes cleared her throat, drawing his attention back to her. "Is there something else you need, Mr. Foster?"

"No."

There was only one person who could give him what he needed now, and it wasn't Agnes. She frowned but said nothing more as she turned back to her computer, leaving him to his own devices.

Just the way he liked it.

He found Sebastian Albright leaning against the frame of his open office door. Even though it was August in D.C., Albright wore his usual khaki pants and lightweight sweater vest. With his rolled-up sleeves and crooked tie, he looked more like his bookstore manager persona than the controlled facilitator Cade knew him to be.

"I wasn't expecting you until tomorrow," Albright said, studying him in a way that was somehow more invasive than the retinal scanner.

"Caught an earlier flight."

"You look like hell."

"I came from the airport."

"I wasn't referring to jet lag."

Cade shrugged. "I'm good."

"Right." After a moment, Albright turned, and Cade followed him into his office. "I've got a kidnapping in San Juan, an import and export issue in the Balkans, and a car theft in Acapulco."

"A car theft?" It wasn't exactly a job that warranted their level of expertise, but stranger things had happened.

"Potential link to a drug cartel," Albright clarified as he sat behind a desk piled high with papers. "Six months undercover. Want it?"

"You're giving me a choice?"

"Yes. This time."

Cade narrowed his eyes as he sat down across from Albright. "No, thanks."

"What about San Juan?"

"Too hot in the summer." It was, but that wasn't the reason he declined.

"Import, export it is," Albright said, lifting the receiver on his desk phone. "Someone's smuggling contraband into Turkey. I can get you a line into our contact there, and he'll brief you."

Before he could dial, Cade leaned forward and slapped a hand on the base, cutting the connection. Albright sighed. "You're not here for a job."

Now or never.

"I'm here for Jack Doyle." Saying it out loud was like sandpaper scraping up the back of his throat, and Cade clenched his jaw against the burn.

"Where did you hear that name?" Albright asked grimly.

"From a friend."

It wasn't a lie. Victoria Chapman *was* a friend he'd met up with at a hotel in Paris a couple of weeks ago who was also a securities agent. It wasn't his fault she'd taken his request for a favor the wrong way. He still maintained her reaction had been extreme, even though he was unlikely to get an apology for tossing his clothes out the window onto browsing shoppers on *Rue Cler* anytime soon.

"What do you know?"

Cade shook his head. "You first."

"Let me remind you that you work for me. Not the other way around."

"I want to find him."

"And I want to vacation in Cabo San Lucas, but we don't always get what we want."

Cade bolted from his chair, toppling it as dizziness assailed him. He gripped the end of Albright's desk for support.

Not here.

He squeezed his eyes shut and didn't open them again until he felt the ground under him. Then, he met Albright's cool gaze. "He has to answer for Beck."

"Criminals don't answer to anyone, Cade, least of all government agents. You're too close to this to be objective."

"Does that mean you know where he is?"

As if realizing his error, Albright bowed his head. "Not exactly."

"But, someone does?"

"That's none of your business."

Cade sighed. If this were the only way he would get through to Albright, then so be it. "I only know his name and that it was Doyle's men who hijacked Juarez's shipment in Miami that day."

The shipment was AKs and grenade launchers bound for Cuba and then repackaged for distribution. Cade could name at least ten countries that would benefit from that kind of inventory.

"There's no proof Doyle was even involved."

Cade grunted. "Not even the fact that every man detained after the ambush worked for one of his shadow companies?"

"Companies led by employers with no ties to Doyle himself."

Cade looked away. No, there wouldn't be. Doyle would have made sure of that. But there was some evidence linking him to *something*, and Cade would find it. Beck's life was the one thing Doyle wasn't getting for free.

"Give me the job."

"Cade…"

"I can do this."

Albright folded his hands on the desk. "Ok, let's say you find Doyle and get him alone, away from his expert and highly compensated security team. You corner him in some alley on some street in some city, and he's miraculously unarmed. You have him at gunpoint. Will you be able to stop yourself from pulling that trigger?"

Cade curled a hand into a fist at his side, imagining cool metal against his palm. "I've done everything you've asked of me."

"You've done your job."

"I have to do this."

"That's not an answer."

"I can't give you an answer."

"Then I can't give you what you want."

Cade spun away from the desk and gripped the back of his neck so hard he felt the pressure at the base of his spine before letting it go. "I know you want me to say I don't want Doyle dead and buried instead of Beck. I can't say that because I do. Putting a bullet in that son-of-a-bitch would make my day; you know it would. But if you want Doyle to live and breathe another day, he will," he said, forcing the air from his lungs. "You have my word."

"And if I say no?"

"Like I said," Cade said, lowering his voice. "I have to do this."

Albright's eyes widened in shock and then narrowed. Even if his handler gave the orders, Cade had never thought of himself as a soldier. Soldiers fought and died for their countries. He was just the one who made sure it didn't come to that. He'd never challenged Albright before, but this time was different. Beck's family deserved justice, and they would get it.

He wouldn't fail them, too.

"Okay," Albright said, finally.

Relief flooded Cade's chest. "Thank you."

"Don't thank me yet. This is an assignment, and like all other assignments, you will follow protocol."

"No problem."

"I mean it, Cade. I'm calling the shots on this one."

Cade smirked. "It almost sounds like you don't trust me."

"As of late, your methods have been…unconventional. Especially this latest job."

"How was I supposed to know the bank was being monitored?"

"You're lucky the distraction caused by your arrest also resulted in the target's apprehension, or you'd still be sitting in a cell."

"Thanks for the bailout, by the way."

"You can thank me by not acting like a teenager with something to prove." Albright sighed. "It's been almost a year."

"I know how long it's been," Cade said, his throat tight.

"I've been more than tolerant, but my patience only goes so far."

"I understand," Cade said. "Where to?"

"Not sure yet. Sit tight. I'll let you know."

"But I—"

"I said I'll let you know."

Dismissed.

Now wasn't the time to push his luck. When Albright's attention returned to his computer, Cade turned to go. At least he'd gotten what he came for.

"Cade?"

"Yeah?"

"Promise me you'll be careful."

Cade only nodded. He wouldn't make promises he didn't know if he could keep.

2

Then

The crinkled brown paper bag was soft, the way paper gets when handled too many times. Cade didn't know how many times he'd used it, but it didn't matter—not as long as the travel-size cereal box inside was new. At least it had been that morning before he'd eaten half of it for breakfast on the walk to school.

He shook out a few loops and popped them into his mouth, the sugary sweetness doing little to ease the ache in his stomach. It was better than nothing, and he could still have the box of chocolate puffs he had at home for dinner.

If Dad didn't eat it first.

A shadow crossed over Cade's lap as he tipped the cereal box again. "Anyone sittin' here?" Without waiting for an answer, a boy plopped down next to Cade, setting his metal Superman lunch box on the grass between them.

"Are you lost?" Cade asked.

"The school is that way, and the playground is over there," the boy said, pointing left and then right toward the throng of kids swarming the tire swings. "So, no. What about you?"

"I ain't lost. I eat here every day."

"I know. I've seen you," the boy said, pulling the visor of his baseball cap sideways over a mop of hair the color of wet sand. "What's your name?"

"Everybody knows my name."

"I don't."

Cade looked into his cereal box and shook it. Frowning, he shoved the empty box back into the brown bag. "It's Cade."

"Cade, what?"

"Foster."

"My name is Beckett Easton III, but everyone just calls me Beck."

"Ok."

Beck reached into his lunch box, carefully divided into compartments, each containing fresh food. He slid a sandwich out of its plastic bag and held out half to Cade.

"What's that?"

"Turkey on rye with pickles."

Cade shook his head. "I mean, what are you doing?"

"Giving you half my sandwich."

"Why?"

Beck shrugged again. "Why not?"

"No, thanks."

Beck shoved it into his hands. "Just take it. If I come home with the other half, Mom'll be mad." Cade took it, and Beck balanced his half on one knee as he reached for the juice box lying on its side in the box. He detached the straw, removed the plastic, and shoved it into the hole at the top, placing the drink down on the upturned lid between them. "Why doesn't anyone like you?"

Cade stiffened and glared at Beck, who didn't seem to notice as he slowly chewed and watched a group of kids chase each other on the blacktop. "My dad's an asshole," he said before finally taking a bite of his half of the sandwich. He tried to remember the last time he'd tasted anything so good.

"Mine's dead."

A piece of bread lodged in Cade's throat, and he coughed. Reaching for Beck's juice box, he took a sip.

"We just moved here from Somerset, Illinois. Do you know it?"

Cade shook his head. Wherever it was, it sounded like it was far from Lakehaven.

"Yeah, well, nobody really does," Beck continued. "Mom said she wanted a change, so she picked New York. She works at an office now. Sloane, that's my sister, is too young to care where we go. She's six." Beck turned to look at him. "How old are you?"

"Nine."

"Same as me." Beck swiped the juice box from Cade's hand, gesturing with it to his face. "Where'd you get that?"

Cade touched the swollen black and blue skin around his eye and winced. "A fight."

"With who?"

"Some kid."

"Why'd you fight?"

"Do you ever stop asking questions?"

"Not really. Mom says if I keep at it, one of these days someone's gonna say something I don't like."

"Why do you do it, then?"

"Can't help it, I guess," Beck said, turning his attention back to their classmates on the blacktop.

Cade kicked a rock with the heel of his shoe. "He made fun of my mom."

"What'd he say?"

"That she was sick." Bobby Renfro said more than that before Cade shut him up.

"Was she?"

"No," Cade spat, rising to his knees.

Beck just watched him, one eye squinting against the sun. "Is she dead?"

Cade opened his mouth to tell Beck of course his mom wasn't dead, but stopped. The only thing he knew for sure was that everything had changed when she'd gone and left him with the asshole.

"I don't know."

Cade braced himself for Beck's reaction and for more questions that he wouldn't be able to answer, but Beck only nodded. It was a full minute before he started eating again, their combined chewing mingling with the cries of the other kids on the playground. After a while, the bell rang, signaling the end of lunch and recess.

Beck launched himself to his feet, swiping his palms on his jeans. "So, baseball tryouts are Wednesday."

"Ok."

"I gotta practice. Meet me after school, and we'll throw the ball around, okay?"

Cade stared at Beck. The sun had changed position enough for him to see Beck's face, and even though he looked for signs of jest or malevolence, Beck's expression remained earnest. So, despite never having swung a bat in his life, he answered in kind.

"Okay."

3

Sloane Easton hated theme songs. She didn't like jingles either, but at least she could do something about a jingle stuck in her head. Her mother's cleaning closet at home was proof of the effectiveness of catchy advertising. A theme song just made you want to poke your own eyes out with a plastic fork.

"If you don't stop humming that God-awful tune, Gig, I swear I'm going to lead these guys right to you."

"It's the Superman theme," her partner, Marvin Giggler, Gig, said into his communications device.

"So?"

"It will motivate you to run faster."

"I think the two men shooting at me are motivation enough, don't you?"

Two shots rang out, and Sloane hunched over, dodging right as the bullets hit a nearby building. She resumed her punishing pace, zigzagging through dark streets that were thankfully deserted at such a late, or *early*, hour.

"Debatable," Gig said.

If Sloane had any breath left in her lungs, she would have groaned. "Where the hell are you?"

"Two minutes out. Just stick to the side streets, keep your tracker on, and I'll find you. Don't worry."

Sloane wasn't worried; she was ecstatic. Or she would be once Gig downloaded the contents of the flash drive in her pocket, information that would confirm the location of the man responsible for her brother's death.

A bullet whizzed by Sloane's head as she rounded another corner. "Uh, Gig?"

"Yeah?"

"We have a problem."

"What kind of problem?"

The plunging-to-her-death-into-watery-depths kind. Sloane swallowed down her panic as she approached the end of the street, which, like most streets in Venice, ended at a canal.

"Is now a good time to mention that I'm not the best swimmer?"

That wasn't exactly true. Sloane had never submerged herself in water, so an accurate assessment of her swimming ability wasn't possible. Still, it was probably something her partner deserved to know.

"Jesus," Gig said. "*What?* Wait, never mind. Incoming on your left." Sloane stopped short as a van pulled out from a side street at full speed, fishtailing before cutting her off right before the bridge. "Get in!" Gig yelled from the open front passenger window, but Sloane didn't need any encouragement. She yanked the van's door open and jumped inside.

More bullets rained down on them as the men chasing her realized she had a means of escape. Sirens sounded in the distance, and Sloane shifted to her knees, throwing all her weight against the door to close it as Gig sped away.

"Are you okay?"

Sloane held onto the door for a minute, breathing hard. "I think so."

"Good," Gig said, checking his rearview mirror. "I think we lost them," he said, his eyes still on the road. "Do you have it?"

"Yes," she replied, joining him in the front. Sloane shifted to face him, briefly drawing Gig's attention away from the road.

"Why are you staring at me like that?"

"Like what?"

"Like you're the Cheshire Cat, and Alice just fed you lunch."

Sloane reached into her jacket pocket for the drive. "I got it."

"I know. You just told me."

"No, I mean, I got *it*."

A look of confusion passed over his features before realization dawned. "Doyle?"

She nodded. "I think I know where he is."

It was the reason she'd gotten caught. Sloane had been just about to leave with intel on their actual target when she'd seen the reference to one of Doyle's aliases and his location. She had studied the list of Jack Doyle's aliases so often during the last six months that she'd memorized them.

"Seriously?" Gig said.

Sloane nodded again. "I mean, I'll need confirmation, but I think so."

"We'll send it in for verification as soon as we get back," Gig said, sounding as excited as she was.

Five minutes later, they pulled into the warehouse garage that had been home base since they'd arrived in Venice. Sloane jumped out and tossed the drive to Gig as he exited the van.

"Get that uploaded. I'll be right back."

"Sure."

Sloane headed to the back room where they kept their stuff and stepped over her sleeping bag in the half-light. Having packed light for their brief stay in Venice, she only had to rifle through a backpack for a change of clothes. Spies didn't exactly have the luxury of carrying a full set of luggage around with them on every mission. Now, she kept a go bag ready at both the small apartment she kept in Lakehaven and her mom's house, just in case. She'd done the same when she was younger in anticipation of taking a last-minute trip to the lake.

But that was then.

She peeled off her ripped black jeans and hoodie and reached back into her bag for a pair of sweatpants and an old Lakehaven

Lions T-shirt. Her stomach turned as her fingers grazed the sealed envelope at the bottom of the bag. She pictured her brother's lazy handwriting on the front and hesitated for only a moment before shoving it aside. Now wasn't the time.

She dressed quickly and found Gig in the gated enclosure where he'd set up shop. Monitors and wires covered every square inch of the space, and Gig sat in the center of it all, hunched over a metal desk. Before Sloane could call out to him, she heard a sultry voice purr through the speakers.

"What are you wearing?"

"I can't talk right now," Gig replied in a hushed tone.

"But I'm wearing those glasses you like. You know, the ones that make me look like a hot librarian."

"I can see that, but now's not really a great time."

"But your library books are overdue. You've been a very bad boy."

"I told you, I can't—"

"Hi Jess," Sloane said, poking her head into view of the camera. "Nice glasses and nice…uh…uniform?"

Her outfit *resembled* a uniform, even if it wasn't one any school in the U.S. would mandate that students wear. Still, Sloane had to admit Gig's analyst girlfriend looked hot in the red pencil skirt and white tank top with a red and white striped tie looped around her neck.

"Hey, Sloane," Jess said with a bright smile. "I thought you were done for the night."

Sloane glanced at Gig, whose face had turned the same shade as Jessica's skirt. She smirked. "Almost."

"Well, don't let me keep you. And thanks for the compliment. I just bought it," Jessica said. "I couldn't believe my luck when I found a Halloween pop-up store open in August!"

"Well, it was money well spent."

"I wasn't sure about the skirt, but I think it works. My ass doesn't look big in this, right?" Sloane held back her laughter as Jessica set down her computer and turned her back to the camera.

Gig cleared his throat. "You look great, babe, but I really gotta go."

"Oh, right," she said, turning back around. "We'll continue this later." She blew him a kiss. "Bye S—."

Sloane had just lifted her hand to wave back when Gig cut the connection. "Sorry about that," he said sheepishly.

This time, Sloane didn't hide her smile. "I'm not."

"Don't start."

"If you guys are into role-play, I have a couple of ideas."

"Don't you dare."

"How can you deny me this fun after what I just went through?"

"By reminding you we're supposed to be working."

Sloane pouted. "Fine. Did you upload the data?"

No sooner had she said it than Gig's laptop pinged with an incoming video call notification. "It's him."

Sloane pulled up a chair just as Sebastian Albright's image appeared on the screen. "Team," he said in greeting, nodding at the two of them. "I take it the job went well?"

"Define *well*," Gig said, flinching when Sloane elbowed him in the ribs.

"It was successful," Sloane said. "Did you get the information?"

"I did."

"And?"

"It's legit. Jack Doyle is in the South of France under an assumed name."

Sloane had to stop herself from jumping out of her chair and fist-pumping the air. It had been nearly a year, but she'd finally found him.

She exchanged an excited look with Gig before standing. "We'll pack up and be on the first flight out of Venice."

"Not so fast," Albright said, his voice hard. Sloane dropped back into her chair. "Jack Doyle is of utmost importance to the agency."

Sloane knew more than anyone the havoc Doyle had wreaked, and not just in the last several months since her brother's death. It had been decades. Decades of crime, thievery, and a line of victims as long as her mother's grocery list.

"I know."

"Then you also know there's no room for error."

"Of course."

"Frankly," Albright said, "I have my doubts that you're right for this job." Sloane opened her mouth to protest, but Albright held up a hand. "But I'm willing to make an exception. Under one condition."

Sloane said the only thing she could. "Anything."

"There will be no surprises. We're doing this by the book. Do you understand?"

"I understand."

"Good," Albright said, leaning back in his chair, satisfied. "You both leave for Nice in the morning."

"Is there a safe house on site?" Gig asked.

For the first time since the call began, Albright hesitated, and Sloane felt a niggling sensation in her gut. But then he nodded. "You'll have everything you need when you get there. Get some sleep tonight. You're going to need it."

The screen went dark, and Gig stood. "Well, Easton, you heard the man."

Yes, she'd heard him, but Sloane knew she wouldn't sleep.

Not until Jack Doyle was where he belonged.

4

Then

Sloane skipped down Main Street, an envelope filled with cash burning a hole in her pocket. Mrs. Levinson was partially blind but still insisted she'd given Sloane the right amount. According to her, Cuddles had never been so happy. Was it normal for a person to understand as much about their cat? She wasn't sure, but Mrs. Levinson and Cuddles shared a special bond. She also enjoyed having Sloane around, which made her mom happy. Faye Easton practically shoved her out the door every time Mrs. Levinson called them for a favor. Sloane didn't mind. The woman smelled like peppermints, and she was kind, which was why she probably wouldn't mind if Sloane donated to a church on her behalf, even if she was Jewish.

Sloane stopped on the church steps and reached into her pocket for the money, pausing when she noticed Cade Foster walking toward her. At least, she *thought* that was Cade dragging a burly older man down the sidewalk with one arm around the man's waist. The man stumbled and threw an arm around Cade's shoulders, weighing him down, so it was almost impossible for Cade to keep them both upright. It was late evening, and the few people on the sidewalk gave the two of them a wide berth as they trudged along, the man grunting with every stomp of his booted foot.

"If you didn't spend your whole life in that hellhole, you would have remembered the rent was due last week."

"Watch your mouth," the man slurred, shaking himself free of Cade. "I didn't raise you to be disrespectful."

Cade straightened and leveled him with a glare. "You didn't raise me at all."

The man lifted a hand in the air, and Sloane was already halfway down the stairs before she realized what she was doing. "There you are," she said when she reached the sidewalk. "I-I t-thought we were meeting in front of the library?"

"Who are you?"

Sloane turned toward the large, imposing man and stuck out her hand, locking her knees to keep them from shaking. "Hi, I'm Sloane."

The man slowly lowered the hand still hanging in mid-air and wiped it on a pair of dirty jeans before closing it around her palm. "Sloane," he repeated. His eyes were the same black as Cade's. Black like Mrs. Levinson's cat, but with no life at all.

Sloane slipped her hand from his sweaty grip. "Yes, sir. Sloane Easton. I'm a f-friend of Cade's."

Beside her, Cade scowled.

"Tom Foster." His curious gaze darted between her and Cade. "I wasn't aware my son had friends."

This was Cade's father? Sloane hid her surprise with a high-pitched laugh. "We are. Um…he does. Have friends, I mean." Sloane cleared her throat and turned her attention to Cade, pulling the envelope from her pocket. "Mom said to say thank you for fixing her sink. It works great now."

Before Cade could reach for it, Mr. Foster swiped the envelope from her hand. "What's this?"

"It's what my mom owes Cade for the work he did in our kitchen. She didn't have money when he came by last week, so she said she would pay him later."

Mr. Foster's eyebrows lifted as he flipped through the bills in the envelope. "There's one hundred dollars in here."

"Cade's been helping around the house since we don't know many people to help with that sorta thing."

"What about your dad?"

Sloane shuffled her feet. "He's…not around."

Mr. Foster stared at her. He stunk like a musty old liquor cabinet, but Sloane just smiled like he smelled like freshly folded laundry.

He looked at Cade. "Is this true?"

It took a long time, but eventually, Cade nodded, playing along. Sloane's grin widened.

"Thank you, kindly, little lady," Mr. Foster said, sounding like a cowboy in the old westerns Beck liked to watch. He pocketed the envelope and gripped Cade's shoulder. "You help this young lady's mother whenever she asks, okay?" Cade nodded again. "Don't let me hear that you ditched her."

"Cade comes over whenever we ask Mr. Foster. He's very polite."

Cade frowned, and Sloane kept right on smiling.

Mr. Foster slapped Cade on the back. "That's my boy." He patted the pocket that held the envelope. "Nice meetin' you, Sloane."

"You too."

Mr. Foster pointed a finger at Cade. "Now, remember what I said and don't embarrass me. Understand?"

Cade stood still and silent, hands fisted at his sides. His jaw worked like he was chewing gum, even though he wasn't. Instead of waiting for an answer, Mr. Foster turned and staggered back the way they'd come.

When he was gone, Cade whirled on her. "What'd you do that for?"

Sloane flinched. "You're welcome."

"Do you think you did me a favor just now?"

"I heard what you said."

"You heard me arguing with my dad about paying our rent, so you decided to donate to the cause?"

"Well, I—"

"What do you think he's going to do with that money, huh?"

"I don't know," she said, some of her bluster fading at his tone.

"I do. He's going to dig himself into another hole like the one I found him in and drink it away. Our landlord won't see a dime."

"He was going to hit you."

"So?"

Sloane jerked back. "He can't hit you."

"Why? Because he's my dad?"

Her stomach dipped the way it always did when she rode a rollercoaster. "I can help."

"I don't need help from a nine-year-old."

"I'm ten."

Cade rolled his eyes. "That's so much older."

"It's old enough to have a job."

"Cat-sitting isn't a job."

"Says who?"

"Me," he said, squaring off in front of her. "I don't need your help, okay? I know Beck and I hang out, but you and I are not friends."

Hurt and anger flared in Sloane's chest. "Alright," she said, marching past him. "If you want to be an idiot, then go ah—"

A horn blared as she stepped down from the curb, and Sloane felt the wind rush between her and a passing car. She cried out as Cade grabbed her arm and pulled her back onto the sidewalk, the car whizzing by them down the street without stopping.

"Asshole!" Cade yelled at the fading tail lights before looking down at her. It wasn't the same icy stare as his father's or the angry one he'd given her a moment ago. It was more like the way Cuddles looked at a new ball of yarn before he batted at it with one of his paws. "Are you okay?"

She nodded as she caught her breath, and he dropped his hand from her arm. The skin where he'd touched her tingled the way it did when it fell asleep. "Thanks."

"Yeah, sure." He made a face, his mouth twisting into a half-frown as he stepped down from the curb. "Come on," he said over his shoulder. "And look both ways this time."

Sloane did and hurried to catch up. "Where are we going?"

"You just told my dad that I'm working for your mom."

"So?"

Cade stopped short, causing Sloane to plow into his back. He turned to face her, his expression hard. "I'm not a liar."

"But I don't know if Mom has anything for you to do."

"You should have thought about that before you told my dad I was the hired help. I'm not some charity case."

"I know."

"Either you pay me for doing actual work, or I go home and tell Pop that *you* lied."

"You can't do that."

"Why not?"

Sloane clamped her mouth shut. Did he think she was stupid? If Cade's father was ready to hit him just for challenging him, what would he do if he found out that Cade hadn't actually earned the money Sloane had given him?

As Cade stared at her, head half-cocked like a puppet, Sloane realized he *wanted* her to call him out. He expected it. And that, more than any other reason, was why she didn't say what was on her mind.

Instead, she moved past him. "Let's go. I'm sure Mom won't mind if I have a *friend* over."

"We're not friends," he said as he fell into step beside her. "We're just... even."

Sloane hid a smile and stayed one step ahead of Cade the entire walk home.

5

Cade drove up the circular drive of the safe house and cut the engine. Frowning, he pulled out his phone from inside the console and scanned the text Albright had sent him three days ago. It was the right address even if the place looked nothing like any safe house he'd ever seen.

Six windows spanned two stories of the stone villa, each framed with pale blue shutters. Ivy cascaded down one side of the house from the roof to the ground, and wildflowers lined the walkway to the door. There was a grimy, chipped fountain in the grassy courtyard to the left of the entrance, across from a decrepit iron bench that was likely an antique somebody had paid big bucks for.

Not that Cade knew anything about that. What he did know was how to follow his instincts, and right now, those instincts were telling him he wasn't alone.

He leaned over and retrieved a Glock 19 from the glove box before getting out of the car, taking care not to slam the door behind him. The pistol had come with the Aston Martin he'd rented, and he knew he would get shit for later. He'd used his own money for the car, but somehow, he doubted that would stop Albright's impending lecture.

Worth it.

Not wanting to risk being seen before he could assess the situation, he headed around to the back, dipping low when he reached the side of the villa to avoid the mounted cameras.

Albright was going to be pissed. Hell, Cade was pissed, too, and he was looking forward to venting his anger on the trespasser.

He sidled up to the stone wall at the rear of the house and peeked around the corner. A woman with cropped brown hair and slim shoulders stood on the patio looking out over the lawn that lay beyond a giant lap pool. She wore a white T-shirt and pink running shorts, the spandex pulling tight over a shapely ass.

Cade shook his head to clear the image from his mind, as well as the random feeling of déjà vu that came over him when he saw that ass. He noticed the buds in her ears when he was halfway to her and heard the music blaring so loud that there was no way she could have heard him approach. He smirked. Taking her down would be easy. He'd even reward himself afterward with a swim.

He lifted the gun, cocked it, and touched the barrel to the back of her head. The woman stiffened. Without turning around, she slowly reached up to remove an earbud from one ear. Cade waited until he was sure she could hear him.

"Don't move."

She moved, immediately crouching low and swinging one of her legs under his to knock him off balance. But Cade was rarely off balance, and he did little more than stumble back, barely having time to right himself before she kneed him in the stomach. The gun skittered to the patio floor as Cade doubled over, pretending to be more hurt than he was. It was a hard hit, but not hard enough. The woman lunged for the gun, but Cade shifted his weight to his core as he half stood and caught her around the waist, hiking her over his shoulder. He carried her to the grass at the edge of the patio, where he dropped her unceremoniously to her back.

She continued to struggle, her moves strong but textbook. Cade had written the book. He laid himself on top of her and shoved her arms over her head, clasping both of her hands in both of his. Then he looked down, his gaze colliding with familiar amber-colored eyes.

"Bullet?"

She stopped struggling. *"Cade?"*

Somewhere in the distance, a screen door slammed, and Cade jumped to his feet. He crossed the patio in three strides and grabbed his gun, aiming it directly at the guy, the *kid*, who had just come through the back door. The kid's eyebrows lifted into a mop of brown hair, his eyes widening behind black, thick-rimmed glasses as he held up both hands in surrender.

"Stop," Bullet said, stepping between him and the kid. "He's with me."

"What does that mean? And what the hell are you doing at my safe house?"

"I could ask you the same question."

"Uh…you two know each other?" The kid said.

Sloane sighed. "Gig, this is Cade."

"Cade?"

"Yes."

"Cade *Foster*?"

Sloane rolled her eyes and looked back over her shoulder. "Yes."

"Who are you?" Cade said.

"Marvin Giggler." He started toward Cade with an outstretched hand, then stopped, wisely opting to wave a hand in greeting instead. "Nice to meet you."

Cade glanced at Sloane. "Talk."

"Let's go inside. We'll talk there."

"We'll talk here."

Without another word, she turned her back on him and started inside. The kid merely shrugged and followed, leaving Cade with no choice but to do the same, especially if he wanted answers, and he definitely wanted answers.

There was nobody in the kitchen, so he continued to the front of the house. A long hallway to his left revealed three closed doors, with an adjacent living space that was furnished but also empty of occupants. A set of stairs to his right led up to the second floor, but Cade didn't take the stairs. Instead, he made his way to the room just beyond it. And what he saw inside nearly stopped his heart.

Someone had shoved aside all the furniture in the room except for a large dining table topped with more electronic equipment than he'd ever seen. Half-eaten plates of food and file folders also littered its surface.

What the…

"What is this?"

Cade looked across the table at Sloane and then over her shoulder at the back wall, which displayed an array of multi-colored sticky notes and images. They were all images of one man. A man who had haunted Cade's dreams since he'd learned his name. He tightened his grip on his gun. He wasn't planning to use it, but the metal against his palm was something stable amidst the turmoil surging in his chest.

Sloane gave him a sardonic look. "*This* is probably Albright's idea of a joke."

She couldn't know that name. Nobody but him and Beck knew that name. "What did you just say?"

"If it makes you feel any better, he didn't tell me either."

Nothing about this situation made Cade feel anything but rage. "What are you doing here, Bullet?" Before she could respond, one computer on the table pinged with a notification.

"It's Albright," the kid said, taking a seat in front of the open laptop.

Sloane nodded and moved to the kid's side. On autopilot, Cade did the same on his other.

"Good," Albright said once the kid accepted the call. "The gang's all here."

"You didn't have to call him," Sloane started. "Gig and I can handle this job."

"What are you talking about?" Cade asked, trying hard not to lose his shit. "Albright, what is she talking about?"

"Sloane found a solid lead on Jack Doyle a few days ago. I confirmed it."

Cade couldn't have heard that right. "What do you mean *Sloane* found a lead?"

The kid leaned toward Sloane. "Is he always this slow?"

Cade glared at him before turning his attention back to Albright. "There's no way Sloane could have found a lead. It's impossible because Sloane isn't an operative. Is she, Albright?" Sloane was right. This had to be some kind of sick joke. But if it was, the look on his handler's face was proof enough that Cade was the punch line. "How long?" He asked through clenched teeth.

"Six months," Sloane answered.

"Six mo—" Cade dropped the gun on the table with a thud. The room spun, and he gripped the top of the kid's chair with one hand.

"Technically, it's been nine months, but a few of those don't count because I needed to complete my field training before joining Albright's team."

"This isn't happening." Any minute now, Cade was going to wake up from the nightmare he'd just walked into.

"Oh, it's happening," the kid said, and Cade sent him another murderous look.

"Finally," Sloane said with a sigh.

Cade looked at Albright. "Why didn't you tell me?"

"Since when are you on Albright's recruitment team?" Sloane said. "He can do anything he wants. He's our boss."

"No, he's *my* boss. And this job is mine," Cade said to Albright. "You gave it to me."

"Like hell," Sloane said. "Gig and I did all the work. It's *our* job. The door's that way," she said, waving a hand. "You can leave any time you're ready."

"You're the one who's leaving."

"Not a chance."

"Enough!" They fell silent, and all three sets of eyes swung to Albright. "This isn't some after-school dodgeball game where the team captains get to choose their own players." He leaned closer to the camera, resting his forearms on the surface of his desk. "You are not captains. And this isn't a game. You are all in France at my behest, on a mission *I* sanctioned because it's what *I* want. If you don't like it, then you can both leave. Do you understand?" Cade ground his teeth, nodding along with the other two. "Now, if it's alright with you, can we please get back to the matter at hand?" More nods. "Gig," Albright said. "What did you find out?"

Gig minimized Albright's image and tapped a few keys on the keyboard. "It's what we thought. Barnes Junior's death was ruled a heart attack, but the item was definitely missing from his personal collection."

Sloane swore. "That's two of three."

"At least we know where the third is," the kid said.

"Right."

Cade looked from one to the other of them, confused. "Two of three, what?"

"Sloane?" Albright said, arching a brow.

Sloane sighed dramatically and flipped her hair. Her *dark* hair, Cade now realized. The strands were so dark they were almost black. When had she dyed her hair?

"Two of three emeralds," she said. "A set."

"So, Doyle's a jewel thief now?"

"He's whatever his clients need him to be," Sloane said. "You'd know that if you'd done any research on him at all."

Cade turned to face her, his toes bumping against the kid's chair. "Who do you think was out catching the bad guys while you were busy reading files?"

"Gig will brief you on the research later, Cade," Albright said before Sloane could reply. "For now, all you need to know is that the third emerald is here."

"Where?"

"*Le Centre de Feu*," Gig said, with a fake French accent.

"The City of Fire?"

Gig shook his head. "It's not an exact translation. The Passion Center is a museum in town."

"So, Doyle's planning to steal the emerald from the museum?"

"Likely," Albright said.

"Who's his buyer?"

"Unknown."

"What's the play?"

"You'll go in undercover, get close to Doyle, and find out who his buyer is. If we can get some leverage on the buyer, we might get him to give up Doyle."

"I'm on it," Cade said.

"Not you." Albright gestured to Sloane. "Her."

Sloane's eyes widened, also surprised. Then, a wide grin spread over her face. "I'm in."

"No," Cade said. The anger he'd tamped down at Albright's earlier reprimand morphed into something else in his gut. His blood pressure rose, his pulse quickening to a steady gallop. "I'll do it."

Albright nodded to the kid, who pulled a folder from the top of the pile to his right. He dropped it in front of Cade. "The museum hired a curator from an agency a few days ago to assist with their upcoming exhibit. *Elena* Caldwell starts next Monday."

Shit.

"We can say she got sick. They'll send someone else."

"No," Albright said.

"But she knows nothing about art."

Sloane raised an eyebrow. "And you do?"

"She doesn't have the experience," Cade tried. "I've been undercover." In fact, he'd likely been undercover more in the last few years than he'd been himself. "I know what to expect."

"I know, which is why you're the perfect person to help Sloane navigate that world. She has knowledge of the target, and you have experience in the field."

"I know the target."

Sloane looked at him. "Really?"

"Yes."

"Okay, then. What alias does Doyle use when he's in France?"

Cade opened his mouth. Closed it.

"Exactly," she said, looking way too pleased with herself.

Cymbals clanged in Cade's ears. "This is a mistake." He looked at Albright. "You can't actually be considering this."

"It's done," Albright said in a tone that left no room for argument. "The museum is hosting a benefit off-site this Friday. It's a charity event to raise money for the arts. Sloane will rendezvous with the target, and you and Gig will be backup."

Friday. Backup.

One week. Not even. In five days, Cade would play backup to Sloane Easton when she met a suspected murderer for the first time.

The room spun again, faster than before. The edges of Cade's vision blurred as Albright droned on, a bee buzzing around Cade's head.

One, two, three...

He tried to breathe, tried to pull air into his lungs, but there wasn't space. He needed more space.

Sloane turned to him and said something, but whatever it was pinged off the walls of his mind. Cade shook his head, muttering something unintelligible as he stumbled out of the room.

6

Sloane found him on the patio where she'd been earlier, staring into the pool like he was ready to dive in and swim far away from her. He could have if he wanted to, and not only because she wouldn't step one pinky toe into that water. Cade Foster was just good at leaving.

"What's your problem?"

He slowly turned to face her, and she sucked in a breath at his ashen complexion, the angles of his face suddenly jarringly sharp. A thin sheen of sweat shone on his brow, and the shadows under his eyes made him appear almost ghostly in the fading light.

"Excuse me?"

"Are you alright?" She asked before she could stop herself.

"I think it's safe to say I am as far from alright as I can get right now."

Sloane sighed. "I'm not happy about this either, but you can't just—"

"Happy?" Cade barked out a laugh. "The only thing that would make me happy is putting you on the first plane back to New York."

"That's not happening."

"What Albright said in there was true. This isn't a game. These men are dangerous."

"I know who and what they are."

"Do you honestly think that a little internet research will tell you what kind of man Jack Doyle is? You have no fucking clue what you're up against."

"Don't swear at me."

"Why?" Cade said, stalking up to her, so close that she had to fold her arms over her chest to ward off contact. "Because Faye wouldn't like it? This isn't a world where you can add five dollars to your mom's swear jar to make yourself feel better."

"I'm staying."

"Really?"

"Yes." Sloane lifted her chin. "I know what you're thinking."

"I doubt that."

"You think I'm not ready for this."

"You're not."

"I've spent six months preparing to take Doyle down."

"You've spent the last six months breaking into abandoned buildings in the middle of the night. This isn't the same thing."

"That's not all I've done."

"Shit, Bullet. I was kidding." Cade swiped a hand through his hair and gripped the back of his neck. "What else?"

Sloane didn't think surveillance and helping Gig with database mining would help her case, so she said the next best thing. "That's classified."

"I have higher clearance than you."

"So? I'm not required to give you my resume. All you need to know is that I'm trained as a field agent."

"You're a glorified errand girl. Have you ever even been undercover before?"

She hadn't, but she wasn't about to admit that to Cade. Besides, there was only one thing that mattered. "I'll do whatever it takes."

"Even if that means taking a life?"

"I've shot a gun before."

"But have you ever shot a *person* before?"

Sloane swallowed hard. "That's…not what this mission is about."

"But it could happen. Are you ready for that? Are you ready to stare into someone's eyes and take their life if you have to? Has your field training prepared you for that?"

"Don't be an asshole," she said through clenched teeth.

Cade clucked his tongue. "Where's that swear jar when you need it? Faye would be so disappointed."

"Don't you talk about her." Sloane seethed. Something flashed in Cade's eyes and she pounced, the anger she'd felt when she'd first stepped foot outside returning with a vengeance. "You gave up that right when you *left*. Just like you gave up the right to know anything about me and my life since you disappeared from it."

"This isn't about that."

"You're right. It's not. I get you don't want to work with me. Trust me when I say I want to work with you even less. But you don't get to dictate what I can handle. Albright assigned me this job, and I will work it, with or without you. Nothing you say or do will change that."

Sloane spun on her heel and started back toward the house. Tears stung her eyes, but she blinked them back and choked down the sob that swelled in her throat. She would not cry. Not now, and not in front of *him*. She was almost at the door when his voice stopped her.

"Beck wouldn't want this for you."

Sloane looked over her shoulder. He hadn't moved from where she'd left him, his blank expression one she recognized. Shielding emotion was another talent Cade had adopted over the last couple of years and might even be the reason he was so good at his job. But Sloane played by different rules. Her experience had taught her that emotion, when wielded properly, could be a powerful weapon.

"Beck is dead," she said, with all the ire she could muster. "He can't want anything anymore."

7

Then

"Do you have anything to say for yourself?"

Cade slouched in the chair across from Principal Fisher's desk and shook his head, wincing as pain radiated through his temple.

Principal Fisher sighed. "We've tried calling your father but can't seem to reach him. Do you know where he might be?"

"No."

It wasn't exactly a lie. Cade didn't have any idea which bar his father was at that afternoon.

"You'll have to stay here until we can get in touch with him."

Cade shrugged. He didn't particularly like Principal Fisher, but it was better than sitting in class. Someone knocked on the door, and Cade twisted in his seat as the principal's secretary entered the office.

"What is it, Mrs. Bryce?"

"Mrs. Easton is here to see you."

"Faye?" Principal Fisher flipped through a notebook on his desk. "We don't have an appointment today."

"She says it's important," Mrs. Bryce said, looking down her nose at Cade. "Should I tell her you're busy?"

"No, it's fine. Send her in."

Cade couldn't remember much about his mother before she left, but what he did recall was that she was nothing like Mrs. Easton. Becca Foster was a wisp of a woman with long, thin hair, the same inky black as his. She'd liked dresses, the long, flowy kind, with skirts that billowed around her when she twirled, reminding Cade of a bird in flight.

He couldn't imagine Beck's mom, in her khaki slacks, white shirt, and black cardigan, twirling like that and even if she did, he doubted it would have the same effect.

Did looking like a mom make you a better one?

"Faye," Principal Fisher greeted, rounding his desk to meet her.

"Hi, Stan."

"Gerald didn't tell me you'd be stopping by."

"Oh, he doesn't know I'm here. Like he said, you'll have the copies of those papers he's filing for you on the sale next week."

"I appreciate your help," Principal Fisher said. "Now that Mom's gone, it's a relief to know that someone trustworthy is handling her estate."

Mrs. Easton waved a hand. "Gerald's the attorney. He does all the work. I just handle the filing."

"You do more than that. He's lucky to have you."

Mrs. Easton's cheeks flushed pink, and Cade shifted in his chair.

"I brought these," she said, presenting the tray she'd walked in with.

Principal Fisher took it from her hands and peeked under the foil wrapping. "You came all this way to bring me chocolate chip cookies?" He smiled, and Cade glanced at the open door, considering how much more trouble he could get into if he made a run for it.

"Actually, no. I'm here for Cade."

Principal Fisher glanced between them. "For Cade?"

"Yes."

"We have a call out to his father."

"Whom you haven't been able to reach?"

"Yes, but I'm not able to discuss the situation with anyone but Cade's legal guardian."

"And by *situation,* you're referring to Cade's argument with the Renfro boy?"

"It was more than an argument, Faye," Principal Fisher said, gesturing to Cade's split lip and black eye.

Both were no big deal to Cade. Bobby had gotten it much worse. Just as he always did when he tried to start shit.

"I know. My son explained everything."

"He did?"

Mrs. Easton nodded. "You do realize that Bobby Renfro has been bullying my daughter since the beginning of the school year?"

"Well, I—"

"And that this morning, he attempted to put his hands on her in the middle of *your* hallway during school hours?"

Principal Fisher frowned. "That's not what Bobby said."

"Are you calling my son a liar, Stan?"

Silence filled the room, and Principal Fisher opened his suit jacket and loosened his tie. "No, not at all. I'm merely pointing out that—"

"Good." Mrs. Easton moved past him and placed the tray of cookies on Fisher's desk. Then she looked at Cade for the first time since entering the office. "Cade, honey, can you please wait outside while I talk to Principal Fisher?"

Fisher blanched as Cade nodded and slid out of his chair, moving toward the door. It closed behind him, and he leaned against the far wall, too stunned to do anything but stare at it.

Mrs. Easton had come to the school *for him?*

Mrs. Bryce made a sound at her desk, and Cade glanced over just in time to see her giving him the evil eye. Instead of looking away, he stared back at her, the same way he had stared at Bobby right before he threw the first punch. Cade knew a few things his classmates didn't. Like how bullies came in all shapes and sizes and ages. Just because Mrs. Bryce was old didn't mean she wasn't one.

It took a minute, but eventually, Mrs. Bryce huffed and turned her attention back to her desk, frowning at it so hard that Cade wondered if her face would stay scrunched up like that forever. A couple of minutes later, Principal Fisher's door opened, and Mrs. Easton strolled out.

"Come on, Cade," she said. "Let's go."

Cade glanced into the principal's office to find Fisher sitting in his chair, tie slightly askew, as he slumped over his desk. He wore a tired smile as he stared at Mrs. Easton's back but didn't stop Cade as he trailed after her, past Mrs. Bryce and through the office's double doors. She didn't pause once as she walked down the hall toward the school's exit.

"We're leaving?" Cade asked. It wasn't even lunchtime yet, and everyone was still in class.

"I suppose you can stay if you want to," she said breezily, holding open the door. "Beck mentioned you have an English quiz this afternoon?"

Cade walked outside.

The car ride was quiet, punctuated only by Mrs. Easton's intermittent humming along to the radio. Cade sat in the passenger seat, stealing glances at Beck's mom, who didn't say a word as they drove through town. Cade clenched his hands into fists as they passed the corner of Walnut Street and Main, but she didn't stop at the tiny apartment he shared with his dad. Instead, she turned right on Maple and pulled into her own driveway before cutting the engine.

"I'm not sorry," Cade blurted.

Even if she hand-delivered him to his father right now and told him everything, he would never be sorry. Mrs. Easton reached out with a single finger and lifted his chin. He saw none of the disappointment and ridicule he expected to see in her gaze, only a kind of softness that made Cade's own eyes burn. She glanced at the bruise along his jaw and swept a hand over his forehead, brushing away a stray hair. It was the briefest of touches, something a mother would do, something he'd seen her do to Beck and Sloane a hundred times without ever really imagining how it felt.

Now he knew.

Mrs. Easton pulled back. "Can you help me with something in the garage?"

Without waiting for an answer, she got out of the car and shut the door behind her. Cade watched through the windshield as she opened the garage door and waved for him to join her before he opened his own door. If Mrs. Easton wanted his help cleaning the garage, he supposed he owed her that much, though he didn't know what she would have him do. He'd been in the Easton's garage, and it was more organized than Mrs. Bryce's desk.

He stepped into the half-dark space to find her dragging something bulky and cylindrical across the floor. Cade jogged over to the help, and the two of them dragged the large sack to the center of the garage.

"What is it?" Cade asked.

"What does it look like?"

"A punching bag."

It was old and faded and covered in dust, but it was a punching bag, alright. She nodded and stood the bag upright, holding it in place with one of her forearms.

"You know that Beck's dad was a police officer, right?"

"Yeah." Beck had told him as much.

"On his off days, he used to coach at a boxer's gym in Illinois when Beck was little. He enjoyed teaching the kids something new. Then he got sick and, well..." She trailed off and gazed past Cade toward the yard. "I suppose I know now why I kept it all these years."

"What are you gonna do with it?"

Her smile returned. "It's not what *I'm* going to do." She tipped the bag toward Cade, and he wrapped his arms around its middle, stumbling a bit at the weight. Mrs. Easton walked away and returned a minute later with a step stool. "See that?" She said, pointing to a metal ring attached to the ceiling of the garage. "I'm not sure what this was for, but we'll attach it here." She stepped onto the stool. "You lift the bag, and I'll make sure it holds."

Cade did as he was told, bending at the knees to support the weight. It was heavy, but the months of outdoor work he'd done for Mrs. Easton had made him strong.

"Okay now," she said when they'd secured the bag. "Let it go." He did, and the bag swung off the ground, the center of it almost at eye level. Beck's mom got off the stool and moved to the far wall. "I don't have any gloves," she said, returning with a box that she dropped in a cloud of dust at his feet. "You can wrap your hands in some of this for now."

Cade looked at the rolls of unused boxers tape. "This is for me?"

Beck's mom placed a hand on his shoulder and looked him in the eye. "You're smart, Cade. Too smart to be using your fists on others when you can use your head. Anytime you feel like hitting something, you come here and hit this instead. Any time, day or night. Got it?"

"Okay."

"Try it now."

"Now?"

"Right now."

She stepped away, and Cade swallowed hard. He shifted on his feet before awkwardly raising a fist and throwing a punch. The bag barely moved.

Mrs. Easton frowned. "You punched Bobby Renfro harder than that. Put your weight into it. Like this."

To Cade's surprise, Beck's mom landed a punch that had the bag swinging on its anchor. She let out a loud whoop and jumped from foot to foot like a real boxer, with both fists in the air. "See? It's easy. Try again."

Cade stared at her.

"Go on," she prompted. "Show me what you've got."

Still slightly embarrassed but having little choice in the matter, Cade again squared off in front of the bag.

"Focus," Mrs. Easton said.

Cade squinted hard and flexed his fists. He imagined Bobby Renfo pulling Sloane's hair and grabbing her arm, and he saw himself intervening by blocking Beck and pushing Bobby away.

Thunk. Thunk. Thunk.

The bag swung wide and kept swinging as Cade punched it. More of Mrs. Easton's cheers echoed in the garage. "That's the way!" She settled the bag as Cade stepped away. "How does it feel?"

Something buoyed in his chest as Cade caught his breath, feeling calmer than he had all day. He glanced down at his red knuckles. "Good," he said, and meant it.

"Good." Mrs. Easton repeated, her expression turning serious. "There comes a time in every boy's life when he has to decide what kind of man he wants to be. Now's your time, Cade. Are you ready?"

Cade looked at the bag and then at Beck's mom. "Yes."

"And don't think this entitles you to become some kind of professional fighter. If I ever see you in a boxing ring, I'll drag you out by your ears. Understand?"

"Okay."

"Promise?"

"I promise," Cade said.

8

Cade blinked his eyes open and flipped onto his back, listening. When the sound came again, muffled as it was, from the other side of his bedroom door, he rose from the bed, threw on a shirt and shorts, and followed the sound to the kitchen, half sure he was still asleep. But then he heard it again, and he knew it wasn't a dream.

It was Bullet.

Laughing.

She sat on a stool at the kitchen island in the same pink running shorts he'd seen her in the day before, cradling a mug of coffee like it was any normal day. The wave of nostalgia that crashed into him was so strong that he gripped the door frame as he stood there and reveled in the sight of her smile.

She hadn't seen him yet, and neither had the kid, who was too busy putting on a show to notice Cade lurking in the hall. He wore a white apron imprinted with the phrase *Kiss The Cook* as he danced to French music playing on an old radio. He tossed a spatula from one hand to another, singing into it, as he whirled back to the stove to flip a pancake before resuming his performance. The second time he turned back around, the batter stuck to the spatula, and the half-baked pancake dropped to the floor with a splat, sending Sloane into hysterics.

The kid laughed, too, but then he stopped and watched her, his eyes roaming her face with something like appreciation. No, it was worse than that, Cade realized. Hearing what Sloane had said about Beck the previous night had been a sucker punch to the gut, but seeing the way the kid looked at her now, with admiration and pride, was a kick in the balls.

When Sloane swung the full force of that warm smile in the kid's direction, Cade knew he'd been wrong about them being just partners. Relationships between agents were rare but not unheard of. Cade knew a few couples who had made it work. Were *they* making it work? Had they made it work last night?

The thought made him want to pummel something. Shit, where was a punching bag when you needed one? He decided he was going to string one up the first chance he got, if only to stop himself from doing something else he'd regret.

A low growl rose above the music and when Sloane looked his way and their gazes locked, Cade realized the sound had come from him. Her smile instantly faded, and she looked into her mug, staring at the contents like she expected a genie to appear any second. If it did, Cade had a feeling he knew exactly what she'd wish for.

"Good, you're up." The kid said. He disappeared from view and then reappeared, pinching the fallen half-cooked pancake between his thumb and forefinger. "Breakfast is ready."

He dropped the mangled pancake into the sink before plating two more and sliding the dish next to the empty place setting beside Sloane. The cocky bastard arched an eyebrow and smirked as if daring him to decline the invitation. Instead, Cade crossed the small space and sat down in front of his plate, returning the kid's knowing smile with a glare.

They ate in awkward silence as the radio blared on in the background, giving Cade the mother of all headaches. "Can you turn that off?"

"I like it," Sloane said.

"Do you even speak French?"

"Do you?"

Cade looked at her. "I've been to over twenty countries in seven years. What do you think?"

"Prove it," she said, bringing the mug to her lips. "Tell me what he's singing about."

While they were eating, the song had changed from the high-pitched, catchy tune the kid had butchered to the soft croon of a male vocalist. He cocked his head, listening for a second, then shook it.

"I thought you knew how to speak French," she said.

"I do."

"Then translate the song."

"No."

"Why not?"

Cade sighed. "He's singing about a woman."

"What about her?"

"Does it matter?"

Sloane shrugged and looked out the window above the kitchen sink, adopting an air of nonchalance that did nothing to hide the smug satisfaction on her face. Hell, he was going to regret this.

Cade shoved his plate away and shifted on his stool, angling his body toward hers. Their knees brushed, and he didn't miss the way she slid hers away as she crossed one leg over the other.

"He's singing about his lover."

Sloane dipped her chin. "What about her?"

"About how he had her and then lost her to someone else."

"Why?"

"Because he kept a secret that he shouldn't have."

Sloane's gaze softened as she swept a stray hair behind her ear. Her hair had been pin-straight when it was longer, but it curled at the shoulders now, likely from the humidity she'd encountered on her morning run. Cade had the sudden urge to touch the now-dark strands to see if they still felt the same as they had before.

"What was the secret?" She asked.

"He doesn't say."

"Does he tell her the truth?"

Cade let out a breath. "Yes, and she leaves him anyway."

"For lying to her?"

Cade nodded, not trusting himself to speak. Sloane's brow furrowed, and when she looked at him again, it was with an expression he didn't recognize, something cold and hard that gave him a chill.

"Good."

One word. That was all it took to make Cade wish he'd stayed in bed. The sound of a throat clearing brought him back to the present.

"Sooo," the kid said. "Should we…um…get to work?"

Cade swiveled on his stool again, trying to hide the fact that he'd forgotten the kid was there. But he was, *they* were, and this was France, not Lakehaven.

He nodded and forced himself into work mode. "Bring me up to speed."

The kid retrieved his laptop from under the counter and pushed their plates aside. "It will be better with visuals."

"For Christ's sake, I don't need a flowchart. Just give me the facts."

"Typical," Sloane muttered.

Cade stood. "If you want to sit through a PowerPoint presentation, be my guest," he said. "I'll let you know when Doyle's in custody."

The kid tapped a few keys and spun the laptop so Cade could see the screen. "This is Edmund Barnes. Well, it's Edmund Barnes II. Barnes Senior died twenty years ago."

Cade sat back down and stared at the image of a stout, bald man who looked to be in his early sixties. "This is the guy you said died of a heart attack?"

"That's the official story."

"But that's not what happened?"

"We don't think so," Sloane said. "Barnes Junior died in London ten days ago. We have information that places Doyle in the city at the same time."

"Information from whom?" Cade asked, the thought of Sloane pumping some lowlife for information not sitting well with him.

Sloane frowned. "Not important. What *is* important is that one item—an emerald—was missing from Barnes' private collection."

"Just because Doyle was in London at the time doesn't prove that he was the one who stole it or that he killed Barnes to get to it."

If they had that proof, Doyle would be in custody, and none of them would be here. He would be off on another mission and maybe so would Sloane. For the first time since he'd heard the name Jack Doyle, the thought of finishing what he'd started didn't bring Cade any comfort.

"No, it doesn't," Sloane said. "But it's convenient when you consider his connection to the other two jewels."

"What do you mean?"

Sloane looked at the kid and nodded, their silent conversation doing little to quell Cade's desire to punch something.

"There isn't much information about the emeralds from before 1945 when we began recovering items the Nazis stole during the war," the kid said. "Nobody claimed them, and Barnes Senior purchased them at auction." He pulled up another article, this time an obituary of a man with a long white beard and bald head that resembled his son's. "The stones were worth a small fortune back then but still didn't make a dent in Barnes' net worth." Cade sent him an inquisitive look, and the kid responded to his unasked question. "The Barnes men descended from a long line of shipbuilders and merchants dating back over a century. Not that Barnes Junior took any ownership of the family business."

"What did he do for a living?"

"He retired from his position as a history professor at Oxford almost three years ago," the kid said.

"Okay, so if one emerald went to Junior when his father died, what happened to the other two?"

"Barnes Senior donated one to the National Museum of Ireland and the other to the Victoria and Albert Museum in London. The one bound for Ireland never made it."

Cade glanced between Sloane and the kid. "Are you telling me you believe Jack Doyle stole that emerald?"

"Twenty years ago, Jack Doyle was eighteen years old and working for Harry Callahan, a small-time mobster in Dublin," Sloane said. "There's proof that Callahan's operation intercepted that shipment. A couple of his guys went down for it."

"But not Doyle?" Cade asked.

Sloane shook her head. "And the others didn't have the emerald in their possession. Doyle disappeared not long after that. He became a ghost until his mid-twenties when he started campaigning hard."

"Campaigning, how?"

"He took a page out of Harry's playbook and started granting favors. Then, he started cashing them in."

"It didn't hurt that he allied himself with some of the most well-known men and women in the States and abroad," the kid said. "We've seen him with actors, bankers, even senators. Doyle doesn't discriminate. As long as they have money and influence, they're worthy of his time."

The company he kept had protected Doyle so well that Cade hadn't even heard of him until last month. That was one hell of an operational model.

"And now we're supposed to believe that Doyle coincidentally arrived here in the same city where the third emerald ended up?" Sloane said. "It's obvious that he planned it. We just don't know why."

"Management transferred the third emerald from the Victoria and Albert Museum to *Le Centre de Feu* last week for an upcoming exhibit. The event they hired Elena to coordinate," the kid clarified. "Donations from the town's elite keep the museum up and running, and Luc Dubois is one of its most generous benefactors."

"In case you were wondering, Luc Dubois is Jack Doyle," Sloane said.

Cade rolled his eyes. "I got it. Just how much are the emeralds worth, anyway?"

The kid switched the image on the screen to one depicting all three together. "That can vary based on the color and clarity of the gems, but the estimated value of these is at least three million per stone."

"And we still don't have any idea who Doyle's buyer is?"

"Not yet," Sloane said. "But Gig and I are going to research the list of the charity benefit attendees this week."

The event where Sloane would make her undercover debut. Cade looked at her, noticing for the first time that something had changed since she'd started talking about the case. For one, she wasn't staring daggers at him like she'd been before. Now her eyes were bright, her cheeks flushed, and she looked like she was ready to jump out of her seat and go for another run. She wasn't nervous at all. She was…excited.

It was then that Cade realized two things. One, Sloane Easton was even more beautiful than he remembered, and, two, he really needed to leave.

Now.

He stood and pushed back from the table so abruptly that their dishes clattered on the counter.

"Where are you going?" Sloane asked.

"Into town."

"Why?"

"Doyle might have paid a visit to one of the local jewelers," he said, as if it was entirely plausible a career criminal like Doyle would make such an obvious error in judgment. "Someone might know something."

"I'll go with you," Sloane said.

"No!" Sloane paused halfway out of her chair. "You…uh… shouldn't be seen in town before Friday."

"He's right," the kid agreed, and Cade looked at him in surprise. "Elena Caldwell can arrive early for the event, but not five days early. It's best if you stay out of sight for now."

Cade held his breath and waited for Sloane to put up a fight, but she slumped back down in her chair. "Fine."

Any gratitude he'd felt for the kid immediately fled in the wake of Sloane's agreement. If there had been a time when Sloane had done what he'd asked, Cade couldn't remember it. Jealousy surged as the kid looked at him and nodded once like they'd made some kind of pact.

I know what you want the look seemed to say, *Sloane will be safe*. The problem was Cade didn't know whether that look meant the kid would keep her safe from Doyle or from him.

"Let me know what you find out," Sloane said in a tone that left no room for argument.

And even though Cade had plenty of arguments, he turned and left without voicing a single one.

9

Then

Cade looked out at the Eastons' backyard, seeing everything and nothing at the same time. He didn't notice the tire swing that hung from the tallest tree or the fence that wrapped around the yard, but he knew they were there. Just like he knew his father wasn't.

Shingles cut into his back as he leaned against the house, shifting position to slide both legs out in front of him on the deck. He took a drag from his cigarette and listened to the voices of the mourners Faye had invited to her home drifting to him from an open window.

Such a shame…

He wasn't ever the same after…

That poor boy…

Except he wasn't a boy anymore. At least his dad had waited until Cade was legal to croak. He'd narrowly avoided being placed in foster care by a few months. That was something. Or, it would be once Cade could bring himself to summon the appropriate amount of gratitude for such a selfless act.

Today wasn't that day.

The back door swung open, and Sloane emerged from the house dressed in the same sleeveless black dress she'd worn to the funeral. When she saw him, she moved to his side and sat next to him, pulling her knees up to her chest. "I'm sorry about your dad."

"He was a bastard."

"Maybe, but he was still your dad."

Cade shrugged, and Sloane waved a hand in front of her face, crinkling her nose as she eyed his cigarette with distaste. He rolled his eyes but stubbed it out anyway, knowing she'd tell Beck if he didn't. The two of them had been riding him hard over the habit for months.

"Do you have any memories of your dad?"

Cade scoffed. "Plenty."

"I mean, from before."

"Not really."

"Okay."

They sat in silence for a while, and it was the silence that helped him remember.

"There was one time Dad took me to the shop with him. He did that a lot when Mom was…not feeling well." Cade recalled those dark, early mornings when his mother couldn't get out of bed. Sometimes, she was still there when they returned in the evening, and they would find the breakfast dishes they'd used that morning still in the sink. "There was this car," Cade said, the image of an old Mustang with original paint forming in his mind. "I'd never seen it before, but someone must have hired Dad to rebuild the engine because there were parts scattered everywhere."

"Sounds like a mess," Sloane said.

"It was. I mean, it would have been for someone who didn't know what he was doing."

"Did he fix it?"

"We both did. I'd spent enough time at the shop by then to know what some parts were, so he let me help." Cade remembered how his father had smiled every time he named a part correctly, pride shining in his eyes. "We spent all day working on that car." And when they'd returned home to find his mom still in bed, his dad made them both pancakes for dinner. "It was a good day."

"How old were you?"

"Five." He only remembered that because his mom had left that same year. He'd been five years old when he woke in the morning to find his father still in bed that time. Alone.

"It's okay, you know."

"What is?"

"To be angry."

"I'm not angry," Cade snapped.

"Right. Well, if you *were* angry, it would be a good thing."

"I doubt that." At no time in his life so far had being angry resulted in anything good.

"Mom says being angry is better than feeling nothing."

"Why?"

"She says it takes more energy to feel nothing."

"That doesn't make sense."

"It's what she said," Sloane said as if everything her mother said made sense. Not that Cade could argue that fact, as everything out of Faye's mouth pretty much did. "She also said you can love someone and still be angry with them at the same time."

Cade froze. It had taken a while, but he'd thought he'd come to terms with the man Tom Foster had become. It didn't even surprise him when he found his dad in his favorite chair one morning a week ago, gripping a Bud like it was an anchor between this world and the next. Ghosts lived in the shadows, and his father had been a shadow of the man he'd once been.

"He gave up," Cade said.

How else could he explain how his father had let him down by making nothing but shitty choices instead of one right one? How could he tell her that what he felt wasn't anger but rage? Rage that wasn't directed at his dad, but at himself for loving him, anyway.

"But *you* didn't. You're still here."

Cade looked at his best friend's sister. He expected to see confusion, or worse, pity. She was only fifteen, and fifteen-year-olds didn't understand this stuff.

But he saw neither of those things. Instead, he noticed that her hair, which had been down for the funeral, was now pulled back into a loose braid that draped over one shoulder. The odd shade of peach that stained her lips made him wonder if she had rummaged through her mother's makeup just for him. Not for him, he scolded himself. For the occasion. For the occasion of his father's funeral.

"I am," he said, more aware of his presence—and hers—than he'd been all day.

She nodded, and it reminded Cade of the satisfactory gesture Faye made every time she sampled a good batch of cookies made from a new recipe. Then she glanced at the remnants of his cigarette. "You better get rid of that cancer stick before Mom sees it."

He smirked. "Did you just school me, Bullet Easton?"

Her cheeks pinked, and his insides flooded with warmth as she slapped him on the thigh and folded her arms over her chest, feigning annoyance. He nudged her with his shoulder, calm settling over him as he let his head loll back against the house.

"You can stay here for a while, you know. Mom won't mind."

"I know."

"Will you?"

He sighed. "I don't know."

He really didn't know. Until now, he hadn't thought about what would come next. It was his senior year. In two months, he and Beck would graduate, and not long after that, Beck would leave for a state college a couple of hours away. Cade had no plans other than to continue working at Old Man Wilson's garage. His father's business was long gone, but Wilson had taken him in two years ago when he was old enough to work, and Cade was grateful.

"You could go to school, too," Sloane said.

"Maybe."

"It's a good idea."

"Why? Because you thought of it?"

She punched him in the arm. "I'm serious."

"So am I."

"You always do that."

"Do what?"

"Make jokes to avoid thinking about something important."

He frowned. "No, I don't."

She eyed him, seeming to debate with herself before shaking her head. "Never mind. Just promise me you'll think about it, okay?" He nodded. "That's not a promise." She waited, one eyebrow lifted in a silent standoff.

"Fine. I promise."

He had a little money saved. Not much, but he supposed he didn't have to stop working if he went. He just wasn't sure if school was for him.

Sloane rose to her feet. "I better get back in there and save Beck from your Great Aunt Tilda before she stuffs him with more pie."

"I don't have a Great Aunt Tilda."

Sloane looked down at him, the sun behind her casting a shadow over her white-blonde hair and creating a halo effect that would make anyone a believer. Even him. "Would you know if you did?"

"No."

"Thought so," Sloane said, turning away from him. "Coming?"

"In a minute." She nodded and walked across the deck. The back door squeaked open, and he reminded himself to pick up some WD-40 on his way home. "Hey Bullet?" She looked at him expectantly, and he felt a twinge of something deep in his chest at having her complete, undivided attention, even for a minute. "Thanks."

It was lame, but it was all he had. She flashed him a smile, her cheeks once again flushing pink. By the time she disappeared inside, Cade had already decided that today was as good a day as any to quit smoking.

10

"I need some air."

Gig looked up from his computer screen. "We're outside."

Sloane glanced around at the expansive yard with its smattering of lemon trees swaying in the afternoon breeze. The sun sat high in a cloudless sky, warming the surface of the lap pool and the tops of their heads. The villa and property surrounding it were more beautiful than most five-star resorts, but they'd been in deep research mode for four days, and Sloane couldn't spend one more minute in her gilded cage.

"I mean, I need a break," she said as she stood and walked through the back door into the kitchen.

Gig followed her. "Where are you going?"

"Out."

"I don't think that's a good idea."

"I do," she said, grabbing her crossbody bag from the table in the entryway before moving to the door. It suddenly swung open, and Sloane leaped back into Gig's chest, her heel stomping hard on his foot.

"Ouch," Gig said as his arms automatically circled her waist to steady her.

"Sorry."

"Are you okay?"

She turned her head sideways to look at him and fluttered her eyelashes. "My hero."

Gig flushed crimson, and she patted his cheek, laughing when he wrinkled his nose to reposition his glasses on his face.

The sound of a throat clearing had them both turning toward the doorway, where Cade loomed, his sudden presence making Sloane's pulse spike. His obsidian eyes flashed behind thick, dark lashes as he glared over her shoulder like a bull ready to charge. Gig's arm disappeared from around her waist, and she was on her own again, a matador facing fury.

"Where did you go?" She asked.

"Out."

Right. It had been like that all week. She'd ask Cade where he was going or where he'd been, and he'd respond the same way. They stayed in their separate corners of the villa and avoided each other while Gig bounced between them like a human ping-pong ball. When Cade returned from wherever he went during the day, the two of them disappeared into one of the back bedrooms to hold their secret boys' club meetings.

"Did you do that…thing?" Gig asked.

Sloane frowned. "What *thing*?" When neither of them spoke, she looked at Cade. "If it involves the job, I need to know." Silence. "Fine. You two have fun. I'll be back later."

She tried to move past him, but Cade blocked her path, and suddenly, they were chest to chest, his heat enveloping her, the air thick and heavy between them.

She lifted her chin. "Get. Out. Of. My. Way."

He watched her lips as she spoke, and frustration, annoyance, and something else settled low in her belly. She knew what it was. The feeling was as familiar to her as her old Lions sweatshirt, *his* sweatshirt, and she didn't want to feel it. Not for this man. Not anymore.

"Go with her," Cade said over her shoulder, though his eyes remained on her. "Let me know if there's trouble."

"Okay," Gig said.

Sloane huffed. "I don't need a chaperone."

"I wasn't asking," Cade said before slipping past them into the house, disappearing like he'd never been there at all.

***

Two hours later, Sloane and Gig sat side by side on a bench a safe distance from the water, snacking on pastries they'd picked up at a local patisserie. One reason for going into town, her dress for the charity benefit, sat folded on the seat between them in a garment bag. The other reason had been to put as much distance between herself and Cade as possible.

This was as good a place to do that as any. Sloane had been to Paris once on a job for Albright, but this part of France couldn't compare. Paris was beautiful, but it was still a city. Here, the sun filtered through the clouds, reflecting off the water and blanketing everything in soft focus. It was mesmerizing and alluring, almost ethereal. She understood now why celebrities flocked to the area every summer, though its appeal was about more than just the weather. It was the feeling it elicited of being suspended in a place and time that was so different from your own reality that you never wanted to leave. It was a fantasy, though. One pinprick and your entire world could cease to exist.

"So, are you ever going to tell me how you know the legendary Cade Foster?"

Sloane groaned. "He's not legendary."

"He's been involved in more successful operations than I have pairs of socks."

She couldn't even deny it. The two of them had learned of the operations Cade and Beck had been involved in during training. Impressive was the word Gig had used, but she'd found it irritating—especially after their instructors had used their tactics as shining examples of what to do in less-than-ideal situations.

"I told you he was Beck's partner," she said.

"Yes, but you conveniently left out the fact that you two have a history."

Sloane wrapped up the rest of her croissant and shoved it back into her bag. So much for her appetite. "We used to know each other."

"Know each other like you passed him on the street one day or like you used to date?"

Sloane whipped her head in Gig's direction. "What makes you think we used to date?"

"Uh, you mean other than the air in any room the two of you are in together rising to the temperature of the Amazon rainforest?"

"It does not."

"Okay, well, how about the fact that every time I touch you, he looks at me like he's contemplating the best way to kill me and where to hide my body at the same time?"

"That's not true."

Gig threw her a look. "Fine. You can continue to live in denial after you tell me how you know Cade Foster."

Sloane sighed. "We're from the same hometown."

"Excuse me?"

The half-croissant she'd just eaten crept up the back of her throat. "He is…was…Beck's best friend."

"Are you telling me you are *friends* with Cade Foster, superspy?"

"He wasn't a spy when we met."

"But he's still a friend of yours."

"No," Sloane snapped, causing them both to jump. "We're not friends. We're…nothing."

"Really? It doesn't seem that way to me."

"Nobody asked you."

Gig held up both hands, looking affronted. "Okay, then. Just forget I mentioned it, I guess." He slumped back on the bench and stared out at the water.

God, what was wrong with her? Cade had materialized out of thin air barely one week ago, and she was already acting like a crazy person. "Shit, I'm sorry." She shifted in her seat, pulling one leg under her as she faced him. "Cade and I were close growing up. All three of us were."

Gig didn't look at her, but she could tell by the way he crossed his arms over his chest and angled toward her he was listening.

"There was a time when I thought maybe Cade and I…" she trailed off, shaking her head. She didn't want to think about that night. It had changed everything for her, but just for her. "Anyway, it didn't happen. And then Beck died, and Cade just disappeared."

Sloane would never forget the day she and her mother had learned of Beck's death. She'd been grading papers at her mother's kitchen table when Faye answered the phone. Her mother had made an in-human sound, one that Sloane hoped she'd never have to hear again. She'd collapsed while holding the phone, and Sloane had rushed to hold her up, taking the receiver and listening to words she didn't want to believe could be real.

Gig looked at her. "What do you mean he disappeared?"

"He didn't call or come home. He even missed the funeral. We tried to reach him, but he disconnected his phone." She thought nothing could feel worse than burying her brother, but that came close.

Gig's expression morphed from one of curiosity to outrage on her behalf. "Asshole."

Despite her mood, Sloane smiled. "I don't disagree."

"You never told me what happened to your brother."

His tone was soft and careful, but Sloane still blanched at the question. "That's because I don't know."

"What do you mean?"

"I don't know what happened to Beck. After it happened, nobody told us anything. It wasn't until I joined Albright's unit that I even found out Cade was involved."

Gig's eyes widened. "He was?"

She nodded. "They were partners, so I guess I should have assumed they were together that day, but I didn't."

She hadn't realized until then that she'd been holding on to the hope that it was grief keeping Cade away and not that he was involved. With that, and the fact that he'd never come to her with the truth, the last thread holding together their tattered relationship snapped. She still didn't have the clearance to view the entire report, but she knew all she needed to know.

"And now?" Gig asked.

"Now, what?"

"Is he still refusing to tell you what happened?"

"I haven't asked."

Gig gave her an incredulous look. "Why not?"

"Because it doesn't matter." She knew Cade. If he'd wanted to tell her, not her security clearance or even a direct order from Albright to keep quiet could have stopped him. But Cade had chosen silence over her. And because of that, he wasn't the man she thought he was. "Cade made his choice, and I made mine."

She'd chosen this life to finish what Beck started. She wouldn't let Cade or the past derail her from bringing Doyle to justice.

"Are you sure?" Gig asked, looking unconvinced. "The two of you obviously have unfinished business."

"We do," Sloane said. "And his name is Jack Doyle." She stood from the bench and grabbed the garment bag. "Come on, let's go."

"Right." Gig stood, too, trashing their pastry bags in a nearby bin. "Back to work, then?"

"Back to work," Sloane repeated.

It was the work she needed to focus on. There was no longer anything she wanted or needed from Cade Foster.

11

Then

"Come on, Sis. Wake up."

Sloane rolled over in her sleeping bag and squinted at Beck's blurry form at the opening of her tent. "What time is it?"

"Around one."

She groaned. "Unless you're about to tell me a bear attacked the camp, I'm not coming out of this tent until morning."

"It is morning."

Sloane threw a pillow at him. He caught it and tossed it back, nailing her in the face. "Hey!"

"Get dressed. I want to show you something."

Sloane got up from her sleeping bag and grabbed a sweatshirt and pants, even though she doubted she'd be able to see anything in the dark woods at night. Turning her back to the tent's opening, she put on the pants and had just pulled her arms into her shirt sleeves when she heard a noise behind her. She jumped at least three feet and turned in an ungraceful pirouette to find Cade inside her tent.

"Dammit, Cade," she said. "What the hell?"

He held up two hands. "Sorry, I just…" he paused, his gaze traveling down to where she hugged her shirt to her chest. "Beck wanted me to get you."

Sloane felt heat creep up the back of her neck as she hurriedly donned the shirt. "He wanted you to stalk my tent like some kind of creeper?"

He frowned. "What? No, I just—"

"Let's go," she mumbled as she brushed past him through the tent's opening.

This was the last thing she needed after the night she'd had. The worst part was that she didn't even know exactly what about the night had irritated her enough to feel murderous about being woken up in the middle of it. It was their group of friends' yearly camping trip, a weekend Sloane looked forward to every spring. Beck had come home from college for the weekend, and Cade had even crawled out of whatever hole he'd been living in for the last several months to join them. He visited often but only to see her mom while Sloane was at school, which annoyed her.

Of course, she found other things annoying, too. Like Beck's not-so-scary ghost stories or Summer Sanchez sneaking into Cade's tent when she thought nobody was looking. Gross.

"Over here," Beck whisper-hissed from the other side of camp.

She walked toward the shadowy figure at the edge of the camp, not sure why Beck bothered to keep his voice down when everyone else was likely drunk or passed out. Everyone except for her and, of course, Cade. Her, because Beck would have killed anyone who dared give his sister alcohol, and Cade, because he never touched the stuff. It was possible, however, that Beck was drunk, which didn't make her feel any better about following him into the woods.

Sloane marched up to him and stopped short, sighing when Cade nearly crashed into her from behind. "Okay, we're here. What's the big emergency?"

Beck grinned, his teeth glowing in the moonlight. "Follow me," he said before ducking into the woods. A couple of seconds later, Sloane heard a click, and light shone a few feet down the path.

"At least he brought a flashlight," Cade muttered.

Sloane shot him a glare before disappearing into the brush herself. She tried to follow the light, but the glow became fainter the further Beck walked.

"*Beck*," she hissed.

She wasn't afraid of waking the camp, but she *was* afraid of waking whatever slumbered in the woods. She'd only been kidding about the bear attack, but now she thought it was entirely possible one would eat her by the time the night was over. Beck obviously didn't hear her because the light ahead suddenly disappeared, plunging both her and Cade into darkness.

Just great.

Sloane took another step, the toe of her sneaker catching under a root. She flailed, her arms automatically reaching out to brace her impending fall, just as a muscular arm caught her around her middle and hauled her back into a hard chest.

"Careful," Cade said, his hot breath tickling her ear.

Goosebumps rose on her skin, and she froze for an instant before shrugging out of his hold. "I got it," she said. Light appeared at her feet, and she whirled to find Cade holding his cell phone open, his face illuminated by the backlight. "What are you doing?"

"What does it look like?"

"I don't need that."

"So, I should wait until the next time you almost face-plant before turning it on?"

Instead of responding, Sloane turned and stomped in the direction Beck had gone. She was glad she'd thought to put on a sweatshirt. Not only was the late April air cooler by the lake, but the path was dense. Branches jutted in all directions, the edges scraping her sleeves and poking her through the fabric. Cade followed close behind, keeping pace and occasionally reaching ahead of her to swipe the branches away before they could scratch her face.

That was annoying, too.

Eventually, they came to an intersection. Sloane stopped in the middle and spun in a slow circle. Beck was nowhere to be found, and they were so deep in the woods now that she didn't dare call for him. Defeated, she plopped down and sat in the dirt.

"I wouldn't do that if I were you," Cade said.

"Do you have a better idea?"

"Yup. And it involves not getting a snakebite on the ass."

Sloane jumped up so fast she was pretty sure she cleared the air. Cade, apparently not at all worried about waking any woodland creatures, roared with laughter.

"Jerk." She spun and started walking in any direction. It didn't matter where just as long as it was far enough away from Cade Foster.

"Hey, wait," Cade said. He caught up to her and caught her by the elbow, spinning her to face him. "I'm sorry, okay? I didn't mean that. But you've been weird all night."

"No, I haven't."

"You're obviously pissed at me."

Sloane shrugged him off. "Of course I have to be because the world revolves around you, right?"

"Ouch." He lifted his phone so he could get a better look at her, but she swiped his hand away. "Okay," he said. "What's your problem?"

"Mom said you came by the other day."

"I dropped off the van."

Faye Easton had been driving the same van since Sloane was still in a car seat. It was a deathtrap, but Mom refused to part with it. Her compromise was letting Cade pick it up and drive it to Wilson's garage every few months for a "tune-up."

"What part did you replace this time?"

Even in the dark, she could see his smirk. "The engine."

"You know she's going to figure it out, right?"

"She hasn't so far."

Beck hadn't figured it out either, which was likely why Cade still did it. Her brother had a thing about Cade doing favors for their family, so he usually did them in secret.

"You were gone before I got home from school."

Cade cocked his head to the left like he was listening for the crunch of leaves that signaled the approach of a wild animal. Luckily, it was quiet. "I had to get back to work."

Sloane pursed her lips. Old Man Wilson was half-blind, which was part of the reason he'd hired Cade. He could barely see two feet in front of his face, let alone the only hanging wall clock tucked into the far corner of the garage. "You could have stayed longer."

"That doesn't mean I should have."

"So, you'll replace parts in Mom's van without her permission, but you can't be five minutes late for work?" That was the thing about Cade. He did things that made little sense to anyone else but him and, somehow, rarely got in trouble for it.

It was annoying.

"Is that what you're upset about? That I saw your mom and not you?"

"That's not the *only* reason."

"What are the other reasons?"

"I don't know..." she hedged, not at all happy with the direction of their conversation.

"Didn't you tell me you wanted to be a teacher?"

"So?"

"How do you expect to communicate with kids if you can't talk to adults?"

"You mean, like you talk to your girlfriend?"

Cade jerked back. "I don't have a girlfriend. Wait, do you mean Summer?" He laughed. "Summer isn't my girlfriend."

"So, she's a friend with benefits, then?"

"Jesus, Bullet. Where did you hear that?"

Sloane rolled her eyes. "I don't live under a rock."

"You're only sixteen."

"And I have eyes. You two were all over each other at the campfire."

"Correction. *She* was all over *me*."

"Whatever."

"Wait," Cade said, stepping closer. He hovered over her, and she held her breath as he scanned her features in the dark. "Are you jealous?"

"What? No!"

"Are you sure?"

"Yes."

"Really?"

"Yes!"

"I don't believe you."

He was playing with her and despite what she'd said about not living under a rock, she very much wanted to crawl under one right now. Still, she wasn't about to let him win. "Believe what you want. It's true."

In the moonlight, she saw him blink, his lashes fluttering closed before the whites of his eyes appeared again. He inched closer still, and Sloane froze as their feet met, toe-to-toe. The overgrowth was too dense where they were for any kind of breeze to filter through, but even if it had, she wasn't sure she would feel it. The surrounding sounds faded away, replaced by the roaring in her ears.

"You know what I think?"

His voice was low and indistinct, and Sloane could tell he was no longer smiling. Her stomach flipped as awareness flooded her system, rooting her to the ground.

"What?" she whispered, licking her lips as if doing so could ease the dryness in her throat.

"I—"

They both jumped back as Beck came barreling out of the woods to their left. "Seriously, guys," he said, shining the flashlight in their faces. "Can you at least try to keep up? Mom'll kill me if either of you gets eaten by a wolf."

And she'd thought she only had to be afraid of bears. She looked at Cade, but he was staring at the ground, and Sloane wondered if he'd even heard what Beck said. A second later, Beck disappeared through the brush, and Sloane hurried after him, aware of the crunch of leaves and branches behind her as Cade followed them both.

"It's just up here," Beck said, sounding excited.

Sloane wasn't excited. Right now, she just felt…odd and confused. It had almost seemed like Cade had been about to… but no, that wasn't right. She must have misread the situation. Cade was Beck's best friend. She'd only meant to tell him she missed him, that with her brother away at school, she was lonely and missed just hanging out like they used to. But then she'd mentioned Summer. Why had she done that? Sloane had never cared much for the girls Cade spent time with, but he was nineteen and old enough to date whomever he wanted. What did it matter? Why did any of this matter?

Lack of sleep. That was it. After their hike into the middle of nowhere, Sloane was going to crawl back into her sleeping bag and forget all of it.

With renewed determination, Sloane walked faster. The once-level ground suddenly turned steep, and she climbed higher, following Beck and the strip of light that darted over the ground. The sooner they got to their destination, the sooner she could go back to bed. Tomorrow, everything would make sense.

After a few more feet, she stepped into a clearing, her sneakers landing on smooth, hard stone.

And then, she froze.

They were on a ledge overlooking the lake with water surrounding them on three sides. Beck threw open his arms and whooped, the sound carrying into the night. He turned to her just as she felt Cade's presence on the rock behind her.

"Check this out, man," he said, gripping Cade by the shoulder. "Isn't this view incredible?"

Cade murmured his agreement, but Sloane stayed silent. How could she tell Beck she thought the view was incredible if she couldn't see it? She'd shut her eyes the instant she'd seen where they were and had kept them closed. They were up high, but it wasn't the elevation that made her suck in deep lungfuls of air as she tried to ward off the nausea that engulfed her.

"You can't see a view like this back at camp," Beck said.

No, you couldn't, and that was exactly why Sloane liked where they camped. It was far enough from the lake that she didn't run into it every time she ventured down an unfamiliar path. She'd been lucky that she had avoided joining the group on their excursions down to the beach, begging off to read in her tent or take a nap. Apparently, her luck had run out.

Sloane knew she should tell Beck, but she couldn't. Nobody knew. She'd never told a single soul about her fear. How could she when it was so ridiculous? It wasn't like she was afraid of getting wet. She took showers and didn't run for cover when it rained. It was the uncertainty of open water that gave her nightmares. Oceans, lakes, rivers, even swimming pools were off-limits. Large bodies of water that, at any moment, could swallow a person whole.

Beck said something else, but she couldn't hear what it was over the buzzing in her ears. Crap. She needed to get off this rock. She needed—

A hand suddenly closed over hers, fingers entwining with her own. It squeezed, and she squeezed back, gripping it so hard it had to hurt. And still, the hand, Cade's hand, remained where it was, infusing warmth into her shockingly cold skin. Slowly, Sloane opened her eyes and what she saw nearly took her breath away.

The stars. Hundreds of them floated in space around the fullest, most iridescent moon she'd ever seen. She almost reached out to touch it, believing she could. The water's surface, like spilled ink, glistened in the soft glow of the moonlight, tiny ripples gently lapping at the edge of the rock where they stood. Sloane could just barely make out the beach across the water and the outline of trees that stood vigil over it like they likely had for hundreds of years. It was a scene that no photograph could ever do justice, the kind you just had to see to believe.

Cade squeezed her hand again, and she tore her gaze away from the view to meet his gaze. Worry and confusion crossed his face, mixing with something she couldn't name, but that made her heart skip. Cade, who knew nothing of her fear, understood what she needed without having to ask. He might not always do the right thing, but he would do right by her—even when she acted like an ass in the woods in the middle of the night.

She smiled and watched as the crease embedded in Cade's forehead smoothed. He let out a ragged breath, and she followed suit, finally feeling like herself for the first time all weekend.

Beck came around to her other side, hooking an arm around her neck and pulling her into him. He smelled like the woods and like Beck, his steady presence beside her like a soothing balm to her soul.

"What do you think?" Beck asked her. "Was it worth waking up for?"

She looked at Cade and replied with absolute sincerity. "Yes."

It was worth it.

12

Cade tugged at the bowtie around his neck as he paced the villa's entryway. "Report."

"Quadrants one through four are clear."

"And the entrance?"

The kid looked up at him from his cross-legged position on the floor. "I'm not an idiot."

"What about the—"

"Yes."

"You don't even know what I was going to say."

"You were going to ask if we had a view of the outside."

"No, I wasn't," Cade lied.

"The estate's ballroom has an accessible veranda that I can also see. All cameras are online, and I've been able to gain access to all of them. It wasn't even that hard."

"That's what worries me," Cade muttered.

Part of him knew he should be relieved that they hadn't run into any issues hacking into event security. It likely meant Doyle wasn't expecting trouble, which gave them the upper hand, the exact position Cade wanted to be in going into tonight. But something about it just seemed too easy. A feeling of dread had taken up residence in his gut the minute he'd woken that morning. If he didn't think Albright would give him hell for it, he'd abort tonight's mission, but he didn't stand a chance of winning that battle. Not with Albright or Sloane.

"Are you going to tell me why we needed two extra earpieces?" The kid asked.

"Are you going to stop being a pain in my ass?"

"Not likely."

"Then, no." The kid continued to stare, waiting him out, until finally, Cade sighed. "You'll find out soon enough. Just keep a close eye on quadrant three."

"Aye, aye, Captain."

Cade wanted to snap at him to stop it with the sarcasm, but he didn't. He knew what the kid's problem was. It had taken him all of two seconds to sense the change in him when he and Sloane had returned from their excursion the previous afternoon. His playful banter had turned scornful, and his attitude wasn't much better, which meant Bullet had told him. Just how much she'd told him was anyone's guess, but Cade didn't think he wanted to know.

What he *did* want to know was why she'd waited so long to say something. Just how long had they been together? Unfortunately, the kid wasn't talking. Not about Sloane, anyway. That hadn't surprised him, but instead of refusing to work with him like Cade expected, the kid had stayed awake until two in the morning with him, running through worst-case scenarios without complaint, something he and Beck had never done.

Maybe if they had…

Cade shook his head. He and Beck had taken a chance that day, but he wouldn't take any more. Not with Bullet's life. He resumed his pacing, glancing up the stairs every time he passed them, something that didn't go unnoticed by his shadow.

"Relax," the kid said. "She'll be down when she's ready."

"We're late."

"There's plenty of time."

Plenty of time for all their carefully laid plans to go up in flames. "I like to be early."

"You haven't spent much time waiting on women, have you?"

Cade paused his steps. "Have *you?*"

Before the kid could respond, a flash of movement at the top of the stairs caught Cade's attention. He turned, immediately starting a count back from ten. His therapist had told him that counting breaths could help ward off an attack. Nobody had said anything about what to do if he couldn't breathe in the first place.

She descended the stairs slowly in a gown the color of red wine and sin, its bodice hugging her waist and hips before billowing in layers to the floor. Her hair was blonde again and pinned up on one side, revealing an unholy amount of golden skin at the neck and collarbone and a single ribbon of fabric draped over one shoulder like an invitation.

Cade swallowed hard, unable to speak. Unfortunately for him, that was never a problem for Bullet.

"Why are you dressed like that?" She said, frowning at him with lips painted the same ruby red as her dress.

"You didn't think you were going alone, did you?"

"Yes," Sloane said, reaching the last step. "I am."

She crossed to the table by the door and dropped her purse on its surface before lifting the hem of her dress. Bending at the waist, she reached for one barely-there strap attached to gold sandals, swearing under her breath when the dress restricted her movement. Something about the dirty word passing through perfectly made-up lips and the way her palms slid over the smooth skin of her shin had Cade holding back a groan.

The kid jumped to action, scrambling to his knees at her feet like some kind of knight in shining armor. He slid the wayward strap back into place, and she smiled down at him.

Cade gritted his teeth. "I'm going with you."

"No, you're not."

"It's not up for discussion."

There was a swish of fabric, and then she was in front of him, eyes flashing copper like a spark triggered by a flint. "I can take care of myself."

Her chest was just inches from his. Lately, the only time she ever got that close to him was when she was angry. Maybe it was the way she smelled, like mist after rain, mixed with a hint of the lavender that seemed to cling to everything at the villa, or maybe it was just that damned dress, but suddenly Cade didn't care. He didn't care why she was there, only that she was standing in front of him now.

Safe.

A deep, honey-blonde wave fell onto one cheek and without thinking, he reached up to tuck it behind her ear. She flinched at the contact and he dropped his arm, shoving both hands in his pockets. "You dyed it back."

She shrugged. "Doyle likes blondes."

Ten, nine, eight…

"Well, I dig it," the kid said, breaking the awkward silence. "You look like a combination of Marilyn and Julia." They both looked at him. "Monroe and Roberts?"

"Thanks," Sloane said.

Cade glanced at his watch and held out his hand to the kid, who dropped a few devices onto his palm. He gave one to Sloane, and she slid it into her ear.

"Testing," she said into the microphone.

"Loud and clear," the kid said into his own.

"I guess it's time."

Time.

Cade wished he could fast-forward to a time when all this was over or rewind to when he and Beck stood outside Albright's office, ready to start the rest of their lives. But since he couldn't do either, he looked at Sloane. "Ready?"

"Ready," she said.

13

When Sloane was in college, she took an economics class with a professor who had built a successful career in sales.

"Opportunity lies in leveraging demand," he'd said in one of his lectures. "Get to know what your customers want and need. If you engage them at the right time and in the right circumstances, you're golden."

To her, it sounded a lot more like luck than skill, but he wasn't wrong. Sales was a numbers game, but Sloane knew it could also inflate the ego and warp a person's sense of value. You couldn't buy a positive sense of self-worth. Accumulating material possessions didn't guarantee happiness and sometimes, the more lavish the surroundings, the higher the probability someone had something to hide. Just because something looked pretty on the outside didn't mean it wasn't rotten on the inside.

At least, that was what Sloane reminded herself when she walked into the charity benefit that evening. The pristine ballroom dripped with detailed extravagance. Arched entryways led into an expansive space with sweeping views of the grounds. Art or tapestries hung on every available wall, and light from a dozen crystal chandeliers reflected off a marble floor the color of bleached driftwood. Hushed voices and laughter echoed in the room, overlaid by soft music played by a live band tucked into the corner. In place of a formal dinner, servers shuffled past in tuxedos and tails carrying hors d'oeuvres on silver platters.

"Impressive, isn't it?" Gig said in her ear.

"Something like that," Sloane murmured as she swiped a glass of champagne from a passing server's tray.

Only a man like Jack Doyle could create such an epic distraction. The museum had sponsored the event, but as Luc Dubois had signed almost every vendor's statement, it was entirely possible he'd also chosen the venue.

"Remember," Cade said in her ear. "We mingle, Elena makes contact, and then we're out. No deviations. Got it?"

"Roger that," Gig said.

"Bullet?"

"Right," she agreed before downing half the champagne.

If she wanted to get to Doyle tonight, she'd have to do more than just make contact. Debating that with Cade at the moment, though, seemed ill-advised. Instead, she made one round around the ballroom, then a second, stopping once at the table set up along the far wall to peek at the items up for auction. A ski weekend in the Alps, a spa retreat for two, a private wine tasting in Bordeaux—all gifts for the rich and richer. There were also complimentary tickets to the upcoming exhibit at *Le Centre de Feu*.

Eventually, she sidled up to the bar. "Status?"

"Nada," Gig replied.

Sloane tamped down her impatience and shook her nearly empty glass at the bartender. He nodded but then walked to the other end of the bar to help another customer.

"Are you sure that's a good idea?" Cade said.

Instead of responding, she slid her middle finger up the length of her glass and swallowed the last of her champagne. She heard a grunt and then silence as they settled in to wait. A minute later, the couple next to her left and a regal woman with coifed silver hair wrapped in a French twist joined her at the bar. She sighed, her sleek gold gown rustling as she turned to glance at the dance floor.

"I wish they would play something a bit more lively."

She said it in English, but her accent was so strong it took Sloane a minute to understand the words. "I'm almost afraid to find out what would happen if they did."

The woman smiled, her pale gray eyes sparking with interest. "You're American."

"Guilty."

She faced the bar, and Sloane was about to tell her not to bother when the bartender immediately appeared in front of them. He bowed in deference to the woman, who slipped easily into her native tongue to order a drink before glancing expectantly at Sloane.

"I'll have another," she said, placing her empty glass on the bar. The bartender was gone in a flash, heading to the other end to open a fresh bottle even though there were already a few open. Sloane lifted an eyebrow at her companion. "Friend of yours?"

"You could say that. Of course, everyone here is a friend of *Le Centre de Feu*." She held out a hand. "Celeste Armand."

"Your new boss," Gig said into her ear.

Right. *Elena's* boss and also the museum's director. Sloane returned the smile and took the woman's hand.

"Madame Armand, it's a pleasure. It seems I won't have to wait until Monday to make your acquaintance, after all." When the woman glanced at her, confused, Sloane continued. "I'm Elena Caldwell."

"The new curator. How lovely," Celeste said politely as the bartender returned with their drinks. "The agency wasn't able to confirm your arrival date."

"My apologies. I wasn't sure if I'd be arriving early until just this afternoon."

She waved a hand. "I'm sure the information is sitting in my email."

"On it," Gig said in Sloane's ear, followed by the clicking of keys.

"Thank you again for the opportunity, Madame."

"Celeste, *s'il vous plaît*. We are going to be working closely together, after all." Her expression remained pleasant but assessing. "Is this your first visit to France?"

"It's my first visit to Nice," Sloane said, vaguely, before gesturing to the wall of glass that separated the ballroom from the veranda. "The grounds are lovely. Have you been here before?"

Celeste turned to the dance floor, where a few couples were already dancing. "Oh yes, many times. It's owned by one of our most distinguished benefactors. I'm sure you'll meet him soon. Since you'll be working at the museum, I mean." She looked at Sloane, her eyes flashing with something Sloane couldn't read before she pursed her lips. "I look forward to working with you, Elena. If you'll excuse me, there's someone I must see." Then she abruptly turned, leaving her untouched drink on the bar as the crowd parted and then closed ranks behind her retreating form.

Cade's voice echoed in her ear. "What the hell was that?"

"I don't know," Sloane said into her glass. "Something."

"Later," he said.

She nodded, mentally filing away her interaction with Celeste to dissect another time. At the very least, she'd discovered Doyle hadn't simply chosen the estate, but that he owned it, information that might prove useful later.

"Incoming," Gig said.

Sloane placed her glass on the bar and pivoted on one heel, her breath catching when she saw Jack Doyle at the ballroom's entrance. He was prettier in person, debonair like an old Hollywood actor, with the self-assured stance of a man who knew he belonged. He'd skipped the tuxedo and opted for a black-on-black suit and dress shirt. Sophistication with an edge. Sleek, like a viper slithering toward its prey.

"There are three more men in the hall, and two more cars just pulled up," Gig said.

An entourage. They'd expected as much, though the news did little to quell the burning anticipation in her gut. Two bodyguards dressed like the staff flanked Doyle as he inched around the edge of the circle the dancers had made, his gaze sharp as he scanned the crowd. Now was her chance. All she had to do was introduce herself. She stepped forward and instantly came up against a hard chest.

"Dance?"

Cade towered over her, his tuxedo fitting over broad shoulders and sinewy muscle as though someone had painted it on. James Bond didn't look better in formal wear, an observation she'd made when she saw him waiting for her at the bottom of the stairs at the villa. Not that she'd admit it now, as he stared at her with Bond's signature cocky grin.

"What are you doing?" She hissed, forcing a smile when she saw a woman to Cade's left watching them. "You're supposed to stay out of sight."

Instead of responding, he pulled her hand from her side and led her out onto the dance floor. She could either follow or make a scene, so she followed, squeezing Cade's hand until she saw the tips of his fingers turn white. When they got to the center of the dance floor, he flattened a palm to her lower back and pulled her into him.

"This isn't the plan," she said, leaning away from him. "What happened to no deviations?"

"I'm not deviating. I'm executing," he said, tugging her close. "Stacey Clearwater."

"Am I supposed to know who that is?"

"You *do* know who that is."

"You can't expect me to remember every girl you—"

"Stacey Clearwater," he said, "was my tenth-grade biology tutor."

"I was only in 7th grade when you were a sophomore. How would I remember that?"

"Because we met for our study sessions at your house."

That made sense. By high school, Cade was practically living at her house. She thought about it, digging deep until a fuzzy image of a petite, well-endowed redhead came to mind.

Sloane snorted. "Right. Your tutor. I imagine she had no problem getting you to pay attention to her anatomy lessons."

"It wasn't like that."

She rolled her eyes. "Please."

"It's true. We only pretended to date for a couple of weeks."

"Why would you do that?"

"Because she was into the captain of the chess club, Lance Fielding. He was too much of a pussy to ask her out, so I hung around her and made it seem like I was interested."

"So he would make a move?"

"Exactly."

"Did he?"

Cade grinned. "They dated until the end of senior year."

"I suppose you're going to take credit for that too, Romeo?"

"You're missing the point."

"I think I understand perfectly," Sloane said.

The music changed, and a female singer joined the orchestra, her smooth croon accompanying the instrumentals. Cade's palm was hot on her back as he pulled her even closer, his mouth hovering just above her ear.

"You can't understand because you're not a man."

She wanted to laugh, except the sound that escaped her wasn't a laugh at all but a cross between a hiccup and a whimper.

Cade leaned back, his gaze dark and intense. "Every man in this room noticed you the second you walked in the door, but not one of them has approached you. Do you know why?"

His breath ghosted over her skin, and Sloane's gaze dropped to his mouth. She slowly shook her head.

"Because they're afraid," he said.

"Of what?"

"Getting too close." Cade's palm flexed once, twice, then slid down her lower back, leaving a trail of goosebumps in its wake. "But right now, I have you."

The low tone of his voice spilled over her like motor oil from a drum, heavy and viscous. She dipped her chin as he led them into a full turn. Her back had been to Doyle before, but now she could see him, just over Cade's shoulder, staring right at them.

"And nothing makes a man crazier than wanting something he can't have."

A wave of ice-cold clarity crashed into her, and Sloane stiffened against the chill. She paused her steps, stopping the dance, as she looked up at him. "So, you dangle the carrot and hope that he bites?" She let out a humorless laugh. "I guess that makes me the carrot."

His face fell. "Bullet."

"Don't call me that," she snapped, a lump the size of a baseball beginning to swell in her throat.

A couple dancing beside them looked their way, and she tapped him on the shoulder. Cade led them back into a gentle sway, though she kept as much distance between them as possible this time.

"It's your name," Cade said, frowning down at her.

But it wasn't. It was just *his* name for her. And she wasn't his.

"Right now, my name is Elena Caldwell." Sloane glanced back over Cade's shoulder and watched as Doyle lifted a finger to one of his goons, who quickly approached. They whispered to each other and then Doyle gestured at her and Cade. The man shook his head, and Doyle tugged at the sleeves of his suit jacket before taking a step onto the dance floor. "And Elena is about to meet *Le Centre de Feu's* most distinguished benefactor."

Cade spun them again, his mouth drawing into a hard line as he watched Doyle's approach. "We don't have a lot of time."

"Looks like your plan worked."

Cade glared at her so hard that his left temple twitched. "Your two o'clock."

Confused, Sloane looked to her right. A tall, blonde man with blue eyes stood beside a striking dark-haired woman at the edge of the crowd. She'd never seen them before, but as soon as the female caught Sloane's eye, the woman winked at her, a wicked smile curling her lips.

"Who are they?" She asked.

"Backup."

"Albright approved backup?"

"It was my call."

Sloane felt sick. "You called in reinforcements without telling me?"

"We need the support."

"What you really mean is *I* need the support, right?" Cade didn't respond, and his temple continued to twitch. "I'm not sure why I'm surprised. You've never had faith in me."

"That's not wh—*shit*." Cade looked over her shoulder. "He's here."

As if on cue, the song they'd been dancing to ended, and the audience applauded their praise. Sloane reached up to smooth her hair and discreetly pulled the device out of her ear.

"What are you doing?" Cade said as he took the hand holding the earpiece and brought it up to his mouth, brushing his lips over her knuckles.

Heat traveled up her arm, starting a fire that she let burn. His eyes widened when Sloane slid the device into his palm, and he squeezed her fingers, but she tugged her hand away and stepped back. "Thank you for the dance," she said. "It was just what I needed."

Face red with fury, Cade reached out again, but Sloane turned her back, colliding with another hard chest.

"Oh!" Sloane said, bracing herself with a palm against cool Italian silk. She lifted her chin and stared directly into Jack Doyle's piercing jade-green gaze. "I'm so sorry," she said, dropping her hand. "Excuse me."

Then she brushed past him and off the dance floor.

14

Sloane descended the stone stairs that led from the ballroom to the lawn and walked the short distance to the gardens, her stomach in knots. The proof that Cade didn't trust her had been staring her right in the face, and she'd refused to see it. Given their history, she should have, but once again, she'd given him the benefit of the doubt. She'd thought he had finally accepted the situation they were in, but he'd only been waiting for the right moment to take control. Well, Cade Foster didn't control her. If he could make plans without her, then so could she.

And that was exactly what she'd done. While Cade and Gig held their secret meetings, she'd been busy researching their target. She and Gig had tracked Doyle's movements for months, but this week had been about getting to know Doyle, the *man*. No detail was too insignificant. Sloane wanted to know his shoe size, drink of choice, and, especially, who he dated.

Turned out, the latter wasn't as difficult to find as she thought it would be. The women on Doyle's arm were mostly celebrities or high-ranking figures, even daughters or ex-wives of mobsters. She recognized nearly every one of them and those she didn't, she'd Googled. Most people would find it unusual that a man as private as Jack Doyle would ever consider dating women who led such openly public lives. But hiding in someone else's spotlight was a lesson in deception that would have made even his old boss, Harry Callahan, proud.

After that, it was just about narrowing down his type, and Doyle definitely had a type. He preferred women who were tall, blonde, and put together. They showed composure and an even temperament and appeared unflappable. So, that's what she would be. Of course, a man who had gone to such great lengths to steal two highly coveted jewels over decades also liked a challenge.

Which was how she knew Doyle would follow her.

The garden's labyrinth led Sloane to a clearing, and she stopped at its center, where an enormous stone statue stood. Lights in the grass illuminated the figure of a woman looking over her left shoulder, her right arm raised as if reaching for something.

"It's beautiful, isn't it?"

Satisfaction bloomed in her chest at the sound of the voice behind her. His accent was vaguely European, lacking any trace of the brogue of his home country. It could have originated from anywhere or nowhere, just like the man himself.

"It is," she said, keeping her gaze fixed on the statue.

"The woman was the wife of a French aristocrat. He had the gardens built in her honor centuries ago."

Sloane moved to the statue's other side to get a better look at the woman's face and to keep Doyle in her line of sight. "Love?"

"Desperation. He had them made as a gift to win back her favor."

Sloane met Doyle's gaze for the second time that evening. "That implies he had it to begin with."

Doyle smiled. "Such cynical words from such a beautiful mouth."

"Would you think I was cynical if I was a man?"

"I think that a show of this magnitude wouldn't impress you if you were a man or a woman."

"You'd be right."

"Why?"

"You said it yourself. Grand gestures are about desperation, not love."

"Shakespeare might disagree," he said. "Consider Romeo and Juliet, for example."

"A forbidden romance does not equate to love."

"And yet, they paid the ultimate price for it."

She bit back a laugh and crossed her arms over her chest. He could wax poetic all he wanted, but nobody had paid a higher price than Beck. "They were also narcissistic, hormonal teenagers with too much time on their hands."

His grin widened, revealing two rows of brilliant white teeth. "To think that ten minutes ago, I thought this party dull."

"I thought the same. Though, there's always the view."

"Yes, there's that." He crossed the courtyard, edging closer until they faced each other, the statue standing vigil over them both. "I thought I knew everyone on the guest list, but it seems I'm at a disadvantage."

"Something tells me that's a foreign concept for you."

"I like to stay informed."

"Well, knowledge is power."

"Do I have to beg?" He said, his tone falling just short of teasing.

"My name is Elena."

"Elena," he repeated, letting the name roll off his tongue. "A pleasure."

He moved into her space, forcing Sloane to step back. "Likewise, Mr. Dubois."

"Luc, please."

"Luc."

"*Vous* êtes *américain.*"

"Oui." It was one of a handful of French words she knew, not that she cared. At the moment, apparently, not even Doyle seemed to care whether she could string two sentences together. Sloane told herself that was a win, even if she suddenly found it difficult to breathe.

"What business brings you to France?"

"I could be here on vacation."

His laugh was light. "Nobody would subject themselves to a party like this if they were on holiday."

"As the host, you seem to have a rather low opinion of the event."

"I seem to remember you agreeing it was dull."

"Why have it then?" She asked.

"Some things are necessary."

Like schmoozing with buyers of stolen property?

Because Sloane couldn't ask that question, she opted to answer his. "Celeste Armand hired me to assist *Le Centre de Feu* with their upcoming exhibit."

"I see," he said. "It's rare to meet a lover of art who isn't a romantic."

"As rare as it is to meet a pragmatist who reads fairy tales?"

"Perhaps that's true, though I would hardly call Romeo and Juliet a fairy tale. Not that it matters. There's still much to learn about human nature in tragedy."

Doyle advanced again, and Sloane retreated, nearly stumbling when the heel of her sandal scratched the base of the statue. How had he cornered her? She cursed herself for forgetting the first rule in Albright's secret agent handbook *and* for leaving her purse on the bar in the ballroom. The only thing valuable in it was the small switchblade sewn into its lining. Not having it was inconvenient, but she was still in control. She could do this. She just had to keep him talking.

"How so?"

"As humans, we are uncharacteristically blind to our true selves. We might think we know our limits, but then, suddenly, we're standing on the edge of a cliff with no recollection of how we got there."

He stared at her, unblinking, and she felt suddenly exposed. There was no way he could know who or what she was, but his words still felt like a chastisement rather than a general comment.

The need to defend herself rose swiftly out of nowhere, and she lifted her chin. "But some of us know. Some of us go to the edge willingly because we know exactly what we want."

"Perhaps," he said. "And sometimes, that's a mistake."

Sloane shook her head. "It's not a mistake for the strong, but the weak will—"

She yelped in surprise as Doyle came at her, and she flung herself back into the cold, hard edge of stone. Pain shot down her left side, and she bit her lip to suppress a cry as Doyle gripped her hip and held her firm with bruising force.

"The weak will fail," he said through clenched teeth.

His fingers dug into her injured side, and panic flooded her chest, mixed with fear and the realization that she'd somehow underestimated him. She shifted slightly, preparing to knee him in the balls when a second realization struck her. Sloane Easton knew self-defense, but Elena Caldwell probably couldn't even throw a punch. If she wanted to keep her cover intact, she couldn't use force. She would have to play this out. Doyle was right, after all. There was only weakness in failure, and she wouldn't fail.

Sucking in a ragged breath, Sloane swallowed her fear and tried to conjure an air of annoyance rather than rage. Fear would only fuel his fire, and rage was something *she* felt. For Elena, this was a minor inconvenience, a blip in an otherwise uneventful evening.

She met his fierce gaze with one of her own. "I couldn't agree more."

She waited, wanting to see how he would react to the challenge she'd just posed. But before he could say anything, a man appeared in the clearing behind them, his face semi-obscured in the dark.

"Monsieur Dubois?"

"I said, no interruptions," Doyle snapped.

To his credit, the man didn't even flinch at his employer's obvious fury. Instead, he stepped into the half-light of the garden, and Sloane recognized him as the man Doyle had called to his side in the ballroom.

"*Je suis désolé*, but there's a situation that requires your immediate attention."

The silence dragged on. But then, just as quickly as he'd grabbed her, Doyle let her go, causing her to pitch forward. She caught herself at the last minute, just in time to see him roll back his shoulders and re-button his suit jacket. She stared, transfixed, as he slid his facade back into place like a robot resetting its own programming.

"If you'll excuse me," he said as if he hadn't just accosted her.

Then he was gone, disappearing into the gardens in the direction they'd come with all the dexterity of a panther skimming through the jungle grass. His bodyguard didn't follow right away but watched her as she righted her dress. He was a giant of a man, but with a baby's face that made him appear non-threatening, almost benign. He could be anyone—her next-door neighbor, the town barber, a bank teller—and it suddenly occurred to her that was probably the point.

Babyface squinted hard at her a second longer before following his boss into the shadows. When he was gone too, Sloane slumped against the statue, allowing herself one deep, steadying breath before walking back through the maze. The walls surrounding the estate prevented her from reaching the front without going back into the ballroom. Of course, there was one side that wasn't blocked, but she wasn't going anywhere near the ocean.

The only way out was through.

The first person she saw when she slipped back inside was the woman who had winked at her earlier. She looked like a model in a black satin dress that hugged her curves and black hair tied back in a slick, tight ponytail. She stood by a table looking bored, but her posture and focus on the glass suggested otherwise.

Sloane passed her on the right, brushing her shoulder as the woman shoved something into her palm. She continued on her way without looking back, and Sloane casually slid her once-abandoned communications device back into her ear.

"Exiting front," she said.

"Too hot." Gig's voice was sharp and insistent. "Move to the foyer, then left to the study."

She altered her route and was almost out of the ballroom when three loud booms echoed in the hall. It couldn't be thunder. She'd just been outside, and the night was clear enough to see stars. "Are those fireworks?"

"Just keep moving," Gig said.

So she did. Four more of Doyle's guards rushed past her, too preoccupied by whatever was happening out front to notice. Her only thought as she climbed through the large bay window at the rear of the study was of Gig's first words to her.

Funny that he would say it was too hot when all she felt was cold.

15

Then

Shit, it was hot.

Cade stepped away from the popped hood of the Ford Bronco and cleaned the grime from his hands with a grease-stained rag. The Bronco likely needed a new transmission, but hell if he'd replace it before exhausting all his options. The truck belonged to a buddy of Wilson's, a widower who barely had two dollars to scrape together after using the last of his cash to bury his wife a few months earlier. Cade didn't want to have to give the man any more bad news, so he'd spent his afternoon making sure he didn't have to. He didn't mind. He liked the challenge and figured the old man didn't mind either because Wilson didn't needle him about wasting time.

He crossed to the other side of his terminal and flipped the switch on a standing fan. It would only blow hot air around, but it was better than nothing. He reached for a bottle of water, downing half of it, and looked up just in time to see Bullet stroll into the garage in a white tank top and the shortest shorts he'd ever seen on a woman.

Maybe that was the problem. At seventeen, Cade could no longer consider Sloane Easton a girl. She'd grown up and out in all the ways he found most appealing. He'd thought of little else since the night of their camping trip months earlier. He shouldn't have provoked her, but she'd been all piss and vinegar and so damned cute that he just couldn't help himself.

And he needed help, alright.

Apparently, he wasn't the only one. He watched as Ed Stevenson, one of Wilson's other mechanics, slid out from under a vehicle to check her out as she passed his terminal. Ed was twice her age, with a wife and two kids at home, a message that Cade tried to get across with the glare he sent his co-worker when Ed glanced his way. The mechanic's face turned a healthy shade of lobster red before he disappeared under the car once again.

"Hey," Bullet said, stopping in front of him. She held up a brown paper bag. "I brought you lunch."

"Is that what I think it is?"

She nodded. "Turkey on rye with pickles. Your favorite."

It was his favorite, but even though he'd skipped lunch to work on the Bronco, Cade wasn't hungry. At least, not for a sandwich.

"Uh…thanks," he said, yanking the bag from her hand and dropping it on his workbench. "What's up?"

Sloane shrugged. "Nothing. I just finished camp for the day and thought I'd stop by."

Cade pursed his lips to keep from smiling at her feigned nonchalance. She was so ridiculously transparent, but, God help him, he enjoyed playing with her. "Were there any last-minute trips to the emergency room?"

"Luckily, no. But there was a gum-in-hair incident that caused some drama."

"So, DEFCON 5, then?"

"At least a three. Do you have any idea how difficult it is to remove gum from hair?"

Cade pointed to his shaved head. "Can't say I do."

"Right." Sloane shifted in place, stuffing both hands into the back pockets of her shorts. She gestured to the Bronco. "What are you working on?"

"A transmission."

"Oh."

She moved to the front of the truck, and Cade closed his eyes to keep from checking out her ass. As far as he was concerned, Bullet didn't have an ass. She was ass-less.

Cade finished the water and crushed the plastic in his hand before tossing it into the trash. On his way back to the front of the car, he reached inside the open driver's side window and retrieved a white box wrapped tight with red and white string. He'd planned to give it to her later, but what the hell?

When he got to her, Sloane was bent at the waist, peering under the hood like it held the answer to all of life's problems. The answer to Cade's problem would be to pretend that Sloane also didn't have breasts. He'd just think of her as a female version of Gumby. Was Gumby gender-specific? He'd look that up later.

Sloane glanced up, her smile so bright it could have lit up all of Lakehaven in a blackout. "You remembered," she said, lunging for the box.

"Happy Birthday, Bullet."

She tore at the string, and he laughed before reaching for the blade he had kept in his back pocket. He cut the string, and she opened the flap.

"Mmm," she moaned, making Cade wish he had a grandmother to think about. Or maybe he could think about baseball. Baseball would work. He'd think of baseball.

"Is that what I think it is?"

Cade hurriedly glanced down at his crotch before looking back at Sloane. The cupcake. Right.

"Vanilla with strawberry frosting," he croaked.

"My favorite."

"Your favorite."

She beamed at him before removing a cupcake and handing him the box. Could astronauts see that kind of thing from space? While he debated the merits of enhanced satellite technology, Sloane peeled the paper off the cupcake and took a bite. She closed her eyes, savoring the taste, another moan escaping her as her tongue flicked at the frosting on her lips. Even though he'd never been to a church in his life, Cade wanted to pray. Or go to confession. Or pray *and* go to confession.

Instead, he put down the box, reached for a wrench, and bent over the hood. Sloane finished her cupcake and leaned against the truck to his left, squinting out the open door into the July sunshine. Cade frowned as he worked. Something was off. He could tell by the way she hunched her shoulders and idly tugged at the ends of her hair, something she only did when she was deep in thought.

"How's your mom?" He hadn't been by the house in a couple of days and hoped whatever was bothering her had nothing to do with Faye.

"She's okay. I told her it's too hot to cook and that I'd be fine with a birthday barbecue, but she insisted. Beck will be home in a few hours with his roommate from school. You're coming, right?"

"I'll be there."

Even if being around her confused him, he didn't dare pull another disappearing act. The last thing he needed was another scene like the one they'd had in the woods. Even if he wasn't worried he'd make the same mistake again, he'd never been able to say no to Bullet, and he wasn't about to start on her birthday of all days.

She let out a breath that he recognized as relief. Did she actually think he wouldn't show? He wanted to ask, but also didn't, so he put down the wrench and reached for another tool.

"Can I ask you a question?" she asked.

"Sure."

"How do you know when…*if*...you should have sex with someone?"

Cade shot upright, banging his head on the lifted hood. He groaned.

"Fuck, are you alright?"

"Swear jar."

Sloane rolled her eyes. "Not you, too."

No, not him. But if he didn't say it, he'd have to admit just how much he didn't mind hearing that word come out of her mouth. He must have hit his head harder than he thought.

"Are you really okay?" she asked, standing on tiptoes to inspect his injury. "That looked like it hurt."

He pulled away and cleared his throat. "I'm fine. You were saying?"

Sloane flattened her feet on the ground and pulled her hair over one shoulder, slowly stroking the ends again as she bit her lip. She'd given up wearing her hair in a braid months ago and now wore it long and loose. He missed the braid. At least when she wore her hair in a braid, he didn't think about what it would feel like wrapped around his fist.

"I just…well…there's this guy I know."

"And?"

"And we're sort of dating."

Cade lifted an eyebrow. "Sort of?"

"I mean, we *are* dating."

"Does Beck know?" There was no way Beck would be okay with any guy dating his sister.

"No! And you can't tell him."

"Bullet, I can't just—"

"Please," she said. "He's too overprotective. He wouldn't let me go out with Chad once, let alone date him for two months."

"Two *months*? Shit, Bullet."

"Swear jar."

Cade growled his frustration. This was no time for games. "Do I know this guy?"

"Not really."

"What does that mean?"

"Can you please just answer my question?"

He shook his head. "Bullet, I don't really think I'm the best person to answer that question."

"Yes, you are."

"What about your mom?"

She jerked back, clearly disgusted. "I can't talk to my *mom* about this."

"Why not?"

She crossed her arms over her chest, which had the unfortunate effect of pushing her breasts further into his line of sight. "Do you really think I want to hear about her escapades with Principal Fisher? He's coming to my birthday party. That would be weird."

She had a point. Cade didn't much care for Fisher either, but he was good to Faye, Beck, and Bullet, and he didn't mind Cade hanging around the house. Beck also seemed to like him, which was really all Cade cared about.

"I still think you should discuss this with another female."

"But you've had more females than anyone I know." Her cheeks pinked. "Wait, what I meant was you've had more *girlfriends* than anyone I know."

Heat crept along the back of Cade's neck. "Yeah, but I'm a guy."

"So?"

"So, I don't really know when a woman is ready for…umm…"

"Sex?"

Forget confession. Cade was ready to drop to his knees right now in the garage if it meant he wouldn't have to have this conversation. "Uh…right. That."

"Is it because, as a guy, you're always ready?"

Cade nearly laughed but choked it down when he saw her expression. If he laughed now, she'd take offense, and offending Bullet was the last thing he wanted to do.

He dropped his tool on the workbench and leaned against the Bronco next to her. "Not exactly."

"Then, how do you know?"

Cade looked at her. Bullet could be a brat. She was brazen, impulsive, and, his favorite, deliberately argumentative. But she was sweet, too. And sometimes, that sweet naivety made her vulnerable in ways that only the people closest to her ever got to see. Not for the first time, Cade wondered if being in Bullet's inner circle made him the luckiest or unluckiest bastard alive.

"You know when you know."

"I knew you wouldn't take this seriously." She whirled, nearly whipping him in the face with her hair.

"Wait," he said, wrapping a hand around her wrist and tugging her back. "I *am* serious." He swiped his free hand over his head in frustration, his gaze dropping to his fingers circling her wrist. Her skin was soft and, despite the nearly suffocating heat in the garage, cool to the touch. It felt good. So good that he didn't let go. "It's not something you can analyze; it's something you have to feel." He searched for a way to explain that wouldn't royally screw this up. "It's like when you're driving, and you know when to brake without having to think about it. Or when you're running, you automatically know what pace to keep. What do you call it?"

"Hitting your stride?"

Cade nodded. "Exactly. It's a feeling you get in the moment with someone when you just *know* it's right. You're ready and he's ready and you're both just…ready."

It was lame, but also all he had right now. Sloane lifted her chin, seeming to mull over what he'd said, the action drawing his attention to the stretch of skin from her neck to her collarbone.

"Do you love every girl you sleep with?"

Cade coughed, letting go of Sloane's wrist to pound at his chest. "Sorry," he said. "Swallowed wrong."

"Well, do you?"

"Do I what?" Sloane threw him a look. Yes, he was stalling, but what guy wouldn't be in his situation? "No," he finally said. "I don't love every girl I sleep with."

"Have you loved *any* of them?"

"No," he answered honestly. It was a truth he'd shared with no one else. No one except for Bullet.

"But you must have felt something otherwise you wouldn't have done it."

He'd felt something, but what he'd felt had been purely physical, absent of the emotional connection that came with strings. Strings meant expectations, and Cade sucked at fulfilling the expectations of others.

Just ask his parents.

But Cade didn't want that for Sloane. She would have it better than he did because she deserved more. She deserved everything. He stepped closer to her, flexing his fingers to keep from reaching for her like he had before.

"What I felt doesn't matter. What *you* feel is. If this guy…"

"Chad," she supplied.

Cade gritted his teeth. "If Chad doesn't make you feel special, and I mean, like the queen of this entire universe, then he's not the one. And, even then, it's your choice. Not his. Remember what I said about being ready?"

"Yes."

"Well, that works both ways, but it can't happen at all if you're not. If you say no, then it's *always* no."

"I know."

"Do you?"

"Yes."

Even hearing her say it and believing her didn't make Cade feel any better. If the thought of some guy's hands on Bullet drove him insane, then the idea that the guy might also disrespect her made him positively murderous. But what choice did he have? She'd come to him for advice, and he had to give it. He even tried to convince himself that Beck would approve, but the odds of his best friend not kicking his ass for talking to his sister about this were slim.

"Hey, Cade?"

Oh, for the love of... "Yeah?"

"Thank you."

She launched herself at him, wrapping her arms around his neck like he was her birthday present and not the damn cupcakes. His arms automatically came around her waist, tightening as she melded her body into his. She smelled like strawberries and cream and sunshine and summer, and he wished he could bottle that scent, even though he knew in his bones nothing would ever be as sweet as the real thing. She pulled away from him, his senses slowly coming back into check as she dropped her arms.

"Do you have any more questions?" He asked.

Okay, so maybe he didn't have *all* his senses in check. But it was a valid question. The last thing he wanted was for her to ask someone else because she didn't get what she needed from him. Someone like Chad.

"No," Sloane said, straightening her shoulders.

Was it his imagination, or did she look more confident than she had before? Cade almost gave himself a figurative pat on the back for being the best advice-giver the world had ever seen. And he would have, had it not been for the next words out of her mouth.

"I know what I have to do now."

Before he knew what was happening, she was telling him she'd see him later at Faye's. Then, she skipped out of the garage, leaving Cade with no choice but to resolve never to give anyone advice ever again.

16

Sloane spent the entire ride back to the villa shifting in her seat in the Aston, trying to find a position that didn't set her ribs on fire. Cade's erratic driving didn't help, nor did his refusal to look at her even once since they'd left the estate. Neither concerned her more than the fact that he hadn't said a single word to her since she got in the car. Not that she'd tried to engage him in conversation, either. She wasn't that stupid.

The instant they pulled into the villa's circular drive, Sloane threw open the door. She got out carefully and started up the path, barefoot, her sandals dangling from her fingers, as she hiked up the dress that now felt like a potato sack. Cade followed silently behind, the tapping of his shoes on stone beating in time with her pulse.

Just as she reached the front door, it flew open, and she jumped back, dropping her shoes and wincing as her injured side connected with Cade's stomach. She bit her lip to stop the whimper that escaped anyway, and she felt him stiffen behind her, every muscle that grazed hers growing instantly rigid.

Damn.

Oblivious, Gig reached for her, grabbing her hand and pulling her into a hug that, thankfully, didn't put any added pressure on her side. She relaxed into him, grateful for his presence after such a long night.

"Are you okay?"

She nodded into his shoulder, and Gig finally stepped back, letting her go. He looked at her, and she recognized the grin spreading over his face. She knew that look and the rush of adrenaline that came with it. The only thing she felt at that moment, though, was tired.

"It went well, didn't it?" He said.

"It did." Even if there had been a few surprises, she'd still achieved what she set out to do.

"I mean, your disappearing act was a bit of a setback, but…"

He trailed off, his face paling by degrees as he looked over her shoulder. Sloane turned, too, swallowing hard at the sight of Cade in the doorway. He stood as stiff as a piece of furniture, the night cloaking him in black, save for white-knuckled fists clenched at his sides.

Gig cleared his throat and retreated further into the house. "Well, I'm wiped. Debrief tomorrow?"

Without waiting for an answer, he turned and hustled down the hallway. A second later, the door to one of the back bedrooms clicked closed, leaving her alone with Cade.

Double damn.

Sloane moved slowly to the door. She paused in front of her shoes before gingerly lowering herself to the floor, working to keep her spine straight as she crouched low and reached out an arm. Beside her, Cade growled and swiped the sandals from under her nose before yanking her up by the elbow with his free hand. His touch was gentle but firm as he guided her into the bathroom across from his bedroom and flicked on the light.

"Take it off." He met her reflection in the mirror above the sink, his eyes boring into hers, blacker than black, his face a mask Sloane couldn't read.

"No."

Cade turned her to face him and dropped both hands on the pedestal sink behind her. His forearms pulsed against her hips, caging her in as he leaned forward, his mouth hovering just inches above hers. "If you don't take that dress off now, I will. And if I do, there will be pieces of it all over this floor." He straightened again and squared off in front of the door, arms crossed over his chest.

"I'm fine." Another growl rumbled through the confined space, and Sloane reluctantly reached for the zipper at her back. Pain shot through her at the movement, and she winced, dropping her arm before making a second attempt. Cade made a move to help her, but she slapped his hand away. "I've got it."

"Let me help you."

She looked up, the frustration and disappointment that had been bubbling up in her throat ebbing when she saw the imploring look on his face. Her hands shook.

"Please," he said.

Sighing, she nodded and held her breath, clutching the top of the dress as he reached behind her. She stared at a crack in the ceiling as Cade's hand slipped under the fabric.

"How bad is it?" She asked when she couldn't take it anymore.

Cade's fingers brushed over her skin in response, making it tingle. Her breath hitched when he gently flattened his palm against the side of her ribs in the same spot where Doyle's had been.

"He did this?"

His voice was so low and menacing that she winced again. "It was me. I fell back, and he came at me, and I—"

"He *attacked* you?"

"No."

"An imprint of his hand is on your skin. Don't lie to me, Bullet. "

"He came at me, but I shoved *myself* backward."

"And then?"

She sighed again. "Then, yes, he touched me, but the damage was done." Cade stormed out of the bathroom and was halfway down the hall by the time she managed to re-zip her dress and catch up. "Where are you going?"

"To call Albright."

"No!" She grabbed his elbow. "You can't do that."

"He put his hands on you."

"I can handle it."

"You can handle him smacking you around?" Cade said, shaking her off. "Good for you. I can't."

"I told you, it was my fault. He caught me off guard and—"

"Of course he did! That's what criminals do."

Sloane stiffened. "I know that."

"Then why would you put yourself in danger?"

"Gig was watching. There were cameras everywhere."

"And you were out of range of every one of them."

She paled. "What do you mean?"

"There were no cameras in the gardens. We were blind the entire time you were out there."

Shit. "Oh."

"What made you think you could go off half-cocked without so much as a warning?"

Blood pulsed in Sloane's ears as anger surged. "Like the warning you gave me?"

"That's different."

"How is that different?"

"Because Jean-Paul and Bianca have been officers for longer than I have. They're trained to handle situations like these."

"So am I!"

Cade tore out of his suit jacket as he paced the narrow hallway, chucking it to the ground before clawing at his bowtie. "If I told you about them, you would have refused their help."

"I guess we'll never know, will we?"

"Bullshit."

"Call it what you want, but you still decided without me."

"Hi, Pot, I'm Kettle."

Sloane shook her head. "It's not the same thing. I didn't plan what I did. I made a call in the field."

"What you did wasn't about the mission, Bullet. You cut off communication to piss me off."

"Why would I do that?"

"You tell me."

"Okay, fine, yes! I did it to piss you off. Is that what you want to hear?"

Cade stalked toward her. "Why?"

"You used me."

"I *helped* you."

"I don't need your help. You or your merry little gang of spies."

"We saved your ass. When are you going to stop acting like a teenager with a score to settle?"

"There *is* a score to settle."

The vein in Cade's temple bulged, ugly and angry. "Don't."

But Sloane refused to let him continue dictating every move she made. "Okay, then maybe I'll remind you that you don't get to decide how much or how little I'm involved in this job. I won't stop."

He fumbled with the buttons at his neck and ripped open his shirt collar, eyes red-rimmed and blazing. "No."

"It's not your call."

"No!" Cade said right before he slammed his fist through a wall.

17

Right before his mom left, Cade's parents fought.

He still remembered the sound of the vase hitting the wall, the glass shattering into a million pieces at her feet. Cade stood against the wall outside his bedroom, palms over his ears, and screamed for them to stop. They did, eventually, and he watched as his mom slid down the living room wall, disheveled and spent. It took Cade a minute to realize she'd collapsed on the broken glass and a split second more to register that something was wrong. She clutched her hand to her chest as she rocked in the glass, her eyes wide, breaths harsh and uneven. Terrified, he ran and then crawled to her, scraping his hands and knees on the shards. His dad tried to pick him up, but Cade fought and flailed until the older man threw up his hands and left them both.

His mom grasped his hand so tight that he cried out, but he didn't let go. They sat there, holding on to each other until his mother stood suddenly and walked to the coat closet for a broom. He could still see her there, scratched up and bloody, hunched over her task like she wanted to fold into herself and cease to exist.

Now, Cade thought he knew how his mom must have felt that day. Her anxiety had gotten her in the end. At least it had affected her enough to cause her to turn her back on her life and her family. It was ironic that of all the things Mom could have given him, it would be this that would be her legacy.

He tensed when he felt a light touch between his shoulder blades. He flexed his back into the warmth of Sloane's palm, his breaths evening by degrees, as he dragged his fist from the wall.

"How long have you been having panic attacks?"

Of course, she knew. It wasn't like he was doing an outstanding job of hiding them. He'd even had an audience for the first time. He'd been on a plane filled with passengers on his way to a job, his first without Beck. The plane hit turbulence for a minute or two, and he'd thought he was dying. When it was over, Cade found himself with his head between his legs, gasping for breath. It was one of only a handful of times in his life that he could remember being truly afraid.

He turned to face her. "A while."

Sloane only nodded and reached for his throbbing fist. She held it in both of her hands as she gently pried his fingers free. Cade stopped breathing all over again when she swept a thumb over his ruined knuckles.

"You know you didn't have to hurt yourself, right? I would have been more than happy to do that for you."

For the first time since their godawful night started, Cade smiled. "Where would the fun be in that?"

"I guarantee you, that would be very fun for me."

"I bet."

She continued to work her magic over his ruined skin, the two of them falling silent as she massaged circles around the fresh scrapes. "Does it hurt?"

He looked at her. "More than you know."

She nodded again, as if she understood, and he realized she was probably the only other person in the world who did.

"I'm sorry, Cade, I really am, but I have to keep going. You know I do."

He did. That was the hell of it. He couldn't stop her any more than she could stop him. But he'd be damned if she was going to do it alone. "I know, but you're not doing this without me."

"Okay."

"I mean it, Bullet. You need to tell me everything. No more stunts like you pulled tonight. I have to know you're okay."

"I understand."

Cade shook his head. "I mean, I need to know *everything*."

Bile rose in his throat as he thought about what that meant, but he swallowed it down. If they had any hope of navigating this hell, he'd have to treat this like any other job. He'd have to put aside his personal feelings and focus on what had to be done, and he could only do that if he had all the information.

Sloane pulled her bottom lip between her teeth, her gaze darting to the ground and back up to meet his. "I'll tell you about everything that concerns the mission." He opened his mouth to protest, but she held up a hand. "No more changing the game without advanced notice, I promise, but you have to stop excluding me from your plans and start treating me like a partner."

A partner.

Cade had only ever had one partner, and he'd screwed that up worse than either of them could have ever imagined. A sliver of fear shot through him at the prospect of taking on another one, especially *her*. But what choice did he have? With Beck gone, it was Cade's responsibility to keep his sister safe.

"Okay," he said.

"I mean it. No more secret boys' club meetings."

"It's not a boys' club."

"Tell that to Gig. I'm pretty sure he already has a password."

Cade groaned and shook his head. "Fine. We'll take the *No Girls Allowed* sign off the door."

She smiled a genuine smile that hit him harder than he'd hit the wall. "Come on," she said, leading him away from the mess he'd made. "Let's get you cleaned up."

PART 2

If I saw the in-between,
I wouldn't plead, or beg, or scream,
or hold my breath and lie in wait,
for the heavens to choose my fate.

18

Cade woke the next morning with a hangover.

At least that's what he *thought* had caused the head-pounding, body-aching weariness he felt until he remembered he didn't drink. He blinked his eyes open, his bedroom at the villa slowly coming into focus as he rolled his head. The muscles in his neck protested, and he winced, reaching out a hand to ease the tension before realizing that, too, was in pain.

He moved slowly, shifting on the bed where he still sat in an upright position, dressed in last night's clothes. Bullet lay to his left, facing away from him, the steady rise and fall of her shoulders matching the rhythm of her breath. He could tell by the way the sun streamed through the open blinds it wasn't early, but they'd gone to bed too late last night for him to care.

Last night.

The images came one after the other, burning into his mind like brands. He saw Sloane's indignation at seeing him dressed up for an event she thought she would attend alone and the way every man stared at her as she entered the ballroom in that dress he'd think about until the day he died. He remembered her surprise when he'd asked her to dance and the look of betrayal that crossed her face when she saw Jean-Paul and Bianca. The panic he'd felt watching Doyle follow her out to the garden was nothing compared to the rage that consumed him when he saw what that bastard had done to her.

He thought he'd taken every precaution, but nothing had prepared him for seeing Bullet's flawless skin marred by bruises.

His control had slipped after that, and he'd spiraled, unable to stop the inevitable.

His knuckles throbbed as he flexed his damaged hand, loosening the bandage Sloane had applied the night before. She had stuck to their deal, only giving him a few details about her chat with Doyle, despite Cade's insistence for more. The worst part was he couldn't do a damn thing about it. Nothing, except trust her like she'd asked and like he knew he needed to if they had any hope of ending this once and for all.

Rising from the bed, Cade stripped off his clothes and left them in a rumbled mess on the floor next to Sloane's dress. He rifled through his duffel until he found a T-shirt and shorts and pulled them on, glancing at Sloane as he moved to the bedroom door. He paused there, watching her as she slept in one of his old Lions' hoodies. A sheet covered her lower half, and one arm was slung over the mattress, hanging in midair close to a plastic bag filled with water that had once been ice.

Were her bruises worse this morning? Cade scanned her face, looking for any sign that she was in pain, the knot in his gut loosening when he saw she slept peacefully. She shifted in her sleep, one bare thigh edging out from under the sheet, and Cade tore his gaze away, fleeing from the bedroom like it was on fire. Or maybe the heat he felt was just him, burning alive from the inside.

There was a fresh pot of coffee waiting in the kitchen, and Cade poured himself a cup before walking out onto the patio.

Gig looked up from where he sat in front of his laptop at a nearby table. "I'm monitoring the feed from outside Elena's apartment," he said in greeting. "The view isn't bad, but I'd like to add a few more cameras outside, just in case. There's also one camera inside that's not working and needs to be replaced."

"We'll take care of it this afternoon," Cade said. "Did you sleep?"

"Some."

Cade nodded and swirled the contents of his mug, waiting for commentary on the hole in the hallway wall he must have seen coming out of his room that morning, but it never came. "You did well last night," he said. "The surveillance was on point, and you didn't hesitate when I changed the game."

The kid had an innate ability to adapt to any situation with a clear head, which was imperative in their line of work. Cade wasn't sure he could have gotten Sloane out of there without Gig's help. As much as he hated to admit it, he couldn't be in two places at once, and helping Jean-Paul create a diversion had taken precedence. He'd left Gig to be Sloane's eyes and ears on the inside, trusting him to navigate her to safety. He hated that too, but he'd had no choice.

Gig stared at him, mouth agape.

"What?" Cade said.

"That sounded like a compliment."

"Don't let it go to your head."

He expected the kid to smile, but his expression turned serious. "You know, I'm not *with* Sloane, right? I have a girlfriend back home."

Cade sighed. "I know. Not about the girlfriend, but I figured."

He'd known the instant Gig had left them alone the night before that they weren't a couple. If they had been, Sloane never would have spent the night in Cade's bed. Unfortunately, knowing they weren't together didn't bring Cade the relief he expected. Instead, it made him twitchy, like the nicotine withdrawals he had when he quit smoking in high school.

"Is she going to be okay?" Gig asked.

As long as he drew breath. "Bullet is strong. She'll be alright."

"Why do you call her that?"

"Bullet?"

Gig nodded. "I can't tell if she likes it or not."

He never could, either. Of course, that didn't stop him from using it. At first, it had been just to annoy her, but then he'd gotten so used to it that calling her by her real name just didn't feel right. He thought about that day years ago when she'd earned her nickname and smiled.

"When we were kids, her brother and I broke into our school after hours. We ended up in our science classroom where our teacher kept a pet."

"Like a mascot?"

Cade nodded. "It was a turtle. Terrence." He couldn't remember why they'd broken into the school in the first place, but he still remembered the name of that damn turtle. "Anyway, Sloane's school was right next door, and she came looking for Beck so their mom could take them home and found the two of us and Terrence. She took one look at the turtle and decided she had to save it."

Thinking back on it now, Cade realized it was less of a decision and more of a mission. She'd gone to the back of the room, found some of the turtle food the teacher had stashed in a drawer and went back for Terrence.

"Bold move," Gig said, amused.

"When Bullet wants something, she usually gets it."

He'd often wondered if that was because she didn't waste time thinking about the ramifications of her choices like he did. Well, that wasn't entirely true. He hadn't thought really hard about knocking Bobby Renfro flat when he'd laid a hand on her years ago. Maybe they had more in common than he thought.

"So, she did it, then?" Gig asked.

"Yep. She took him out of his case and walked right out of the classroom." He and Beck had followed close behind like two completely inept turtle bodyguards. "About halfway to the front door, a janitor came around a corner and saw us. He came after us, and Sloane took off running." Cade smirked, thinking of her running in her pink dress and Velcro sneakers, her arms outstretched, hands gripping Terrence's shell. "When we finally made it outside, she was already halfway across the parking lot and still going, running as fast as a—"

"Speeding bullet," Gig finished. He sighed. "Well, I guess that explains her aversion to hero-inspired theme songs."

"She also hates comic books."

"Noted."

The sound of the screen door opening caught Cade's attention, and he turned to find Sloane walking through it. Her face was scrubbed clean, and her wet hair clung to her neck from a recent shower. She had replaced his Lions sweatshirt with jean cut-off shorts and a white T-shirt, and a sudden memory struck him of her standing on the bleachers at their high school in the same outfit, cheering him on as he rounded third base.

"Hi," she said, stopping just inches from him. "Good morning."

"Morning," he mumbled, instantly distracted by her scent. Lavender again but with a hint of citrus this time, like he'd woken her from her slumber on a bed of wildflowers under a lemon tree in the villa's backyard. He held back a groan, not sure if it was worse that he'd constructed a fairy tale in his mind or that he'd imagined himself in it.

As if she could read his thoughts, one corner of her mouth tipped up in a half-smile before she reached for his mug. He let her have it, already too jumpy for more caffeine.

"What'd I miss?" she asked as she took the seat beside Gig.

Her wince as she sat was subtle, but Cade noticed. He tensed and made a move toward her, but she subtly shook her head. Nobody hated coddling more than Bullet, and even though he didn't like it, he let her be.

"You missed Cade singing my praises," Gig said.

Sloane peered at Cade over the rim of the mug, her eyes twinkling with amusement. "Is that so?"

"I don't sing."

"It sure sounded like it to me," Gig said. "Though, since nobody else was here to witness it, he'll probably deny it."

"Probably," Sloane said.

Cade cleared his throat. "If you're both done, can we please talk about something useful?"

Gig tapped a few keys. "You got it, boss," he said, his gaze darting to Bullet as he worked.

She nudged him with her shoulder. Even though Gig had just told Cade there was nothing going on between him and Sloane, a fresh wave of jealousy rolled through Cade at the look that passed between them.

He was in so much trouble.

"What did you find out about Celeste?" Sloane asked.

Gig clicked a few more keys. "Celeste Armand, 68. Born and raised in Nice. Studied in Paris. She actually interned at the Louvre and was the youngest intern they'd ever had at the time. Married Maxime Armand, heir to a large real estate development firm in Paris. They moved back to Nice not long after so Maxime could expand his business."

"She obviously didn't give up working in the art world."

Gig shook his head at her. "Just the opposite. She fought for additional funding for *Le Centre de Feu* and got it. In those days, the museum was little more than a protected landmark, a stop for tourists on their way to the beach. She made it what it is today." He stopped tapping and scrolled. "She's connected to almost every formal exhibit since the museum's grand reopening."

"When was that?" Sloane asked.

"Almost 30 years ago."

"And she's still on the payroll?" Cade asked.

"I think she's more of a consultant and part-time curator now, but I don't know for sure. She holds a seat on the board of directors, though," Gig said.

Sloane bit her lip and placed her mug back on the table.

"What?" Cade asked.

"I'm not sure," she said, shaking her head. "It's probably nothing."

"Do you think she's working with Doyle?" Cade asked.

"I want to say no because partnerships aren't exactly Doyle's style, but I don't know. I know I only spoke to her for a few minutes, but I got the feeling she's hiding something."

"Well, then I guess it's good that you start work on Monday," Gig said.

Cade nodded. "See what you can find out, but be careful. If she is working with Doyle, then too many questions too soon will tip her off."

"Really?" Sloane said. "Because I was thinking I should lead with the stolen emeralds and follow that up with, 'Are you working for a psychopath?'"

"Bullet," he chastised.

"Relax," she said. "I know what I'm doing."

It was the same retort she'd been throwing at him for days but without the same bite. Cade was almost relieved. He looked at Gig. "Have you checked the recorded footage for any sign of Doyle's potential buyer?"

"Yes, but there was nothing suspicious."

"Check it again. I want a download of everyone he talked to when he wasn't with Sloane."

"He wasn't doing business," Sloane said. "If he was, I doubt he would have spent so much time talking to me."

"You don't know that."

She rolled her eyes but said nothing.

"What else did the two of you talk about?" Gig asked.

Cade caught Sloane's eye before she glanced away. "Honestly, not much. I mean, nothing besides art and…Shakespeare."

Gig frowned. "Shakespeare?"

Sloane nodded. "We talked about Romeo and Juliet, which led to a discussion about tragedy. He said how a person reacts to tragedy can tell you a lot about them." She gazed out at the lawn like she was back in that moment with Doyle, and Cade wished he could reach into her head, find that moment, and rip it out with his bare hands. "Then he just... lost it. One minute, we were talking Greek tragedy, and the next, meltdown mode. It was all very..."

Psychotic. Perverted. Evil.

"... strange," Sloane finished.

"You need to watch yourself," Cade said.

She finally looked at him. "Isn't that what my backup is for?"

This time, there was an edge to her teasing tone, a weight to her words that reminded Cade of the pact they'd made. His response caught in his throat.

"You bet," Gig said, answering for him. "Just call me your personal recovery server. The Cloud is everywhere."

Sloane's smile was brief. "Honestly, it didn't go exactly as planned. We might need a Plan B. Doyle might not even remember my name, let alone want to see me again."

"I don't think that will be a problem," Gig said. He clicked a few keys and turned the computer to face them. On the screen was a live feed from the outside of Elena's apartment. On the front step was a long, narrow black box tied with a red bow.

"You're in," Gig said.

"I'm in," Sloane replied in a hushed voice.

She blinked up at Cade, and his stomach dropped like he'd just launched himself from the roof of a twenty-story building.

She was in.

19

"I think I should go with you," Sloane said, leaning her good side against the door frame. "The apartment is technically mine."

"No, thanks. Gig and I can handle it."

"Are you saying you actually enjoy installing security cameras?"

Cade smirked. "It's my job as backup."

"How convenient that you've chosen this moment to embrace your role."

"You're just pissed you drew the short straw," Cade said, his tone just cocky enough to be annoying. He leveled her with a stare. "You know it has to be you."

She knew, but that didn't mean she had to like it. "Can't I just send him an email?"

"Sure, if you want him to get it next year. You've seen the phone in his office, right?"

"Would that be so bad?"

"Yes."

"But—"

"Bullet," Cade said, taking a step toward her. "Albright is fair. Just tell him what happened. He'll understand."

"That's easy for you to say. You're not the one he's going to crucify."

"You're right," Cade said, flashing her a grin. "I'm not." He slapped her on the back and then started down the stairs on his way to the driveway, where Gig already waited in the car. "I'd wish you luck," he called over his shoulder, "but it won't do any good."

She gave him the universal sign she gave all assholes when they pissed her off.

"I saw that," Cade called without turning around.

As soon as they were gone, Sloane cleaned their breakfast dishes. Then she organized a closet that wasn't hers, read press releases about the upcoming exhibit at the museum, and skimmed a few art history articles to prepare for Monday. When she couldn't stall any longer, she powered up one of Gig's laptops.

Albright responded to her video chat request immediately. "Sloane," he greeted tersely.

"Hi."

His gaze darted to either side of her chair. "The boys?"

"At the apartment doing a security sweep."

"Good. And Doyle?"

"He made contact. We're in."

"Your cover?"

"Safe."

"Are you sure?"

Sloane frowned. "Pretty sure." She was used to getting the third degree from Albright, but something about the way he asked put her on high alert.

"And Cade?"

"He's fine." It wasn't a lie. Minus a bruised hand and ego, Cade *was* fine. Sloane stared at Albright. Did he know about Cade's panic attacks? She decided it was none of her business.

"You look tired," Albright said.

Drained was more like it. She'd felt like a train had hit her when she woke up in Cade's bed. Taking a shower made her feel better, but the evening had been emotional and filled with revelations she still needed to process.

"I could say the same about you."

Even though it was Saturday evening, it looked like Albright was in his office. The space was windowless and dimly lit, but Sloane could still make out the edge of the framed degree hanging on the wall over his head. He looked drawn and a little unkempt. The usual necktie he paired with his sweater vest was missing, and his graying hair stuck out from behind his ears. Nobody in their profession kept regular hours, but the way he looked and the stubble along his usually clean-shaven jaw gave Sloane pause. Had he even gone home last night?

"My appearance is not your concern. What *should* concern you is how you're going to get to the airport."

What?

Sloane swallowed hard. "I can explain."

"You can explain why you broke protocol and went dark last night without so much as a warning."

"I didn't want to give Doyle any reason to be suspicious. It was a special circumstance."

Albright looked at her like she was a contagious virus he wanted to eradicate from the planet. "There are no special circumstances in this unit other than the ones *I* define. Is that clear?"

"Yes, but I—"

"No!" Albright slammed his hand down on his desk, making Sloane jump. "There are no *buts*. From the beginning, I had my doubts about assigning you this case. Like Cade, I thought you were too close to it to be objective. But, I thought with his help, you might actually learn something."

Disappointment and anger flared inside her, mixing with guilt and shame at his words. She opened her mouth to…what? Rail against Cade? Tell Albright he wasn't being fair? If she did that, she'd accomplish nothing other than to make herself look even more like a petulant child.

"You're a good officer, Easton," Albright continued in a tone that was anything but complimentary. "Nobody can read people the way you can, not even Cade. I know what you've been through. Anyone else in your position would have run as far and as fast from this life as possible, but you ran toward it."

Sloane bit her tongue until she tasted blood. She had. And now, she couldn't imagine her life any other way. Panic seized her as she wondered if she would have to.

"I respect you for that," he said. "You're here because you impressed me. But you, Sloane Easton, are a wildcard. And I don't play poker."

Sloane leaned forward, gripping the sides of the chair so hard her knuckles ached. "I can do better."

"Not can, *will*. You will do better. Because if you don't, if you can't play by the rules, then there's no room for you on this team. Can you play by my rules, Easton?"

"Yes," Sloane croaked. She cleared her throat. "Yes, I can."

"Good. Because if you pull another stunt like you did last night, I will pull you from this job and this unit so fast you won't know what hit you. Am I making myself clear?"

"Yes."

Albright nodded. "Have Cade check in with me on Monday."

Before Sloane could reply, the screen went dark, leaving her with nothing to do but sit back and stare at the wall.

20

Then

Cade bounded through the front door of the Easton house. "Beck?"

"In here."

He followed Beck's voice and the smell of freshly baked cookies to the kitchen. He stopped short, his sneakers squeaking on the tile as he assessed the scene in front of him. A pacing Beck, a harried-looking Faye, a kitchen that looked like the aftermath of an explosion, and Bullet, hunched over the kitchen table in a fancy dress, holding her mother's hand and rubbing at red, swollen eyes.

When she saw him, Sloane groaned and leveled an accusatory glare at her brother. "Why don't you just drive through the neighborhood with a megaphone? It would save time."

"You know I wouldn't do that. Cade's here to help."

"I already told you. There's nothing either of you can do. It's over." Sloane's face crumpled again, and she bowed her head, a tangle of blonde curls falling over one cheek.

Cade's gut clenched. "What's over?"

"That asshat dumped my sister."

"Beckett Easton III," Faye said.

Beck scoffed. "Asshat isn't even a word."

Faye just stared at her son until he grumbled something unintelligible and retrieved two dollar bills from his back pocket. Reluctantly, he crossed the kitchen and dropped them into the overflowing jar on the counter.

"Chad dumped you?" Cade asked.

She nodded. "He's taking someone else to prom."

"Wait," Beck said to Cade. "You knew about this?"

"Of course not."

"But you knew she was dating Chad Renfro?"

"Renfro?"

"Yeah, as in Bobby Renfro's little brother."

Bobby Renfro. Cade's nemesis and the kid who had made their lives hell growing up. Luckily, repeated visits to the Eastons' garage had put Cade solidly in another weight class by high school, and Bobby had left them alone. He'd gone to college out of state, but that didn't mean he wasn't still somewhere out there wreaking havoc. A trait that apparently ran in the family.

"*That*, I didn't know." Cade looked at Sloane. "You lied."

"I didn't lie. I just didn't tell the whole truth." She winced at her own explanation, her expression growing pained again. "And anyway, it doesn't matter anymore."

But it mattered. He should have pried it out of her, asked more questions. Especially on her birthday when she'd visited him in Wilson's garage and asked his advice about…oh, God. "Did he hurt you?"

Beck crossed the kitchen again and came to stand beside Cade. "Did he?"

"No," Sloane said. "Not unless you count making me out to be the joke of our entire senior class. At least I don't have to suffer that humiliation in person."

Cade relaxed slightly, watching as Beck did the same. At least neither of them would have to make Bobby Renfro an only child.

"You have nothing to be ashamed of," Beck said. "Which is something everyone will see when you show up at prom."

Sloane looked at Beck. "I'm not going to prom."

"Yes, you are."

"No, she's not," Cade said at the same time Sloane said. "No, I'm not."

"You have to! If you don't go, that dickwad, *aargh.*" Faye raised an eyebrow, and Beck reached into his pocket for another single and slammed it down on the kitchen table. "If you don't go, Chad will think he won. You don't want him to win, do you?"

It was horrible logic. The worst Cade had ever heard. "You don't have to do this," he said to Sloane.

Beck rolled his eyes. "What should she do instead? Hide in her room all night crying while Chad gets it on with another girl? Sorry, but it's true," he said when Faye gasped. He looked at Sloane. "You're too good to let him see your tears."

Beck had that right. Bullet was too good for Chad. She was too good for any guy, especially him.

Wait. *What?*

"So, what do you say?" Beck asked.

Sloane's brow creased in concentration as she considered his words. Cade knew from the slump of her shoulders what her answer would be even before she opened her mouth.

Ding dong.

For a second, nobody moved. Sloane's hopeful expression as she gazed longingly toward the front door nearly gutted Cade.

Then Faye stood, giving her daughter's hand a last squeeze. "I'll get it."

"I'm coming too," Beck said.

Cade followed suit, exchanging a look with his friend that he could tell Beck understood. If Chad Renfro dared to show up after what he'd done, he was stupider than they'd thought.

"Guys, wait!" Sloane said. She tried to get past them both, but Beck held her back with one arm. Halfway to the door, she hopped onto his back, cursing under her breath when her dress caused her to slide right off.

"I heard that," Faye said over her shoulder, the three of them nearly crashing into her as she swung open the door.

Their visitor, startled by their marching band greeting, took a step back and balanced precariously on one foot as he tipped back. Before he could fall off the porch, Cade fisted his shirt and tugged him forward.

"Thanks?" he said as if he wasn't entirely sure he should thank Cade for anything.

Accurate, considering he didn't have long to live.

"You have some nerve showing up here," Cade said. The kid's eyes widened in fear, but Cade didn't let go.

"Daniel!" Faye exclaimed. "How lovely to see you."

Daniel?

"Cade, stop," Sloane said, breaking through the human barricade. "This isn't Chad."

"It's not?"

Sloane shook her head. "This is Dan. My math tutor."

Cade took another look at the lanky kid whose polo shirt he still gripped. The kid raised his hands in surrender, one of which held a textbook.

"You can let him go now," Sloane said, swatting at his hand. When Cade reluctantly let go, Sloane shoved him aside and looked at Dan. "Sorry about that."

"N-n-no problem."

Sloane reached out to smooth his shirt, but he didn't seem to notice. In fact, from the way he stared at Sloane, Cade doubted Dan would notice if a tornado touched down on the Eastons' front lawn.

"So," Sloane said. "What's up?"

Dan licked his lips, his Adam's apple working as he cast a wary glance at Cade. He inhaled sharply, prompting a coughing fit that had him bending at the waist.

Sloane pounded him on the back. "Are you alright?"

Dan jumped at the contact, eventually straightening and covering his reaction with a shaky laugh. "I'm great," he squeaked and then winced at the sound of his own voice. "I just…uh…you look really nice."

Cade frowned. In a deep green, floor-length gown that clung to her like a second skin, Bullet looked more than just *nice*.

Sloane gave him a tired smile. "Thanks. Is that for me?" She asked, gesturing to the textbook he held.

Dan looked down at his hand, confusion crossing his face as though just noticing it was there. "Yes," he finally said. "You left it at my house yesterday, and I…uh…wanted to return it. You know, in case you needed it to study." He shoved the text at her, and Sloane gave a tiny *harrumph* as it connected with her abdomen. "Sorry."

"It's okay," she said, clearly amused by his shyness.

Cade did not find it entertaining. He glanced at Beck, but his friend's attention was on Sloane and Dan as they awkwardly attempted to make conversation.

"So," Dan said, shifting in place. "I guess you're going to prom?"

Sloane looked down at her dress. "I was, but—"

"Hi, Dan," Beck said, stepping forward. He moved in front of Sloane and stuck out his hand. "I'm Beck. Sloane's brother."

Beck's grin was too wide, and his voice too pleasant to be casual. He also avoided Cade's questioning look, which meant he was up to something.

Before Cade could ask, Dan lifted one of his spaghetti arms and shook Beck's hand. "Uh…nice to meet you? I'm Dan, Sloane's math tutor? But I guess you already know that."

"The pleasure's all mine," Beck said. Dan tried to release his hand, but Beck tugged it back. "Are you a senior?"

Dan shook his head. "A junior."

"Dan's a math genius," Sloane said. "He's good at just about anything that involves numbers."

Dorky Dan blushed, and Beck's grin widened. "Do you have any plans tonight, Dan?"

"No?"

"How'd you like to go to prom?"

"*What?*" Dan and Cade said at the same time.

Beck yanked Dan forward. "Come on in, man, and make yourself at home." He led Dan to the living room and shoved him down on the couch.

"*Beck,*" Sloane hissed. "What are you doing? Dan can't take me to prom."

"Why not? He just said he doesn't have any plans. And you need a date."

"You do?" Dan asked.

"No, I—"

"My sister got dumped today, Dan," Beck said.

Sloane groaned and covered her face with her hands.

"Now, I know we don't know each other, but you seem like a nice enough guy. *Are* you a nice guy?"

"Uh…yes?"

"That's what I thought. Nice enough to want to help my pretty sister make her ex-boyfriend jealous?"

Sloane groaned again, louder this time, and Faye cleared her throat and stepped forward. "Beck, Dan just got here. I think we should give him some time to…settle in." She turned to their visitor, smiling widely. "Do you like cookies, dear?"

Dan shot to his feet. "No!" Faye reared back, and Dan shook his head and nodded. "I mean, yes, ma'am, I like cookies, but no, I don't need more time." He straightened and squared his shoulders. "I'll do it."

"Oh, for Christ's sake," Cade said.

Faye slapped the back of his head and then held out a hand. Knowing he was good for it, Cade slapped a fiver into her palm and rubbed behind his ear.

"You don't have to do this," Sloane said, echoing Cade's earlier sentiment. "I'm not going to prom, anyway."

"Yes, you are." All eyes swung to Faye, who leveled her daughter with a determined stare. "Whether you go with Dan or alone is up to you, but you *are* going to that prom."

"But Mom, I—"

"Your brother's right." Faye grasped both of Sloane's hands. "Go. If only to show that no-good, phony piece of…" Faye glanced around the circle, "*scum*, you're stronger than he is."

"I can't."

"You *can*. You can do anything you want to do." Faye lifted Sloane's chin to meet her gaze. "If you don't do this, you'll regret it. Maybe not today or tomorrow, but someday you'll think back on this night and wish you'd been brave enough. Life's too short to live with regret."

Sloane nodded slowly and turned to Dan, who blinked at her like she was one of the seven wonders of the world.

Cade's stomach twisted. He probably shouldn't have had that burrito for lunch.

"Will you go to prom with me?" she asked.

"Uh…"

"Of course, he will," Beck said. He slapped Dan hard on the back, causing him to stumble forward. "He just said he would, didn't you, Dan?"

"Yes?"

Cade scowled at his friend, a scowl he still wore thirty minutes later as he drove the four of them to the prom in his Mustang.

"Mom could have taken us, you know," Sloane said from the backseat.

"I got it."

Cade glanced at Dan in the rearview mirror. The initial shock of the evening's events had worn off, as had the adrenaline that had fueled his agreeing to the charade. Now Dorky Dan sat as stiff as petrified wood in the backseat, his expression somewhere between startled and constipated. Beck had dressed him in the suit he usually reserved for weddings, though, from the way Dan gripped the door handle, they could have been driving to a funeral. If Cade could find any humor in the situation at all, he'd laugh. Unfortunately, he didn't feel like laughing.

"Can you maybe slow down?" Sloane said. "I'd like to get to prom in one piece if that's okay with you."

"Seriously," Beck said. "Where's the fire?"

Cade eased up on the gas, biting his tongue to keep from answering Beck's question. The fire was inside him, a raging inferno of jealousy he had no right to feel. He didn't get jealous, and he certainly shouldn't be losing it over some math geek taking Sloane to prom. He had no claim on Bullet and never would. Why did that thought suddenly make him want to drive into a tree?

"We're here!"

Cade slammed his foot on the brake and jerked the wheel right. Apparently, he hadn't slowed down as much as he'd thought. The car dovetailed as he jerked the parking brake like a Formula One driver and they slid into the parking lot, screeching to a stop in between two spaces. The rear passenger door swung open and Dan launched himself out of the car, dropping to his hands and knees on the pavement as he gasped for breath.

"Dan?" Sloane asked, stretching over the middle seat for a better view. "Are you alright?" When she received a strangled groan in reply, she unfastened her seatbelt and got out of the car. "Thanks for giving my date a heart attack," she said when she was out, glaring at Cade through his open window and then through the windshield as she rounded the car.

My date.

Cade was halfway out of the car himself before Beck stopped him. "I'll take care of this," he said. "You cool off."

There was no hope of that actually happening, but Cade stayed put, quietly seething in his seat as Beck and Sloane helped Dan to his feet. Bullet fawned over him, straightening his suit and tie and murmuring something to him that put color back into his cheeks. They shared a smile, and Cade's fingers closed around the steering wheel.

Beck ushered them both forward, but Dan hesitated and then, to Cade's utter shock, walked up to the driver's side and shoved a hand through the open window. "Uh…thanks for the ride, sir."

Behind them, Beck let out a half-laugh, half-snort that Cade ignored as he took the kid's hand. He squeezed tight enough that Dan's face paled. "No problem."

He waited until Dan nodded before releasing his hand. Then, Bullet was in front of him, and he forgot all about Dorky Dan.

She'd fixed her hair before leaving the house, the curls now pinned up like a halo atop her head. Makeup hid the remnants of her pain, but her tears had made her eyes so bright they sparkled gold against the green of her dress. Cade's hand flexed on the steering wheel.

"I probably shouldn't be saying this because you almost killed us, but thank you," she said.

"You're welcome. I'll pick you up when it's over."

"Dan's dad said he would come get us."

"Dan's dad can get *him* if he wants to, but I'll be back for you." Sloane opened her mouth, probably to protest, but Cade shook his head. "I'm coming back for you, Bullet."

Instead of complaining, she surprised him with a smile. "Okay." She took a step toward Dan and Beck before turning back. She leaned forward, the folds of her dress rustling against his forearm as she placed a soft kiss on his cheek. "Thanks," she murmured in his ear before straightening again.

Goosebumps rose on his skin as he watched her walk back to Dan, the two of them hurrying to catch up with the group standing outside the venue.

Beck pounded on the car's roof. "Pop the trunk, will you?"

Dazed, Cade reached for the lever, jumping in his seat when the trunk slammed closed again, and Beck slid back into the passenger seat.

"What's that?" Cade asked.

"We can't stay out here all night without provisions." He pulled two cans of Coke free from a six-pack on his lap and placed them in the cup holders before ripping open a bag of barbecue chips.

"We're staying?"

"Of course, we're staying. Did you really think I was going to leave my sister alone with a stranger on prom night?"

For the first time all night, Cade relaxed. He reached for his soda, watching as Sloane and Dan greeted their friends. They were too close together, but at least Dorky Dan had enough sense to keep his hands to himself.

"You know he's afraid of you, right?" Beck said.

"Good."

He laughed and shook his head. "She'll be alright."

"Yeah," Cade said, his attention still on the pair as they made their way to the hotel's front entrance and lined up in front of a row of students holding cell phones.

Bullet *would* be okay because he'd make sure of it. He leaned back and sipped his drink but then quickly sat up when he saw a guy approaching Sloane and Dan.

"That's him," Beck said.

"I know," Cade said because, now that he'd seen him, there was no doubt in his mind.

Chad Renfro looked just like his brother. With his broad, athletic build and dark hair, he could easily have been Bobby's twin. A slight, red-headed girl in a tight black dress that left nothing to the imagination followed close behind, struggling to catch up to his long stride. When he finally stopped, the girl immediately attached herself to his side, but Chad didn't even glance her way. All his attention was on Sloane, the animosity rolling off him in waves so strong, Cade could feel them bounce off the Mustang's hood.

He swung open the door.

"Wait," Beck said.

"*Wait?*"

"Yes."

"Why?"

"Because it's working. Look at him," Beck said. "He's mad as hell."

"That's exactly why we need to be there."

"No," Beck said, in a tone Cade had rarely heard him use. In fact, the last time he'd heard it had been in middle school when he'd mentioned to Beck he wanted to drop out. Beck had taken one look at him and told him if he did that, they couldn't be friends anymore because he wasn't friends with losers. "She has to do this on her own," he said. "If she doesn't stand up to him now, she never will."

Reluctantly, Cade slammed the door shut. He slouched in his seat but kept one hand on the handle just in case. Even with his window open, he was too far away to hear what Chad said to them, but it made Sloane angry enough that she got in his face. Cade smirked. At least she wasn't taking his bullshit lying down.

Still, he watched Chad carefully, making sure he didn't make a move that would shorten his lifespan. Instead, he barked again, and this time, whatever he said made Sloane wince and shrink away from him. This had gone far enough.

This time, Cade had one foot out the door before Beck stopped him. "Just give him a second."

Him?

Cade looked back just in time to see Dan step in front of Bullet, shielding her with his body. He said something to Chad, something else Cade couldn't hear, but everyone else apparently could. The crowd erupted in laughter, and Chad froze at the jeers of his classmates. Then he whirled and stalked away, his date trailing close behind.

"It looks like the kid's got some balls after all," Beck said.

He did, but Cade wouldn't admit it. Nor would he admit what the sight of the grateful smile Bullet gave Dorky Dan did to his stomach.

Damn burrito.

"He could have at least sent Chad home with a black eye."

"Hey, Foster?" Beck said, handing over the chips.

"Yeah?"

"Shut up."

21

Hours after her call with Albright, Sloane stood in the upstairs bathroom and stared at her reflection. The mirror was larger than the one downstairs, which meant that she had a much better view of how awful she looked. A nap hadn't helped, nor had the long run she'd taken that afternoon, during which she'd contemplated the irony of finally being able to do what she wanted without Cade breathing down her neck. He now trusted her enough to leave her alone at the villa but had no intention of treating her like an actual partner.

He'd used her. He'd done it at the charity benefit and then again when they'd returned home, using her concern for him to get what he wanted. Well, if running to Albright with news of her indiscretions was some kind of lesson, she'd certainly learned hers. As far as she was concerned, her agreement with Cade was void.

After a second shower, Sloane slipped into a navy cotton T-shirt dress and padded barefoot to the stairs. She paused at the sound of voices coming from the first floor and inhaled the scent of garlic and olive oil as it wafted to her from the kitchen. Her stomach growled, reminding her she hadn't eaten since breakfast, and she tiptoed down the stairs, her curiosity and empty stomach winning out over a probable confrontation with Cade. On the last stair, she peeked around the corner, surprised to find the two strangers she'd seen last night giving Gig their full attention.

"So, I tell Jess she's crazy, and there's no way the Wall Street suit sitting next to her at the bar would let himself get conned.

Not because she didn't look hot, of course, but because he seemed too smart to let it happen," Gig said.

"Let what happen?" the man asked. Jean-Paul, Sloane assumed, remembering Cade's mention of him the night before.

"I'm getting to that," Gig said, waving a hand. "I only had fifteen dollars in my wallet, so I bet her she couldn't pull one over on him. She winked at me, moved closer, and then slid her hand along his jacket pocket."

"She picked his pocket?"

"Yup. And then she bent over and pretended to find it on the ground. He thanked her by picking up her entire tab."

"*Incroyable*," Jean-Paul said, lapsing into French so smooth Sloane could have spread it on toast.

Gig shrugged. "She got a free meal, and I got a girlfriend. Of course, that was also the last time I made a bet with Jess."

"You should never bet against a strong woman," said their female visitor. Bianca also had a strong accent, but it differed from her companion's. Italian, Sloane guessed, based on the way she gestured with her hands as she spoke. "You will lose every time."

Jean-Paul sent Bianca a hard look that seemed completely out of place on his near-perfect face. In crisp white linen pants and a tailored button-down the same cerulean blue as his eyes, one-half of Cade's backup could have given Barbie's Ken some stiff competition.

Bianca ignored him and glided over to Gig, looking just as heart-stopping as Jean-Paul in a plum-colored maxi dress and gladiator sandals. Unlike last night, her hair was loose, the shiny, silky strands falling over one shoulder as she leaned in and smoothed Gig's hair with one hand. "A handsome man like you has all the women drooling, no?"

Gig stared at her like one of the anime characters he and Jess obsessed over, and Sloane got the impression that was probably the look most men gave Bianca. It wasn't hard to imagine her materializing from a magic lamp to grant a man three wishes, all of them involving her.

"Stop playing with him, *ma petite sirène*," Jean-Paul said. "You'll give him a heart attack."

Bianca pouted. "Why do you always spoil my fun?"

"It's my job as your husband to save the lives of the innocent."

"You're married?" When all the eyes in the room swung to her, Sloane realized she'd spoken aloud.

Bianca's lips split into a blindingly gorgeous smile. "You must be Sloane," she said, crossing the kitchen and folding her into a tight hug. "We've heard so much about you." After another minute, Bianca finally let her go but kept hold of both of her hands. "I'm Bianca, and yes, this is my husband, Jean-Paul Laurent."

Jean-Paul stepped forward and reached out a hand, giving her a similar dazzling smile. "Please, call me JP. It's very nice to meet you, Sloane."

Sloane pulled away from Bianca to shake his hand. "I know who you are. It's very nice to meet you both."

"Is it?" JP asked, his clear blue eyes sparking with amusement. "Does that mean you forgive us for interfering last evening?"

Sloane shifted in place and glanced down at the tile floor. "Uh…sure."

"JP."

She turned at the sound of Cade's voice, noticing him for the first time standing by the sink, stirring something in a saucepan on the stove. He glanced at her and then at Jean-Paul, his brow furrowing in displeasure.

"What? You don't think I know when our presence is a surprise? I've been at this far longer than you have." Jean-Paul looked back at Sloane. "You'll have to excuse my friend for his rather unfortunate behavior. He can't seem to help himself."

Despite her mood, Sloane grinned. "He can't, can he?"

"I'm standing right here," Cade grumbled.

"Well," Sloane said, ignoring him, "I suppose I should thank you for last night. The both of you, I mean." It wasn't their fault that Cade didn't tell her they would be there. The least she could do was show her gratitude for their help.

"It's our job," Bianca said.

"Yes, and where else would my wife be able to wear the dresses she buys to attend such occasions?"

"You say that as if your closet isn't bigger than mine."

Cade laughed. "She's got you there, buddy."

"Yes, well, at least I have only one," Jean-Paul said, giving his wife another pointed look.

Bianca merely shrugged and plucked a tomato out of a salad bowl on the counter.

"Hey," Cade said, approaching Sloane from behind. He handed her a glass of red wine. "Are you hungry?"

She took the glass, swallowing half of it in record time, before smacking her lips. "Starved."

"We're having Spaghetti Puttanesca," Gig said. "Cade made it."

"You can't cook," Sloane said to Cade.

"Since when?"

"Since you started eating at our house when you were nine."

"That doesn't mean I don't know how."

"Cade is an excellent cook," Bianca said. "His spaghetti is the best, and he doesn't even use a recipe."

"I've got it all right here," Cade said, tapping his temple with a finger.

Sloane took another large swallow of wine. "Well, I guess I shouldn't miss out, especially if it's the best. We all know how much Cade likes to be the best, don't we?"

The room fell silent as Sloane slammed the stem of her glass down on the kitchen island. Thankfully, the glass didn't shatter, not even when she gripped it so hard her knuckles turned white.

Cade frowned at her and then turned and walked back to the stove.

"Well," Gig said, his voice an octave too high. "I'm hungry enough to eat just about anything so unless liver is on the menu, I'm not picky."

"Let's *mangia!*" Bianca said as she picked up the salad bowl and started for the dining room. Sloane didn't miss the way Jean-Paul intercepted her to take it from her hands or the way Bianca scrunched up her nose and stalked out of the kitchen ahead of him.

Interesting.

Sloane shook her head. She had enough drama in her life and couldn't afford to add someone else's to an already-full plate.

Cade turned a dial on the stove and lifted the pot off the burner, placing it on the island before facing her with his arms folded over his chest. "I take it things didn't go well with Albright?"

"You tell me."

"What?"

Sloane glared at him. "You must really think I'm an idiot."

"I don't, but something tells me my opinion doesn't matter much right now."

"You're right, it doesn't. Not after you sold me out to our handler to make yourself look good."

"Excuse me?"

"It turns out I didn't need to brief Albright at all about last night because he already knew."

Cade dipped his chin, returning her glare. "And you think I told him?"

"Do you deny it?"

"Yes, I deny it. The last time I talked to Albright was yesterday morning before the charity benefit."

"And then you called him again last night."

"When?"

"What?"

"When did I supposedly give Albright the play-by-play? During our completely silent drive home from the event, or later, when I lost my shit."

Sloane paused at the mention of his panic attack, some of her anger deflating at the reminder. "After I fell asleep."

"You mean after *we* fell asleep in *my* bed?"

Heat crept up the back of Sloane's neck, and she felt her cheeks flame, but she'd come too far to back down now. "You could have snuck out to make the call."

"And then made you call him this morning as some kind of joke?"

"As payback."

Cade frowned. "You'll have to be more specific. I'm having trouble figuring out which of your multiple offenses applies."

"I knew it!" She rounded the counter and met him on his side, fury lacing her words. "You're still holding a grudge. You were just waiting for—"

"What? The right time to screw you?" Cade barked a laugh. "Sweetheart, if I wanted to do that, I would have done it long before now."

Sloane gasped. "How dare you."

"*Me*? You're the one slinging accusations around with no proof."

"I shut you out last night, and you were angry."

"Yes, I was. But then we discussed it and moved on."

"I did. You didn't."

"So I tattled to Albright like some five-year-old?" Cade laughed again. "That's funny."

"It's not, actually."

"No, you're right. It's not funny at all being accused of being a vindictive asshole. It's even less funny that you think I believe the best way to solve our problems is to go to our handler instead of working it out."

"It's obvious you have a different agenda than the one we agreed to last night," Sloane said. "That's fine, so do I."

Cade's eyes narrowed into tiny slits. "What's that supposed to mean?"

"Nothing."

"My agenda hasn't changed. It's the same as it was last night when we agreed to work together."

"That was before." Before she knew where his loyalties lay. Before he'd lied to her about everything that mattered.

"I don't need Albright to fight my battles for me."

"I thought that was the case, but I was wrong."

Cade's jaw ticked, the lines of his face becoming angular and sharp. "Well, at least you've got one thing right with all this bullshit you've been spewing."

"It's not bullshit."

"You *are* wrong," he continued as if she hadn't spoken. "But instead of asking yourself why you want me to be guilty, you're going to take the easy way out."

"That's not true," she said.

"It is."

"Are you calling me a liar?"

"No," he said, shaking his head. "I'm calling you a coward."

She barely registered her hand leaving her side, barely had time to raise it before he caught her wrist in midair, gripping it tight. "Let me go!"

"Calm down first."

Instead, she clawed at his chest with her other hand, growling and tugging the arm he held until her biceps ached. Cade just stood there, still as a statue, watching her struggle.

"I said, let me go," she seethed.

"If you don't stop, you're going to hurt yourself."

She lifted her leg, preparing to knee him in the groin, but Cade expected the move, abruptly letting her go at the last minute. Sloane stumbled back and reached out to brace herself, the palm of her left hand coming down hard on the stove's still-hot burner. Searing pain shot up her arm her, and she cried out, yanking her hand back and hugging it to her chest.

Cade was beside her in an instant. "Let me see."

"Go to hell," she snapped.

"Stay," he said as he walked to the freezer.

Sloane glared at him. "I'm not a dog."

"You're right. Dogs do what they're told." He pulled out a tray of ice cubes and wrapped a few in a dish towel before returning to her. "Give me your hand."

Relenting, Sloane shoved her hand at him, and he cradled the back of it before pressing the towel to her palm. She hissed as he made contact and Cade's touch gentled. They stood there in silence, Sloane's anger fading along with the sting of the burn as the ice numbed her skin. Without meaning to, she swayed on her feet, and Cade turned them, allowing her to lean against the counter for support.

He took her other hand and placed it on the towel, stacking his on top, like they were kids huddling before a football game. "I'm sorry."

"I'm the one who fell on the stove."

"No, well, I'm sorry for that too, but I'm more sorry about what I said. I don't think you're a coward. You're here, doing this incredibly brave and dangerous thing, and I just…" He lifted the hand on top of theirs and grazed her jaw with the backs of his fingers, his touch sending shock waves of heat through her body. "I gave you my word, Bullet. No more secrets."

His word. The one thing Sloane knew mattered to him more than anything. Did she believe him? Could she, when he was still keeping the biggest secret of all?

Cade opened his mouth again, but before he could say anything more, Gig walked back into the kitchen. He stopped short when he saw them, his eyes darting from the ice pack she held to Cade and back again, a slow grin spreading over his face.

Sloane immediately stepped back, gripping the ice pack as Cade's hands fell away from hers.

"I just forgot the bread," Gig said, grabbing the basket on the counter. "Carry on."

It wasn't until he'd left again that Sloane realized her mistake. She glanced at Cade, who, judging by his annoyed yet slightly amused expression, had come to the same conclusion she had.

"I'll talk to him," Cade said.

Sloane sighed. "I'll do it. He probably just wanted to impress Albright." It had never occurred to her that Gig would be the one to brief Albright, but now that she thought about it, it made perfect sense. He'd been worried about her and would have gone to the one person he knew could help.

"Apology accepted."

"I didn't apologize," she said, even though she knew she should.

"You can make it up to me by tasting my sauce," Cade said, dipping a wooden spoon into the pot cooling on the counter.

"I'm not that sorry."

"Would you rather tell me about this grand plan of yours that's so different from mine?"

"No."

Cade held a spoonful of sauce to her lips, his intense stare making her heart skip. "There are no ulterior motives or hidden agendas. Not anymore. We work together, and we succeed or fail *together*. Got it?"

She flushed and inched back half a step, reaching for the spoon. "I can feed myself."

"I need the words," Cade said, tugging the spoon away.

"Yes. I understand."

He nodded. "Now, open." Cade's gaze fell to her mouth as she parted her lips. "Good?" He asked once she'd swallowed.

"Good," she agreed, even though she couldn't taste a thing.

22

Somehow, Cade made it through dinner without throwing Bullet over his shoulder, loading her into the car, and driving her back to the airport. Nothing had changed on that front. He still wanted her the hell away from this mess, even more now after what had transpired last night and today. That probably made him an asshole, but he could live with that. Just like he lived with everything else he'd done and would do to keep her safe.

He brooded as Sloane laughed and joked with Gig, whispered with Bianca like they were old friends, and even, to Cade's annoyance, flirted with Jean-Paul. She also ate seconds of his pasta and had three glasses of the Laurents' French wine, besides the one she'd finished in the kitchen. To everyone at the table, Bullet likely seemed positively jovial.

Everyone except for Cade.

And, by the furtive glances she sent his way, she knew it.

He'd known something was wrong the minute she walked into the kitchen, looking like she used to whenever she went a few rounds with her mother. Faye was a saint but still no match for the hurricane that was Sloane as a teenager. That changed when she became an adult, and even though it had been months since he'd seen them together, he knew they were still close. It was Faye who had taught him how to deal with her daughter. Not that he'd needed lessons. For him, it was simple. He waited her out until she was ready to talk or until he couldn't wait anymore, whichever came first.

Of course, with Bullet, getting what he wanted didn't come with the same level of satisfaction as winning at most everything else. Instead, it came with its usual mix of batshit crazy and mind-numbing frustration. He'd seen the truth in her eyes the minute Gig walked out of the kitchen for the second time and they both realized it wasn't Cade who had told Albright what had happened.

She'd wanted it to be him.

He deserved that and so much more for the things he'd done. So why had he fought so hard to convince her otherwise? Hadn't he already given her every reason not to trust him? If Gig hadn't interrupted them, he would have given her one more. He would have told her right there in the middle of the goddamned kitchen. But no, it was also just as likely that he would have chickened out like he had all the other times he'd tried to tell her, like he had every time he picked up the phone and dialed half of her number, only to hang up without making the call.

Because, even though he hadn't done what she'd accused him of, he was still guilty. Sloane wasn't the coward.

He was.

"So, what's the play?" Jean-Paul asked, breaking into his thoughts.

Cade pushed his plate away. "Albright wants Doyle's buyer."

"Who is he?"

"We haven't been able to determine that yet," Cade said.

"But whoever it is has potentially worked with Doyle for years," Gig chimed in. He gave the Laurents an abbreviated version of Doyle's history with the emeralds.

When he was done, JP looked thoughtful. "So, Albright thinks whoever it is will admit to hiring Doyle."

"He might. With the right incentive," Cade said.

"But, is it enough?"

"If it's not, after working with him for so many years, the buyer likely knows more than one person on Doyle's client list."

JP frowned. "It's not much to go on."

"What if he doesn't talk at all?" Bianca asked.

"He will," Sloane said. All heads swiveled to her, and she sat up straighter in her chair. "All of Doyle's clients have one thing in common. They'll sell anyone down the river to save their own ass."

JP leaned back in his chair. "It's a risky bet."

"It's not a bet. It's the way they operate. Besides, I wouldn't leave something as important as justice for the man who killed my brother up to chance."

Cade winced.

Bianca's eyes widened. "Doyle is the one responsible for Beckett's death?"

Sloane's accusing glare was even worse than the one she'd given him in the kitchen. "You didn't tell them?"

"I was getting to that." Cade sighed and looked at Bianca. "Jack Doyle's men were the ones who raided Juarez's shipment in Miami last year."

"*Mio Dio.*"

"I can't believe you didn't tell them," Sloane said.

"I'm telling them now." Cade stared at her, urging her to read the meaning behind his words.

No more secrets.

It was a half-truth, and they both knew it, but Cade was still grateful when she nodded and relaxed back in her chair.

"It doesn't matter that he didn't tell us," Bianca said. "When Cade calls, we come." She placed a hand over Bullet's arm. "We would have done the same for Beckett."

"How well did you know Beck?" Sloane asked, looking as though she might cry.

"We knew him well enough to know he was a good man. You're so much like him."

"You don't even know me."

"I know all I need to know," Bianca said before turning back to Cade. "We will help you."

"*Mon amour…*" Jean-Paul started.

Bianca shushed him with a look. "We will help you," she said again, clasping her hands together on the table. She inclined her head toward her husband. "Tell him."

Cade glanced between the two of them as they engaged in silent conversation. He knew JP would do anything for his wife, but right now, he sensed his friend's hesitation. "If you want out, now's the time. No hard feelings."

JP gave his wife one last look and rapped his knuckles on the table. "We are here for you, my friend. For as long as you need us."

Cade could only nod, his throat suddenly tight with gratitude. He didn't have many friends. Other than Beck and Bullet, he'd lost touch with almost everyone else. Being a spy usually put a damper on relationships, at least the genuine kind. He'd accepted it, but he'd always had Beck. Now that he was gone, Cade's world seemed much larger and a lot less forgiving.

"Just please don't cook like this every night, or I might have to change my exercise routine," JP said, patting a stomach that was flatter than Cade's.

"Speak for yourself," Bianca said. "I nearly starved when you left Paris. All Jean-Paul can cook is that American dish with cheese and bread."

"Grilled cheese?" Gig asked.

"Yes!"

Cade grinned. "JP makes a mean grilled cheese."

"Thanks for the support," JP deadpanned.

"You were in Paris?"

Cade glanced at Sloane, who had stayed quiet for most of the exchange. Now she studied him as though trying to work something out in her head. "For a bit."

"On a job?"

"Not exactly," he said, settling for vague honesty rather than all-out truth.

She opened her mouth to say something else, but Jean-Paul spoke first. "How confident are you that Doyle doesn't know who you really are?"

Sloane rolled her eyes. "Now you sound like Albright."

JP exchanged a look with Cade, sending him a silent message that Cade didn't miss. If Doyle knew someone was on to him, he would be even more dangerous. Men like Doyle liked to play with their food before devouring it whole—which is why Cade was determined to be at the top of the food chain.

"Albright is a smart man," Bianca said.

"I'm fairly certain he doesn't know who I am. He thinks I am a contract curator hired to help organize the museum's upcoming exhibit."

JP nodded and then excused himself from the table. He returned a minute later with the long, black box they'd seen in front of Elena's apartment that morning on Gig's security feed. "Then I suppose this is for you."

Cade was out of his chair and at Sloane's side before JP set the box down in front of her. He looked over her shoulder as she unraveled the bow and lifted the lid to reveal two dozen blood-red roses neatly packed in black tissue paper. Cade reached for the small white envelope resting on the stems, but Sloane was faster, sliding it out from under his palm before he got the chance.

"Who's Juliet?" Gig asked, peering over Sloane's other shoulder at the envelope.

Cade wanted the answer to that question as well, but Sloane ignored him as she pulled out the card and scanned its contents. When she was done, she looked at Cade the way she'd done when they were kids, and she beat him at a game of UNO, her excitement making his stomach cramp.

Frowning, he plucked the card from her hands.

The Tempter or the Tempted, who sins the most?

"Is this a quote?" Cade asked her.

"Yes."

"Who said it?"

"I think…Shakespeare."

Cade recalled their conversation the night before and that morning about what she and Doyle had talked about in the gardens. He read the note again and then a third time, the slanted, black script blurring the longer he stared at it. Then, without a word, he tore the card to shreds and let the pieces flutter to the ground at his feet.

23

Then

He found her, of all places, on the beach. Well, not exactly *on* the beach. Bullet never actually got that far. Instead, she hovered at the edge, her toes barely breaching the no-man's-land between the grass and the sand. The question of why she never ventured close to the water had kept him up some nights, but that was nothing new. He thought of Sloane whether he was awake or asleep.

Maybe that would change once he left.

As Cade neared the tree stump where she sat, she looked up at him and smiled, her amber eyes twinkling in the late afternoon sun. "Looking for me?"

"We're about to head out."

"Okay," Sloane said, rising.

"Can I…uh…talk to you for a second?"

She glanced toward the parking lot, where their friends were already loading up the cars for the trip home. He followed her gaze to find a lone figure standing on the blacktop, watching them. Beck was too far away for Cade to see his frown, but he knew it was there, just as it had been when Cade told him the news.

"Sure. Is everything ok?"

She sat back down, and Cade joined her, taking a seat on the stump next to hers. "It's great, actually. I…got a job."

After hours of rehearsal, he'd decided enthusiasm was the way to go. Strangely, it had been practicing what he would say that had finally convinced him to take the job. Didn't government agents consider every angle before engaging in a potentially hostile situation? Would *agent* even be his official job title?

Sloane looked confused. "You have a job."

"I mean, a *real* job."

"You have a real job."

It was an argument they sometimes had when he waved off the work he did for Wilson. He'd opted to work instead of going to college, but while his father had made a living owning and working at a garage, Cade hadn't realized until recently that he didn't want it to be *his* life's work.

"This is a different job."

"Doing what?"

"Customer service." Sebastian Albright had given him the same description when they met as if they were in a business meeting instead of standing in a train station parking lot.

"But you hate people."

"I don't hate people."

"So, the reason Wilson sends you into the back to work every time a new customer comes into the shop has nothing to do with the fact that customers are afraid of you?"

"I'm a mechanic, Bullet. I'm supposed to work on cars."

"Right."

"Anyway, a guy—"

"What guy?"

"My new boss. He offered me this job helping him find people and—"

"Oh, so he's a recruiter?"

"Yeah…sure."

Sloane's eyes narrowed. "Why are you being so weird?"

"I'm not being weird."

"Yes, you are. Does Beck know about this?"

"Yes."

"And what did he say?"

"What does it matter what he said?"

"He thought it was weird, too."

"No, he didn't." It wasn't exactly a lie. Beck had said little when Cade had told him about the job offer the day they'd arrived at the campground. He'd just slapped Cade on the back and asked him to help set up their tent.

"Right," Sloane said again. "Okay, well, you're going to take it, then?"

"Yes."

"When does it start?"

"I have to leave soon."

"Leave? You mean, the job's not in town?"

Cade shook his head. "I'll be traveling for a while."

"Where will you go?"

"I'm not sure yet."

"When will you be back?"

"I…don't know."

"This makes no sense," she said, incredulous. "Just last week, you were talking about adding another terminal to the garage so Wilson could take on more customers. Now, suddenly, you want to pick up and leave town just because some recruiter picked your name out of a hat?"

"It's not like that."

"Really? What's so important about this job that you suddenly have to leave?"

Justice? National security? World peace?

"It's just what they need."

"You mean it's what the mysterious boss who found you, hired you, and is making you move to God knows where in a matter of weeks needs?"

"Days."

"What?"

Cade coughed. "I leave in a few days."

"When, exactly?"

"Friday."

Sloane shot to her feet. "*Friday?* As in, five days from now?"

"I know it's fast, but—"

"When were you going to tell me?"

"I'm telling you now."

"What about Wilson? Your apartment?"

"I told Wilson on Friday before we drove up here. He's sad to see me go, but he understands. And your mom said she would take care of the apartment."

"*Mom* knows about this?" Sloane said, her voice rising an octave. "Wow."

"It's not what you think."

"So, you're not abandoning us for some job you know nothing about?"

"Hey," Cade said. He stood and met her on the sand. "I'm not *abandoning* anyone." She sniffed and turned away, but he gently pulled her back around to face him. "I mean it. That's not what this is."

He kept his voice soft but firm, wanting to make sure she heard him. It never occurred to him she'd react this way, and he had to hide his own reaction to hearing her say those words. Cade knew what it felt like to be abandoned. He wouldn't do that to someone he cared about. Ever.

"What is it, then?" She asked.

"It's…hard to explain."

"Try."

Cade slipped his hands into the pockets of his cargo shorts and angled himself toward the water. The sun was still high enough in the sky for it to be hot. He lifted his face to the clouds and closed his eyes, relishing the warmth. Would it be warm where they sent him next?

Sloane said his name, and he looked at her. He hadn't scripted this moment, but with Bullet, he often went off-book. Maybe he could think of it as part of his training, the beginning of a lesson on adapting to the unpredictable.

"The summer after I turned twelve, Dad took me up here to the lake. It was after he started drinking but before it got really bad. We were still spending a little time together but not enough for it to feel normal, you know?"

Sloane nodded, and Cade thought back to that day and the nearly silent car ride. Thinking back on it now, he should have known something was off from the way his father refused to look at him as he drove, his attention fixed on the road ahead.

"He parked, got out of the car and walked into the woods. I sat in the car for a while, not sure whether I should follow, but eventually, I did. We walked for a long time. Long enough that when he stopped, I couldn't see the parking lot anymore or even the lake. I went into the woods to take a leak, and when I got back, he was gone."

Sloane's eyes widened. "He left you there by yourself?"

"He did."

"Were you scared?"

He thought back to that day, to the silence that surrounded him in those first few moments. "I was confused, maybe. Definitely angry, but no, not scared. I think I was almost… relieved."

He shook his head and huffed a laugh. It wasn't funny or sad that he preferred being lost in the middle of nowhere to being with the man who had raised him. It was just the truth.

"What did you do?" Sloane asked like she was interested. When she did that, Cade could almost believe he had something important to say.

"The only thing I *could* do. I kept walking until I hit a couple of marked trails, doubled back to the lake, and found my way back to the parking lot."

His father had been there when he'd made it out, all sweaty, scratched up, and mosquito-bitten. He leaned against the trunk of their car with his arms folded over his chest and a cross expression on his face as if angry with Cade for making him wait.

"What did he say when you got back?"

"He told me it was a man's job to find his own way in the world and that I couldn't depend on anyone but myself to get me where I wanted to go. He said the sooner I figured that out, the better."

"Bastard," Sloane muttered.

Cade chuckled, not at all put off by her speaking ill of the dead. "He was. But he was also right."

His father had died three years ago, and, in all that time, Cade had avoided visiting his grave. He didn't know why, exactly, but something about it felt wrong. *He'd* felt wrong for a while now. Although he never forgot his wallet or to turn off the stove when he left for Wilson's garage every morning, he felt like he did. A feeling like that could drive a person crazy if he let it.

"This is just something I have to do."

Bullet's attention had been on her feet since Cade told her what his dad said to him in the parking lot, but now she looked up at him. Her eyes, alive and bright moments ago, were flat with resignation, the copper of her irises muted to dull lead. He hated seeing her that way, hated causing it, even if a part of him was relieved she understood.

"Your dad wasn't completely right, you know," she said. "There are people you can depend on."

His chest squeezed, and the back of his throat burned as he looked away, stifling his emotion with a laugh. "You guys won't even miss me. Beck's starting that new hotshot job in Manhattan, and you're starting school in a couple of weeks. Are you ready?"

Bullet squinted out at the water. "Dan's ready."

Dorky Dan. Cade shoved his hands in his pockets. The two of them had been dating since Sloane's prom, a fact that Cade rarely, if ever, acknowledged, even to himself. Still, the kid was good to her, and as long as things stayed that way, Dan could live.

"But you're not?" He asked.

"I am. It's just…"

"Just…what?"

She sighed. "Dan knows exactly what he wants to do with his life. He's known since he was ten years old." She held up a hand and counted off on her fingers. "Graduate early. Check. Get accepted to a college with a top-rated math program. Check. Apply for a job as a mathematical modeler for NASA's Aerospace Engineering Program. Pending."

"He wants to work for NASA?"

Sloane nodded. "It's in his five-year plan."

"He has one of those?"

Another nod. "He color-coded the PowerPoint chart by year. *That* was a fun Saturday night."

"Wow." Cade rocked back on his heels. "So, you guys are going to stick it out, then?"

"My school's only an hour from his, so, yeah, we're going to try."

"Trying's good," Cade said lamely.

"I don't have what he has."

"You have a plan."

"Not one that involves having 2.5 children by the time I'm thirty. Two children and a dog," she clarified. "One boy and one girl, of course."

Pushing aside all the mental images her words elicited, Cade cleared his throat. "Yeah, but you want to be a teacher, right? Teaching's difficult. Just ask Principal Fisher."

"You can stop calling him that, you know. He's not our principal anymore, and he's practically married to Mom."

Cade cringed at the reminder. "Not the point."

"What if I change my mind?"

"Then you change your mind."

"But Dan—"

"Isn't you," he interrupted. "And you're not Dan. Just because he has a plan doesn't mean it will happen. Plans change."

"People change too."

The vulnerability in her gaze nearly did him in. He faced her, and even though he knew he shouldn't, he reached out and swept a wayward strand of golden hair behind her ear. "Not that much."

"I will, you know."

"You'll what?"

"Miss you." One corner of her mouth lifted in a smile that was more sad than happy. And yet, as she stood there, with the water, sand, and sun at her back, Cade thought she'd never looked more beautiful.

"Me too," he said.

"Will you be back?"

"Yes."

"Promise?"

"I promise." He didn't know when that would be or where he was going next, but he promised her anyway because, at that moment, doing anything else was impossible.

It was, however, entirely conceivable he'd been wrong before. As they walked silently back to the parking lot, she slipped her hand into his, and he made a mental note to stop by the drugstore before he left town.

He might need some help sleeping, after all.

24

"Lunch?"

Sloane looked up from the folders and documents on her desk to find her assistant, Sophie Trudeau, standing just inside her office. "Sure."

Sophie's smile brightened. "I know this great cafe down the street that sells the best apple and goat cheese baguettes."

"Sounds great."

"You're going to love it," Sophie squealed. "Be back in ten."

She bolted out the door, and Sloane sighed, alone at last. She didn't dislike Sophie. The young intern was competent, enthusiastic, and eager, but Sloane couldn't dig up dirt on Doyle with a shadow hovering over her shoulder. The only upside was Sophie was a California native and, therefore, someone Sloane could talk to without embarrassing herself. If her co-workers had found it strange to work with a curator who wasn't fluent in French, it had shocked them all to learn she barely knew any French at all. Jean-Paul and Bianca knew the language but weren't involved in their day-to-day operations, and Gig knew even less than she did, which left Cade.

Sloane frowned and slumped back in her chair as she thought of the near-perfect French she'd heard from him the night Jean-Paul and Bianca came to dinner. She'd accidentally stumbled on Cade and JP having a private conversation and hadn't been able to hide her shock at hearing Cade speak like a native. Sloane had never heard Cade speak English that well, let alone French. They'd switched to English when they saw her lurking in the hall, but it was too late. Not for the first time, she thought about how much better suited Cade would have been to the role she now played. He moved through the world of secrets and lies like he was born to it. So much so that Sloane wondered if the man she'd known in her youth had ever existed at all.

Her computer dinged with a notification, pulling her from her thoughts. A command prompt appeared on the screen, and multiple random characters depicted an image of a woman wearing a cape.

She smiled and typed. *Is that supposed to be me?*

The reply came a second later. *You have bigger (.) (.).*

She rolled her eyes and entered the password that would give Gig access to the museum's server. The password changed daily, and getting into the system was the only way Gig could run a scan. She stared at the endless code populating the screen just like she had for the past four days and tried not to think about the complete lack of progress they'd made. The emerald that was supposed to be at the museum was missing, and she'd barely seen her boss since the benefit. Even Doyle was MIA. What had happened between last weekend and now? Had Doyle changed his mind about pursuing her? Maybe he already had the emerald. Right now, he could be in some posh hotel suite with Celeste, drinking champagne and plotting their next great heist. She dropped her forehead to her desk and groaned.

"Bad time?"

Sloane shot to her feet, sending her desk chair crashing into the wall behind her.

"Oh, dear," Celeste said apologetically. "I didn't mean to startle you. Your door was open, and Sophie wasn't here, so I just let myself in. I hope that's alright."

"No problem," Sloane said, catching her breath. She bent over her desk and clicked the command prompt closed before rolling her chair back into place. "I was just reviewing our current inventory."

Celeste nodded. "Settling right in, I see."

"I like to be prepared."

"Right. Well, I trust Sophie has assisted you with anything you need?"

"Of course, though, I'm glad you stopped by. There's something I wanted to ask you."

"Oh? Is there a problem with the inventory?"

"I'm not entirely sure." Sloane rounded her desk so she could face the woman with nothing between them. She might not get another opportunity like this, and she was determined to make the best of it. "There are some pieces on the list I couldn't find. The system says we have them, but they're not in storage. I asked Sophie, but she didn't know where to look."

"And you were hoping to select a few for the upcoming exhibit?" Celeste said.

"Yes, but maybe I'm looking at the wrong list?"

"Probably not." Celeste paused. "Do you have a few minutes? There's something I'd like to show you."

"Sure. Just let me grab my bag." Sloane opened the desk drawer where she'd stowed her purse and her communications device.

"You won't need it," Celeste said. "We're not leaving the building."

She looked up, hesitating for only a second before slamming the drawer closed. "Lead the way."

***

Sloane followed Celeste down the long, expansive hall and through the marble archway that led to the main salon. Sunlight shone through the windows, brightening the space and highlighting the display cases of each exhibit. The exhibits at *Le Centre de Feu* included classic-style art and cultural relics from throughout history, some of which were from events Sloane had taught about in class. She'd taken a group of students on a class trip once to a museum two towns over from Lakehaven during a lesson on the American Revolution, but it didn't compare. This venue was a labor of love with a maestro at the helm. Celeste acknowledged patrons and employees alike with a nod and smile as they swept past, addressing the latter by name. Most bowed to her like the bartender had the night of the gala, and Sloane couldn't help being just a little in awe of the woman's celebrity status.

At the end of the main hall, Celeste took a sharp left, and they moved down a hallway Sloane had assumed was a dead end. Instead, they stopped in front of an open elevator with padded walls. A utility elevator, Sloane realized, that hadn't been in the schematics she and Gig had reviewed the week before.

Celeste stepped aside. "After you, please."

Again, Sloane hesitated. Celeste didn't carry a purse, and the thought that she might hide a switchblade in the pocket of her business suit seemed completely out of character. Still, before she stepped inside, Sloane reminded herself not to underestimate the woman. She'd already done that once with Doyle, and she couldn't afford to make the same mistake twice.

Celeste followed her inside and pressed a button for an unnumbered floor. The elevator lowered, and Sloane glanced at her boss questioningly when it continued to descend. The museum was only two floors, and they'd started on the first. Had she read Celeste wrong? Maybe they were in for a fight, after all. But then, the elevator stopped and Celeste lifted the cover of a mounted plate to the left of the door, revealing an ID swipe, a screen, and a touchpad.

"Please excuse the rather clandestine measures," she said, stepping closer to the screen. She pressed a few buttons, and a white light appeared and scanned her features from forehead to chin before disappearing. "Sophie doesn't know where we store *all* the inventory." The system beeped twice, and the sensor below the screen blinked green. The doors slid open, and Celeste snapped the plate shut. "It's better that way." She held the elevator open with one hand and smiled like a grandmother with a secret. The thought of finding out what it was drove Sloane forward.

The lights flickered on slowly, electricity humming as the sensors detected her presence. Then, the space flooded with light, leaving Sloane stunned. Before her were rows and rows of artwork and antiques, a veritable treasure trove of items arranged more precisely than any exhibit she'd ever seen.

"The building is rather old, so I had to make some adjustments," Celeste said. "There's a back entrance, of course, for some of the larger pieces. The cases are temperature controlled and made of special glass to protect against too much light."

Sloane gaped. "It's amazing."

"Yes. I forget sometimes what it must look like to someone who hasn't seen it before. But, in your position, I'm sure you've seen art stored in a variety of ways."

Sloane tensed as she turned to Celeste, who watched her with keen interest. Yes, she would need to be careful around this woman. "I have, but this is still very impressive."

"Thank you." Celeste held Sloane's gaze a moment longer before she pivoted and walked down one of the lit aisles. "This way."

They walked past paintings and sculptures, tools, and preserved documents as they made their way through the maze. Sloane, the teacher, wanted to inspect the relics to learn their origin, but Elena, the experienced curator, kept pace with Celeste. There had to be hundreds of pieces in the room, and though she didn't know how much they were all worth, she could imagine it was no small fortune.

"Are all these on loan?"

Part of the research she'd done with Gig had included details about how *Le Centre de Feu* acquired most of their exhibit pieces. Curators requested loans from other museums, but not all of them approved the requests.

Celeste glanced over her shoulder as she walked. "Most are, but others belong to personal collections."

"Yours?"

"Goodness, no," she said, with a laugh. "I store them for the locals. Men and their toys." Celeste dismissed the subject with a wave of her hand as if they were discussing a mid-life crisis Corvette instead of centuries-old wealth.

"That's very generous of you."

Celeste stopped walking and turned, cocking her head to the side as she considered Sloane. "I suppose it would be generous if the agreements I have with the collectors didn't give me the right to display their pieces in any of my exhibits as I see fit."

Heat rose along the back of Sloane's neck. Generosity had nothing to do with it. Celeste wouldn't hold on to all this out of the kindness of her heart. Not when she had a museum to run. *Elena* would have known that. "Right."

"This is what I wanted to show you." Celeste stepped aside to reveal a section of cases that all held precious gems. Rubies, sapphires, and diamonds of various cuts and clarity glittered in the low light, all somehow paling compared to one.

Sloane moved to the podium that held the object of all her dreams and nightmares. The emerald lay on a velvet pillow, a solitary jewel with no other adornments. Sloane could recite its specifications from memory: Asscher cut, transparent, and an AAA clarity grade. But all of that held no significance now that she saw it in person. The stone gleamed, and Sloane leaned over the glass as if drawn to it by some invisible force.

"Extraordinary, isn't it?" Celeste said as she moved to stand beside her. "It wasn't easy to get, even though I knew the original owner."

Sloane looked at her. "You did?"

Celeste nodded. "A long time ago. His son passed away recently, which is likely why the Victoria and Albert Museum accepted my request this time."

"A sympathy gift."

"I suppose."

"I'm sorry," Sloane said because what else could she say? That Dubois had likely murdered the son of the man she knew and continued to donate to her museum with his blood money? It wasn't like she had any proof. Not yet, anyway. But, at least Doyle didn't have *this* emerald, and if it was up to her, he never would.

"There's a story behind it, you know."

"What kind of story?"

"A legend about three goddesses of the Emerald Isle. That stone," Celeste said, gesturing to the emerald, "is one of a set of three. Gifts from a mother to her daughters."

"They were sisters?"

"Yes. Lea, Agata, and Isolda. Lea was the oldest and cared for her siblings after their actual mother died in childbirth with her youngest. Isolda was beautiful, angelic, and pure. Each of the sisters had inherited some magic, but Agata, the middle child, was different. She was jealous of the attention Isolda received, especially from Lea. When she was old enough, she left home and traveled to other villages to learn more about the dark arts. Eventually, she became a recluse and isolated herself to improve her magic."

"Did she ever go home?" Sloane asked.

"Not until her power reached its peak. Then she went to see her sisters in the Holy Meadow on the tallest hill in Ireland. She went after Lea first, turning her into ash that was swept away by the wind. Isolda huddled in the grass, begging her sister to spare her life, but Agata took one look at her perfect face and unleashed the full force of her power. Instead of ash, Isolda transformed into seedlings that brought new life for years to come."

"Not exactly what Agata had in mind," Sloane said.

"No. She roared to the heavens as rain she had not summoned burst from the clouds. And then she turned her own magic on herself. However, instead of turning to dust or seeds, she became stone. You can still see her there today. A single boulder on a hill in the shape of a woman, hunched over in her grief."

Sloane smirked. "Interesting."

"I know. It's all a bit…"

"Dramatic?"

"Yes, though, there's always some truth to legend. And it's often the story behind something that gives it value. At least that's what my late husband believed."

"I'm sorry for your loss," Sloane said again.

Celeste's response was a faint smile. "Whenever Maxime sold real estate, he used to say that a space was just a space until someone breathed life into it. Then the walls would bear witness to joy, heartache, triumph, and despair for all eternity."

"Is that what you think?"

Celeste seemed surprised by the question, but so was Sloane. She hadn't meant to ask it, but now that she had, she lay in wait for the answer.

"I think true value is based on commitment, dedication, and sacrifice. Everything in this room," Celeste said, waving an arm, "comprises sacrifices made by artists for something they loved."

"Because they were inspired."

Celeste sighed. "Yes."

"Isn't that a good thing?"

"At first, maybe. But there's a fine line between wanting something and becoming a slave to it. Anyone can cross that line. Sometimes, you don't even know you have until it's too late. Then you wake up one morning and realize you can never go back."

Regret. She saw it in the lines of Celeste's face, the way her eyes glazed over as she stared over Sloane's shoulder, reliving a moment only she could see. How much had Celeste sacrificed, and what had those sacrifices cost her?

Celeste blinked, her creased forehead smoothing as she backed away from the glass. "Well," she said, straightening her shoulders. "I just wanted to show you where we keep the additional inventory." She gestured to the other jewels. "I'm unable to give you access, but you can select what you'd like and we will move them to the main hall in plenty of time to be arranged for the exhibit."

"We?"

"The board of directors. It was their generosity, along with a few key investors, that made this facility possible."

"I see," Sloane said, trying to display outward calm despite what she'd just learned.

"Much to the disappointment of a few of our members, the board has to vote on who gets access."

Celeste didn't seem disappointed. In fact, Sloane thought she sensed the barest hint of pride at the board's decision to limit access to the facility to a lucky few. Now that she'd mentioned it, and even though Luc Dubois was on the board, Sloane doubted he was one of them. If he had been, he would have ransacked the facility long ago.

"I understand," Sloane said, eager to get back to her desk and brief Cade and Gig on the emerald's location. At least the day hadn't been a total waste.

"I believe you met a few of our board members at the benefit. Monsieur Dubois, in particular, seemed quite taken with you."

Sloane met Celeste's assessing gaze. "Luc? Yes, we've met, though I haven't seen him since that night." She suspected that asking where he was would make her seem intrusive or desperate, neither of which would impress her boss. Still, she couldn't help the next words that fell from her mouth. "Maybe he's out of town."

"Perhaps, though, if he is, he'll likely return soon," Celeste said as she looked once more at the emerald. "Monsieur Dubois likes to stay informed about all matters concerning the museum."

"I'm sure," Sloane agreed.

Like a moth to a flame, Doyle would be back for his treasure.

25

Sloane froze the instant she closed the door to Elena's apartment, goosebumps prickling the skin down her arms and along the back of her neck.

"It's me."

She whirled on Cade, hand to her heart. "A little warning would have been nice."

He stepped forward, reaching behind her to turn the lock on the door before moving to the window overlooking the street. He snapped the blinds shut and turned to face her. "I could have if…" He trailed off, tapping his ear.

Sloane groaned. Sophie had been waiting for her when she returned to her office, and they'd gotten to work, leaving her with no choice but to put updating Cade and Gig on hold. "If you're here to lecture me again about not wearing that thing, then you can leave now," she said, letting out a sigh as she slid out of her heels.

Cade held up his hands in surrender. "I'm not, I swear."

"Swearing is your favorite pastime."

He grinned. "Fuck, no, it's not."

She bit the inside of her mouth to keep from smiling back. "You shouldn't be here."

"Worried about me, Bullet?" His tone was teasing but with an unexpected edge that begged for truth. Sloane shook her head, deciding now wasn't the time to dissect all the possible answers to that question. Instead, she turned and walked into the kitchen. "What I meant was, *what* are you doing here? I thought we were meeting at *Chez Étoile*?"

The upscale bistro was the strip's latest hot spot and the only one they hadn't yet been to that week. The two of them had been out nearly every night, hoping to lure Doyle out from wherever he was hiding. She stayed out in the open while Cade lurked in the shadows like some stalker surveilling a mark. It should have creeped her out to have Cade watch her while she sipped a drink at the bar. Instead, her insides buzzed with anticipation, like she was on a rollercoaster climbing steadily to its peak before the plunge.

It was just his proximity, Sloane reasoned. For months, she'd had no contact with Cade, and now they were working side-by-side. It didn't matter that working with Cade made her feel like the center line of a tug-of-war, the constant push and pull keeping her just slightly off balance. She'd get used to it. Besides, it wasn't like she had a choice.

"I thought we'd stay in tonight," Cade said, following her into the kitchen and gesturing to a large, grease-stained brown paper bag on the counter.

"What's that?"

"A semi-automatic and two hand grenades," Cade deadpanned. "What does it look like? I thought we'd take a break and eat something that doesn't look like a work of art worth thousands on the black market."

When he opened the bag, the scent of fried food and soy sauce hit her full force. "You found Chinese food in the south of France?"

"It's not like I had anything else to do while you were radio silent this afternoon." He removed the last container from the bag and leaned one hip against the counter. "Are you going to tell me what happened today, or am I going to eat all this myself?"

"So, the food is a bribe, then?"

"I prefer the term incentive."

Sloane rolled her eyes. "Now you sound like Gig."

His expression became suddenly serious. "What happened?"

"What about dinner?"

"Talk first."

Wordlessly, she reached for a bottle of Irish whiskey from the cabinet over the sink. It had been difficult to find in the land of fine wine and champagne, but Cade wasn't the only one with skills. She poured herself a glass and sipped slowly, meeting Cade's gaze over the rim. "Doyle's out of town."

"Confirmed?"

"Not exactly."

"What does that mean?"

Sloane sighed and told him about her afternoon with Celeste.

"It's not much to go on," Cade said when she was done.

"I know, but she did hint that he'd be back, and at least now we know where the emerald is."

"Does he have access to the storage facility?" He asked.

"If he did, he'd have the emerald already."

"And Celeste?"

"What about her?"

Cade lifted an eyebrow. "You don't find it strange that of all the stuff in that basement, she showed you the one thing you wanted to see?"

Sloane hadn't thought of that. "Maybe."

"Do you think she's working for Doyle?"

"Well, she's definitely working *with* Dubois."

"Doyle and Dubois are the same person."

"Yes, but we can't assume Celeste knows that. Luc Dubois is one of the museum's most prominent investors. All I know right now is that Celeste has to work with him, but I don't think she likes him. I'm not buying that they're partners. She can barely look at me when she mentions his name."

"They don't have to like each other to work together."

"I know, but I got the impression that bringing me down there was a play. Almost like she was pulling one over on him." A mental image of prim and proper Celeste giving Doyle the one-finger salute entered Sloane's mind, and she nearly laughed.

"But she waited until he was out of town to do it. Maybe she's afraid of him?"

"Maybe." However, Celeste hadn't seemed afraid. She was confident and self-assured, the complete opposite of a woman who was being threatened. "I just…" Sloane looked up at Cade to find him watching her expectantly. "I can't shake the feeling that she was trying to tell me something by bringing me there."

"Like what?"

"I don't know."

Cade frowned, and for a moment, she thought he was going to ask her if Celeste knew who she was. To her relief, he didn't. If he had, Sloane wasn't sure she'd know how to answer him. Not yet, anyway.

"I'll put Gig on researching Celeste's connection to Barnes," he said. "Maybe there's something there." He plucked the whiskey glass from her hand. "You go take a shower. The food will be warm when you're ready."

Finally, an order from Cade she didn't mind taking.

***

Sloane returned to the kitchen a half hour later to find the whiskey and bags cleared from the counter.

"Food's in the oven," Cade said from the living room, his attention on the small television mounted to the wall.

Sloane grabbed her plate and joined him on the couch, though it was probably generous to call the small settee in the center of the room a couch. The apartment Gig had found for Elena was neat but staged, with none of the comfort and charm of the villa. Subdued watercolor canvases hung on walls that were otherwise gray and white. Crisp, clean, and boring, like the waiting room of a doctor's office. At least, that's how Sloane felt when she was here.

Cade placed his empty plate on the coffee table and chugged half of his water bottle, his eyes still glued to the television. It was only after a couple of glorious bites of fried goodness that Sloane realized what they were watching.

"Is this what I think it is?" She said.

"If you're thinking it's a badly dubbed American soap opera, then yes."

Sloane shook her head at the absurdity of Cade's longtime vice. "I can't believe you're still into that stuff."

"It's so good."

"It's not."

Cade huffed. "It's better than the reality television bullshit you and Beck used to watch all the time."

Her next forkful of orange chicken paused halfway to her mouth. Neither of them had said Beck's name out loud since they'd arrived, at least not unless it was absolutely necessary. Sloane looked at Cade immersed in the show, one hand on the bottle, the other lying casually on his knee, and tried to remember the last time she'd seen him so relaxed.

He turned to her. "What?"

"Nothing." She stuffed the food into her mouth and returned her attention to the screen, where a woman was gesturing wildly to a man who stood with his hands in his pockets. She spoke in rapid-fire French, too fast for Sloane to catch more than a few words—lie or liar, steal, cheat. At that last word, the male actor looked up, crossed the room, and took the woman by her shoulders. He shook her as tears streamed down her face. "Do you actually understand everything they're saying?"

"Most of it."

Sloane thought of the conversation they'd had with the Laurents the night they all had dinner. "Have you spent a lot of time in France?"

Cade shifted in his seat. "Yes."

"And?" When he didn't elaborate, she dropped her plate next to his on the coffee table and moved to stand.

Cade reached for her wrist and tugged her back down. "Alright," he said, angling his body so that he faced her on the couch. "Yes, I've spent some time in France. I've spent time in a lot of countries. It's in the job description."

"I'm not asking about the job."

"What *are* you asking?"

She looked at the hard line of his jaw and his dark gaze as he waited for her reply. They'd formed a truce of sorts over the last couple of weeks, but she'd avoided asking the important questions. Was she ready for the answers? "When were you here last?"

Cade swallowed, and she watched his Adam's apple bob, the lines of his neck growing taut with tension. "Eight months ago."

"So, last December?"

Cade nodded.

"How long did you stay?"

"About five months," he said.

"Were you with JP and Bianca?"

"For some of the time."

"Is that where you learned to speak French?"

He blinked, surprised by her question. "I knew how to speak French before, but, yes. They rarely speak English at home, so I guess I just picked it up."

"What other languages do you know?"

"A few."

"Like?"

"Spanish, Italian, a little German. Some Farsi."

"Really?"

"Yes."

And here she was, barely able to grasp the mechanics of one language, let alone five. She glanced down at her lap, already mentally tallying all her incapabilities, as she had earlier in her office.

"Hey." Cade brushed her skin with his finger as he tilted her chin up to meet his gaze. He frowned as though she'd spoken her insecurities aloud, and she felt her cheeks flush. "I've been doing this for a lot longer than you."

"Still."

He shook his head. "You just started field work. You'll get there."

He said it with the calm assurance she remembered, in the same encouraging tone that had been the reason she always sought Cade's advice. Beck was a kind and protective older brother, always supportive, always urging her to do and be her best. But it was Cade who listened, who had always known what to say to quiet the noise in her head.

Suddenly, Sloane was all too aware of where she was and with whom, Cade's touch sending tingles along her jaw, to the base of her neck, and down her spine. She let out a nervous laugh, pulling away from him as she stood. "Well, it's too bad you don't have an accent to pair with your expert knowledge of foreign languages."

"Why's that?"

"Women would swoon."

Cade grinned at her like he'd won the Mega Millions jackpot. "You think women swoon for me, Bullet?"

To distract herself from the crap she'd stepped into, she retrieved their plates and started for the kitchen. "I said they would swoon *if* you had an accent."

"Same thing."

"It's definitely not."

"I disagree."

"This is a ridiculous conversation." One that she could kick herself for starting. Sloane bent and scraped the remnants of their food into the garbage can, straightening to find Cade blocking the sink. "Move."

"Not until you tell me why I need an accent to get a woman."

He didn't, of course. Cade could have any woman he wanted. That was the problem. She shook her head, searching for another way to dig out of her hole. "You don't. But don't knock the concept. I'm sure if you ask Gig nicely, he'll give you a few tips."

Cade reared back. "You think I'm going to take dating advice from *Gig*?"

"Why not? He has a girlfriend."

"So?"

"He understands relationships."

"All that kid knows how to do is piss me off."

"Admit it," Sloane said, finally shoving her way to the sink. "He's growing on you."

"He's annoying as hell."

"Sounds like someone else I know," she murmured.

"The guy never shuts up," Cade said on a rant. "He has something to say about everything and questions every single instruction I give him."

Sloane gave him a look of mock horror. "How dare he?"

"Come on, I'm not like that."

"Oh, please."

"What?"

"Let's not pretend that you don't have control issues."

"I *don't* have control issues," Cade said and sighed. "Okay, I sometimes, in certain situations, have a problem giving up control."

"And with taking orders from an authority figure."

"Now, wait just a sec—"

"And with not being right *all* the time."

"Are you done?"

"Oh," Sloane said. "I'm just getting started."

It happened so fast. One minute her hands were wet, and the next, she was. Cade grabbed the nozzle, and Sloane yelped as he pulled the extendable cord and sprayed her with a steady stream of cold water. She ducked behind the kitchen island for cover, but Cade didn't let up, and soon, water was streaming over the edge of the counter like a waterfall.

"Cade!" she shrieked as she tried to cover her head.

"Go ahead. I'm listening."

Blindly, Sloane reached an arm over the counter, grasping until her fingers closed over a bowl of lemons. She counted to three and then shot up, cradling the bowl against her stomach with one hand while using the other to launch the lemons at Cade.

The waterworks stopped as Cade dropped the hose in favor of juggling the lemons that pinged against his chest. "You realize you're just giving me more ammunition, right?"

"Not if you have your hands full."

He smirked, rounding the island to the right as she moved left, crouching low. Sloane threw two more lemons, but Cade surprised her by dropping them all to the floor before launching himself over the island like a track and field hurdler.

Sloane let go of the lemon bowl and screeched, turning away only to be tugged backward into his hard chest. "Let go!" She tried to yell, but the words came out in a raspy hiccup because she was laughing so hard she couldn't breathe.

"Surrender," Cade said, changing the inflection in his voice to something low and deep that just made her laugh harder.

"Never!"

"I thought you might say that." Squeezing her tighter, he lifted her off the ground and spun them both in a circle, whirling so fast Sloane feared she might lose her dinner.

And then she had an idea. Shifting her weight to the side that was injured a week ago, she flinched and yelled again for Cade to stop.

He let her go so fast that she nearly face-planted. "Shit, Bullet. I'm sorry."

She gripped her side and watched his face pale as he stood there in soaking jeans. She actually felt sorry for him. Almost. "Gotcha."

The concern on Cade's face morphed into disbelief, and he lunged for her again, this time gripping her hips and hoisting her up onto the wet counter. "Not funny."

He tickled her sides, then her thighs. Even the bottoms of her feet weren't safe, and Sloane squirmed and slapped his back, breathless and hoarse from laughing.

Finally, he stopped, his gaze meeting hers, eyes bright with amusement. Getting Cade to smile had always been like trying to coax an injured animal from a cage. When it came, it was reluctant, even a little defensive. But this time, his smile was genuine, and Sloane's chest swelled with pride at being the one to put it there.

For just a moment, they stared at each other, sinking into the ease of being together. And then, suddenly, Sloane wasn't comfortable anymore but wholly uncomfortable. Cade's jeans were rough against her bare calves, his biceps flexing under one of her palms while the other rose and fell with his breath where it lay on his chest. She shivered, the feeling having nothing to do with being drenched and everything to do with Cade's hands circling her hips.

His grip tightened imperceptibly, and then it was gone. He stepped back and ran a hand through his hair, mussing the ink-black strands.

Slowly, Sloane slid off the counter, her heart beating twice as fast as it had before, even though she barely moved. Not knowing what else to do, she lowered to the floor for the lemon bowl.

"Leave it," Cade said. "I'll clean up. You go get some sleep."

She paused, even though hiding in her bedroom sounded like a great idea. "Are you sure?"

He smirked. "If I can jump from a moving vehicle, I'm pretty sure I can handle drying a kitchen floor. When I'm done here, I'll take a lap and then turn in."

"You're staying?"

"On the couch. If that's ok?"

Maybe it was the fact that he'd asked rather than just assumed. Or maybe it was the way he looked at her, not like he expected a fight, but like he was waiting for her to tell him to leave. But she didn't want him to go, and as she nodded silently and made her way up the stairs to her bedroom, she hated herself just a little because of it.

***

The Exit sign glowed overhead as she entered through the back door. She heard nothing and saw no one as she felt her way along the narrow corridor, pausing at the end of the hall to listen.

"I have to get into that room."

Sloane peeked around the corner. A bar. Stools. A single bulb hanging from the ceiling swayed back and forth above two figures at a table for four. One man and one woman. She knew them. How did she know them?

"Why? So you can take something else that doesn't belong to you?" *The woman said.*

The man laughed. "How do you know it doesn't?"

"Nothing that beautiful could belong to someone so ugly."

Sloane moved into the bar. She didn't want to, but something pushed her forward. Two sets of eyes swung to her, their faces coming into focus.

"What are you doing here?" *Celeste said.* "You're not supposed to be here."

"I'm here for him," *Sloane said, pointing to the man at the other end of the table.*

Jack Doyle smiled a slow, sinister smile. "Ah, so you know who I am."

"You killed my brother."

"No, I didn't," *Doyle said, standing. He pulled a gun from inside his suit jacket and pointed it across the table.* "He's right there."

And suddenly, her brother was there, *in the place Celeste had just been, still and stiff and dressed in the suit they'd buried him in.*

"Beck?"

It was a whisper, barely audible amidst the ringing in her ears. Beck didn't move or look at her. He just stared down the barrel of Doyle's gun until it fired.

"No!"

Beck crumpled to the ground at Sloane's feet, and she fell to her knees beside him.

Blood. So much blood.

She pressed both palms to his chest, but it kept coming. A sob wracked her body as she watched her brother's face slowly drain of color.

No.

She glanced over her shoulder, expecting to see the gun aimed at her, but Doyle had disappeared. Terror clawed its way up her spine as she turned back to the man lying on the ground, wanting to save him, needing to save him. She would this time. She had to.

But it wasn't Beck lying there on the ground. It was someone else.

Someone with cold, dead, coal-black eyes.

26

The first time Cade heard it, he was in the bathroom on the first floor. He lifted his head from the sink, turned off the faucet, and listened. Before it was over the second time, he was taking the stairs two at a time, panic exploding in his chest.

He'd checked the property himself. There was no way someone could have…

Not bothering to knock, Cade flung open the door at the top of the stairs. It banged against the wall as he slapped at the light, the pressure in his lungs releasing almost immediately when he saw there was nobody else in the room. No one but Bullet, lying in her bed, thrashing and gripping the tangled sheets.

Another blood-curdling scream erupted from her throat, and the sound erased all conscious thought from his mind as he went to her. Dropping to the bed, he gripped her shoulders and pulled her up. "Bullet."

Her skin was feverish and slick with sweat. She writhed in his arms but didn't open her eyes. The lids were red and swollen and her cheeks were tinged pink.

Cade gritted his teeth, gripping her tighter. "Bullet," he tried again. No response. Even though he knew it was the single worst way to wake someone from a nightmare, he shook her. Hard. "Dammit, Sloane, wake *up*!"

Her eyes flew open, and blind terror twisted her features. His stomach flipped, and he shook her again, trying to get her to focus on him.

"Bullet." Her gaze darted wildly around the room, and he lifted a finger to her chin and guided it back to him. "It's okay. You're okay. Breathe, Baby, just breathe."

Sloane blinked once and then again. "Cade?"

"Yeah," he said, letting out his own breath of relief. "It's me."

"You're…" she trailed off, her forehead crinkling in confusion as she stared up at him.

"I'm here. I said I was going to stay, remember?"

"You're not…"

"Not what?" He barely had time to get the words out before she launched herself at him, the force nearly knocking him over. He balanced himself with one hand on the bed and wrapped the other around her waist, keeping them steady. "Whoa, it's okay. You're okay."

Both her arms circled his neck, and she squeezed tight, burying her face in the space between his neck and collarbone. She curled into him, the moisture from her leftover tears dampening his skin as he held her close.

Something thick and hot unfurled inside him, enveloping him as he stroked her back and grazed over her cooling skin with his fingertips. He knew what it was, could taste it on his tongue as he whispered soothing words in her ear, his lips against her hair.

Mine.

As soon as it entered his mind, the thought pursued him, chasing him the way he chased bad guys, relentlessly and with single-minded focus. Fearing a panic attack, he counted to ten, but the fog and dizziness that usually preceded an episode never came. In its place was a conviction that balanced the rage inside him with his need to protect.

Bullet stirred in his arms, ducking and sliding out of his embrace like an embarrassed child. The air conditioning clicked on, and cold air from the vent above rushed between them as every one of his body parts she'd touched tingled like a phantom limb.

She scooted back in bed and raised the sheet to cover her chest. Something fell to the ground and Cade bent to pick it up, immediately regretting it when he realized it was her shorts, still damp from their water fight. He swallowed hard as his gaze rose to the bed and up the length of her long, slim legs beneath the sheets.

"Sorry," Sloane said, swiping the shorts from his outstretched hand. "They were wet."

She squeezed her eyes shut and opened them again. They darted left, then right, while he gawked at her like some teenager. He wanted to look away but couldn't make himself, preferring instead to watch the flush that crept up her neck and blossomed on her cheeks. Because of the dream or what she'd said? Probably the dream.

Definitely the dream.

Cade cleared his throat. "Right."

"Sorry for freaking out. It was just a dream."

"It's fine," he said, even though things were the furthest from fine they'd ever been.

He rubbed his palms over his knees so he wouldn't do something stupid like touch her again. His heartbeat thudded in his ears so loud that he didn't realize Sloane had spoken until she kicked him in the hip with her foot.

He looked at her. "What?"

"I said, can you shut the light on your way out?"

Bullet leaned against the headboard, her back straighter than the edge of his switchblade. Those damned sheets were hiked up to her chin, and she looked as though she was about to be eaten by the Big Bad Wolf. He would laugh at the absurdity of it if he didn't already feel like the beast himself.

Without a word, he stood, walked to the light by the door, and flicked it shut. Then he crossed the room and dropped into a chair in the corner, facing the bed.

He braced himself for her protests, but none came. Instead, the sheets rustled as she slid down in bed, and Cade leaned into the silence as the moonlight filtered through the window between them, casting a faded blue glow across her face.

"I'm afraid of the water."

Cade lifted his head from the wall.

"I don't mean, like, a glass of water or running water in the sink or shower, but open water. Oceans, lakes, sometimes pools. They terrify me."

He sighed. "I know."

He could have confronted her about her fear a hundred times, but he knew what it was like when others forced you to talk about something you weren't ready to talk about. The silence went on for so long that Cade thought she'd drop it, but then she spoke, her voice so soft he had to strain to hear.

"Not long before we moved to Lakehaven, Mom took Beck and me to Lake Michigan on a long weekend. It was summer, and even though it was a busy time at work, she wanted to spend some time with us. I was starting kindergarten in the fall, and Beck was eight going on fifteen. Neither of us had ever seen the water. That first day on the beach, Mom had to bribe Beck with ice cream for dessert, just to get him to eat his lunch."

Cade couldn't see her smile, but he could hear it. He remembered all the time he and Beck spent on the sand as kids, even though their hometown lake wasn't as big as the Great Lakes.

"Anyway, on the last day, the hotel we stayed at organized an adventure hike for the kids. Beck had already made some friends and begged Mom to let him go. She agreed, but I was too young, so we went back to the beach, even though the weather had turned. It went from sunny and warm to cloudy and gusty overnight. Mom wouldn't let me near the water's edge, but there were other kids swimming, some closer to the shore and others a little further out."

She paused a moment, and Cade leaned forward, resting his elbows on his knees as he listened.

"One minute, there was laughter, and the next, everyone was screaming. I don't remember if there were any lifeguards on duty, but several people jumped into the water one after the other. A couple of minutes passed, and then I saw one adult get out and walk to shore, a small, lifeless body in his arms."

Cade clasped his hands together and bowed his head, his gut clenching at the image.

"They tried everything, of course. CPR, mouth-to-mouth, but she didn't make it."

"She?"

Sloane nodded. "It was a girl, the same age as me. Her parents only looked away for a second."

He let out a breath. "Jesus."

"After the initial shock wore off, I cried and screamed until Mom had no choice but to carry me off the beach. Not that she wanted to stay after that, anyway. I didn't stop crying until we got to the parking lot, and I couldn't see the water anymore."

He'd survived his fair share of childhood trauma, but Cade might be afraid of the water himself if he'd witnessed something like that. At the very least, it would be something he'd never forget.

"Beck didn't know. I mean, I don't think he knew. Mom might have told him, but we never talked about it."

Which was probably why Cade knew nothing about it, either. Beck would have told him something like that. "Was that what your nightmare was about?"

"No."

Cade waited, but she didn't elaborate, and he finally leaned back again in his chair.

"Do you ever have nightmares?" she asked.

He tensed. How could he tell her that all of his nightmares were *waking* nightmares, that they repeated themselves over and over in the light of day instead of at night when he closed his eyes? "I don't dream."

"Mom tried to get me to talk to someone. You went to therapy, right?"

He contemplated lying. It wasn't like he even thought of the mandated sessions he'd attended as therapy. To him, it was just a place where the people who worked for the people who paid him could speak aloud terms like "PTSD" and "ASD" to make sense of something that had no hope of ever making sense. Just because the light was on didn't mean the monsters weren't there.

Maybe it was because Bullet was in the game now and would know if he lied or just the whole damn night messing with his head, but he told her the truth. "Yes, I saw someone."

"Did it help?"

"Not really."

"Yeah," Sloane said with a sigh. "That's what I thought."

Silence descended again. He could try to convince her to go. In fact, that probably was what he *should* do. Instead, he spoke another truth. "Faye loves you. She was only doing what she thought was best for you."

"Sometimes love isn't enough."

Her words seared him like a fiery brand on his skin. No, it wasn't. Love couldn't make someone stay once they decided to leave. It couldn't change the past, couldn't twist it around and make it something it wasn't.

But it could split a person open, lay him bare, make him do stupid things, like jump in front of a bullet meant for someone else. It could make him believe he was bulletproof when he wasn't.

Sloane eventually fell asleep, but Cade didn't. Instead, he stayed in that chair and listened to the sound of her breathing. He sat awake in the dark so he wouldn't have to wake up in the morning.

27

Then

The bookstore was sandwiched between a nail salon and a custom framing shop in a derelict part of the city, the name *Bookends* carved in scripted gold on a faded wooden sign. With no historical landmarks nearby, the sidewalk where Cade stood was empty of tourists. The White House and the Lincoln Memorial were several blocks away, as were museums and any of the other reasons a person might want to visit Washington.

Anyone except for Cade.

What the hell was he doing? Now that he was there, the reality of the choice he'd made kept Cade rooted to the sidewalk. Last month, if someone had asked him if he'd ever leave Lakehaven, the answer would have been an emphatic no. He wasn't the guy who made plans. Growing up abandoned by one parent and neglected by the other left little room for fancy dreams. You didn't think about much of anything except getting by.

And that's what Cade had done. For years, he'd kept his head down, worked at Wilson's garage, and paid the rent on the dingy apartment he had because his father lost the deed to his childhood home in a bet. He'd barely thought about it until he came home after meeting Albright for the first time, sat on the couch, and felt the same four walls he woke up to every morning closing in on him like a vise.

Albright's lack of surprise at his acceptance didn't faze Cade, since he figured the man probably had only five emotions he displayed on a regular, rotating basis. Was it lack of emotion that made him good at his job? *Was* he good at his job? For Cade's sake, he hoped so.

Lost in thought, he didn't notice anyone was beside him until he felt the slap on his back.

"So, this is it, huh? It's a shithole, but I guess that's the point."

Cade turned to find Beck standing just behind him on the sidewalk, a large backpack slung over one shoulder. It took him a minute to find words. "What are you doing here?"

"Really, man?" Beck said, flashing him a lopsided grin. "Customer service? You hate people."

"I do not ha—wait a minute. You're supposed to be in New York."

Beck shrugged. "The job wasn't what I thought. Besides, I'm much more into this."

"This?"

"You know," he said, waving an arm toward the bookstore. "This. The clandestine government agency stuff is super badass, by the way."

Cade stared at his friend in shock. "How did you even know where to find me?"

Beck shoved his hands in his pockets and glanced at the ground. "I stole your phone."

"*What?*"

"Then I called Albright from it."

"When?"

"On our way back from the camping trip."

Cade thought about the trip home. "When we stopped for food?" When Beck nodded, Cade suddenly remembered him disappearing for a while after they'd pulled into a diner off the highway. Cade hadn't even realized his phone was missing until Beck handed it to him. "You told me I dropped it."

"Well, you didn't."

"Jesus, Beck. Why would you do that?"

"Are you serious?" Beck said, incredulous. "You'd just told me you were leaving town for some job you'd never even mentioned before, to work for some guy you knew nothing about. What did you expect me to do? Throw you a going-away party?"

"You did throw me a party."

Beck rolled his eyes. "That wasn't a party. It even depressed Dan."

"No, it didn't."

"Well, it depressed me. And Sloane, too."

Cade's chest tightened at the mention of Sloane. She'd barely spoken to him in the days leading up to his departure, and he hadn't seen her smile since that day on the beach before he'd given her the news. "How did you even know which number to call?"

"You really should delete your text messages, bro."

Cade groaned. "And Albright just let you in?"

"Yup."

"Just like that?"

"My advanced computer programming degree might have had something to do with it, but yes. If it makes you feel better, he was hesitant at first, but I convinced him that two new recruits were better than one."

"But I had to take tests and fill out paperwork."

"Yeah, man, I know," Beck said, nodding along in commiseration. "That polygraph test was no joke. It's nothing like how it looks on TV."

It wasn't, but that was beside the point. Cade swiped a hand through his hair. "This is a bad idea. I can't let you do this."

Beck's jaw flexed. "You're not *letting* me do anything. If you're in, so am I."

"You have a life back home."

"So do you."

"What about Faye?"

"Mom was a cop's wife, remember? I think she knew this day was coming."

That was bullshit. No mother thought about the day her son might up and leave to join the CIA. Cade didn't call him on it, though. Instead, he asked the one question that had been gnawing at him since Beck had snuck up on him. "And Bullet?"

Beck winced. "She's…not great. But, you know Sloane. She just needs time to get used to the idea. She'll be alright."

Cade wasn't so sure, but even if he wanted to, there wasn't much he could do about it right now. Instead, he looked Beck in the eye. "Are you sure, man?"

It was probably the only question he should have asked. The one Cade absolutely needed the answer to before they walked through the door of the bookstore and started a new life. And, even though it made him a selfish bastard, he knew what he wanted Beck's answer to be.

His best friend squeezed his shoulder. "I'm sure."

Not once did Cade think either of them would ever regret Beck's decision.

28

Meet for lunch?

The text was from an unknown number, but Sloane immediately knew who it was by the flurry of Italian flag emojis that came with the message.

Sure. Where are you?

Bianca's reply was quick, and Sloane grabbed her purse and prepared to meet her outside the museum, glad for the distraction.

Sophie looked up from her desk as she left her office. "You're going out?"

Sloane paused. "Is that a problem?"

"No! It's just…you haven't been out of the office much since you started."

She was right. Sloane hadn't wanted to miss Doyle in case he deigned to make an appearance. He hadn't, though, and they still didn't know where he'd gone. She sighed. Bianca's text couldn't have come at a better time. "Well, I'm going out today."

"Great! Is there something I can do for you while you're gone?"

"No, thank you. I'm just going out for lunch. I'll be back in an hour."

"No rush. I've got things covered here."

"Thanks."

"Have fun!"

Sloane forced a smile and tried not to let Sophie's enthusiasm irk her as she walked into the museum's main hall. It did anyway.

In fact, her patience had been at an all-time low ever since she'd woken that morning to find the chair in the corner of her room empty.

Had he even slept? Unlikely, considering how he'd spent the night. Between the uncomfortable furniture and her rambling, she couldn't blame him. Instead, she blamed herself for the nightmare she hoped never to have again. Coming out of it had been like slogging through fog, but when she did and she saw who was waiting for her on the other side, she'd been beyond relieved. Elation and gratitude had practically consumed her. That, and something else that had caught her by surprise.

Hope.

But that was crazy because hope required faith and trust, neither of which she had in Cade anymore. Still, it grew like a weed inside her until the story of her fear had passed through her lips as easily as a breath. He'd shared, too, but not enough. Not the one thing that mattered.

Sloane shoved open the museum's front door harder than she meant to, nearly hitting her waiting visitor in the face. "I'm so sorry!"

Bianca merely sidestepped, narrowly avoiding the collision with the grace of a cat that always landed on its feet. Then she scanned Sloane from head to toe, her chocolate brown eyes settling on her face. "Bad day?"

"I just didn't sleep well last night."

Bianca lifted one perfectly manicured eyebrow. "That's exactly what Cade said."

"You spoke to Cade?"

She nodded. "He called this morning. Shall we?" She started down the stairs, and Sloane followed, biting her tongue to keep from asking Bianca what they talked about. On the sidewalk, Bianca slipped on her sunglasses. "Don't worry, he's watching."

"I wasn't worried," Sloane lied.

Half of her had expected she'd arrive at work to find him gone. Gone from France, from the mission, and from her life again. That he wasn't, that he was close and monitoring her every move, made her feel raw and even more exposed than she had last night.

Bianca smiled. "Let's go."

They strolled down the sidewalk arm-in-arm, like they were longtime friends, and blended in with the crowd. Well, Sloane blended. Bianca, in her black shades and white wrap dress, resembled a celebrity on holiday. Tourists stared at her, no doubt trying to figure out what movie or TV show they knew her from. Not for the first time, Sloane marveled at how a woman could be that conspicuous and yet so inconspicuous at the same time. Even without seeing her in action, she knew Bianca was a skilled officer. Was the job the reason she didn't bask in or even seem to notice the attention? Or was it just the woman herself?

"I love it here," Bianca said, lifting her face to the sun. "Even though it's not home."

"Where's home, exactly?"

"Palermo."

"Sicily?"

"Yes. Have you been?"

Sloane shook her head, smiling at the genuine enthusiasm on Bianca's face.

"You must come! Though, I haven't been back in a while."

"You live here, now?"

"In France, yes. Paris in the winter, Provence in the summer."

"Sounds like a dream," Sloane said, all too aware of their very different lives. Before she started working for Albright, she could count on one hand the number of times she'd been away from Lakehaven.

"I try to make it home in August, but…"

"I'm sorry," Sloane said.

"Why?"

"If it wasn't for us, you'd be home right now."

"Oh, hush. If it weren't for your brother, I wouldn't have a home."

Sloane glanced at the woman beside her. "What do you mean?"

Bianca pulled them both to a stop. In a move that seemed uncharacteristically American, she removed her sunglasses and tapped them against her fingers as she gazed down at her feet. "The four of us worked a job together a few years ago."

"What kind of job?"

"A difficult one," Bianca said. "The kind you wish you could forget."

Sloane's chest tightened. She'd seen a lot, but it was likely nothing compared to what Beck and Cade had gone through long before Sloane joined Albright's unit. She inhaled deeply and tried to keep her thoughts from spinning out of control.

"We all needed the break, so I invited them both to my home," Bianca continued. "I have four sisters, so Jean-Paul was thrilled to have the guys around."

"And how was it for you?"

"You mean, how was having three handsome men follow me around all day?" Bianca wiggled her eyebrows. "Such a hardship."

Sloane laughed. "I bet."

"I had really never seen my hometown through the eyes of a tourist, and they seemed to enjoy it as much as we did. Then, one night, we all went out for dinner. It was late when we returned, but we stayed up even later, talking, laughing, drinking. It was a perfect night." Bianca's smile faded as her expression grew serious. "We were tired, though, and I forgot about the candles." She paused. "Can you imagine? All those missions, all that danger, only to burn in your own home?"

Sloane reached for Bianca's hand and squeezed. "But you didn't."

"Thanks to your brother. Jean-Paul and I fell asleep and woke to Beck standing over us, shouting in a room filled with smoke. If it wasn't for him…"

Sloane felt a burst of pride for what Beck had done. "I'm glad he was there."

"Me too. Your brother was a good man."

Sloane swiped at a stray tear. "The best."

She had often thought about the man Beck had become. Sloane had pored over his unsealed service records, hoping to catch even a glimpse of the man behind the armor. When Beck was home, she always felt like he was split in two, with each side pulling the other back before either was ready to leave. It was good to know that, at his core, he was still her brother.

"I have a confession to make," Bianca said.

Sloane released the woman's hand. "Okay."

"When Cade called me this morning, he asked me to come today. He's…concerned about you."

Sloane fingered the strap of her purse, more than a little vexed by the thought of Cade sharing their conversation with Bianca. "What did he say, exactly?"

"Nothing so specific. Just that you could use a friend."

"You mean, a babysitter?"

"No, I mean a *friend*. Please don't be mad."

"I'm not mad," Sloane said. "Not at you, anyway."

"Don't be mad at him, either. He only wants to protect you."

"What he wants is to prove that I'm not capable of doing my job, so he can send me home."

"You misjudge him. He might not want you here, but it's not because he thinks you're not good at your job. He just feels… guilty."

"For what?"

Bianca opened her mouth and then closed it again, biting her lip as she shifted from one stiletto-clad foot to the other. Bianca Laurent did not fidget.

"You know, don't you?" Sloane said.

"Know?" Bianca parroted, but it was too late.

"You know how my brother died."

"Sloane, I—" Bianca glanced over Sloane's shoulder, all traces of emotion instantly disappearing from her face. Sloane started to turn, but Bianca grabbed her wrist. "Don't. We're about to have company."

"Doyle?"

Bianca nodded and then gestured to Sloane's purse before releasing her wrist. Sloane dug into her bag for her communications device while watching Bianca watch Doyle.

"Have it?" Bianca asked.

"Almost." When her fingers finally closed around the earpiece, Sloane breathed a sigh of relief and slid it into her ear, re-positioning her hair to hide it.

The voice in her ear was instant. "Bullet?"

"Here," she said in a low voice as she smoothed her skirt.

"Keep it that way."

Sloane barely had time to be annoyed by Cade's tone before Bianca's fingers brushed hers. "*Buona fortuna, mia cara,*" she said before stepping off the curb and into a crowd of tourists crossing the street.

Sloane took a steadying breath and turned, adopting an appropriate expression of surprise as Jack Doyle strode toward her in a light gray suit, sky blue tie, and mirrored sunglasses, his guards one step behind. Babyface's expression turned sour when he saw her, and his frown deepened as Doyle stopped and raised a hand to halt his men. Then he closed the distance between them.

"Ms. Caldwell," Doyle said, bending at the waist in a show of exaggerated gallantry as he took the back of Sloane's hand and lifted it to his lips. "It is both a pleasure and a surprise running into you this afternoon."

Sloane fought the nausea that rose at his touch and forced a smile, delicately slipping her fingers from his. "It's not a surprise when you consider the fact that I work down the street."

Doyle straightened, the arch of one eyebrow visible over the rim of his sunglasses. "I see you believe in chance encounters even less than you do romantic overtures."

"I believe in making your own luck."

He grinned. "As do I."

"But if you prefer to think of our meeting less than half a mile from my place of business as a chance encounter, then I suppose I will concede."

"So soon?" Doyle clucked his tongue. "I didn't think you were the type to give up so easily."

"There's a lot you don't know about me, Mr. Dubois."

"*Easy*," Cade said in her ear.

Sloane cleared her throat. "I'm glad, at least, to have the opportunity to thank you again for the flowers. I sent a note to your office, but they said you weren't in."

"I was away."

"Business or pleasure?"

"Business," Doyle said. He took a step into her personal space, the scent of his expensive cologne settling over her like smog as he trailed a single finger down the length of her arm. "I only regret that I could not see your face when you received them."

Sloane flattened her palms to her thighs and resisted the urge to turn away from him. "They were lovely."

"And, also completely unnecessary?"

"Even I can appreciate a grand gesture once in a while," she said.

"That's good to hear."

"Is it?"

"Yes, because it means you might be more amenable to agreeing to join me for dinner this evening."

Cade's voice was low but urgent. "Not tonight. Need more time."

"And if I have a prior engagement?" she said to Doyle.

Doyle slipped off his sunglasses and folded them neatly into the breast pocket of his suit jacket. "My dear, you may concede on some matters, but I rarely accept defeat when it comes to getting what I want."

That, at least, was something they had in common.

"Until tonight, then, Mr. Dubois."

29

"You could have at least bought us more time," Cade said, glancing at the clock on the wall as he paced the length of the villa's first floor, trying to keep himself in check. It wasn't working. Two hours. In two hours he could watch a baseball game, fly to Paris, even cook a goddamn chicken, but this took planning. This took more…time.

"You're right," Sloane said. "I should have asked Doyle to postpone our date so you and Gig could set up surveillance. If I asked nicely, he might even have lent you a couple of his guys to help."

Cade shot her a glare. "We don't even know where he's taking you."

"I know it's probably been a while since you were on a date, but it's occasionally customary for the man to withhold that information."

"It's not a date."

"Technically, it is," Gig said. "Doyle asked her out, *and* he's providing the transportation, so…"

"It's a job," Cade spat. "One that we're going to be completely unprepared for, thanks to *her*."

Sloane pushed off the wall she'd been leaning against to meet him in the entryway on his hundredth lap. She squared off, the determined set of her shoulders and grim expression telling him all he needed to know about how much patience she had left—exactly none.

Well, that made two of them.

"Thanks to me," she said, poking a finger at his chest. "We are one step closer to catching this bastard and don't have to wait another week while he takes off to God knows where. Every hour, every *second* we waste not taking action is another hour he can spend hurting someone else. Is that what you want?"

"What I want is more time."

"I tried!"

"Not hard enough."

"You heard the conversation. He wouldn't take no for an answer and, anyway, you know as well as I do you don't keep a man like Luc waiting."

Cade couldn't help it. He laughed. He just threw his head back and howled. In front of him, Sloane's expression changed from shocked to appalled, but she didn't back down. Not his Bullet.

"I'm so glad you find this funny," she said.

He kept right on laughing, even though he didn't. It was the complete opposite of funny. If funny lived here on Earth, then Cade was three million light-years away, watching all this go down from another planet.

"What the hell is your problem?"

"My problem?" he asked as his laughter died. "She wants to know what my problem is," he said to Gig, ignoring the kid's disapproving glare. "You, Bullet, are my problem."

"*Me?*"

"So, it's *Luc* now, is it? You're on a first-name basis with the enemy, and you're asking me what my problem is?"

Her eyes widened and then narrowed into tiny slits. "Are you actually implying that there's something between me and that monster?"

Was he?

Cade shrugged. "Like you said, I heard the conversation."

"Only because I let you."

That did it. Forget light-years. He was in another galaxy, an alternate universe, and he was also too far gone. Cade knew it with a clarity he hadn't felt in months. And now that he'd started, he couldn't stop. "For two people who have only met twice, you're already pretty close."

"It's my job to get close."

"It's your job to get Doyle to talk."

"Right, well, if we want to find out who his buyer is, I have to keep him interested."

"Believe me, Bullet. He's plenty interested. Whether he's more interested in fucking you or killing you is anyone's guess."

Even before she lifted her hand, he knew what he was in for. He could have stopped it like he had in the kitchen the other night, but that would have meant that he didn't deserve it, so he let it happen. And after, as he touched a palm to his stinging cheek, the frustration in his gut still didn't abate. He was ready and willing to go another round if it meant doing so would ease the bite of hearing her say that bastard's name, even if it wasn't his real one.

He looked at her, expecting those amber eyes to be boiling over with defiance or resistance. But Sloane wasn't looking at him at all. She was looking at her hand, still hanging in midair, as if she couldn't believe what she'd done, what he'd made her do. And it was that despair and the loathing he knew she felt for him in that moment that drained every last drop of rage from his body.

He took a step toward her, his arms outstretched. "Sloane, I—"

"I hate you," she rasped, her lips quivering as her tears fell hard and fast.

But not, Cade thought as he watched her go, more than he hated himself.

30

Then

She hadn't expected him to come.

When Sloane had mentioned her graduation to Cade on the phone last month, she didn't expect him to show, nor did he tell her he would. But there he was, in her mother's yard, only hours after she saw him across the university's lawn, a lone figure in black standing in a sea of white and gold.

That was the way things were now. Instead of making promises they couldn't keep, they appeared out of nowhere. There were no plans, no notice or warning, nothing at all to expect. At first, finding them waiting in her dorm room, ready to kidnap her away for a camping weekend, had felt like Christmas. Even her mother was thrilled when she arrived at her wedding to Stanley Fisher to find Beck and Cade ready to walk her down the aisle.

It was like a game Sloane looked forward to until she didn't, until their visits became less frequent, and they stopped traveling home together. Beck had visited the last two times and even though Cade hadn't made it back in almost a year, she'd still been glad to see him that afternoon. Any opportunity she had to see either of them was one she took, no questions asked.

If only she didn't have so many.

She watched Cade as he paced the length of the yard, fence to fence, one hand holding a cell to his ear, the other attached to his hip. Sloane had never seen him walk that way before or seen him look so professional and authoritative. It wasn't like anyone would ever mistake Cade for a corporate executive. In his dark black jeans, black T-shirt, leather jacket, and boots, he was better suited for a raid than a board meeting, but there was something about the way he used his free hand to massage the crease on his brow as he moved confidently across the lawn that made him seem *other* to her.

He made the rounds, catching up with everyone at the party. That was different, too. Never one for crowds, Sloane expected him to hang back, but he didn't. Instead, he let Faye fawn over him and even exchanged a few words with Stan. By the time he engaged Dan in conversation, who seemed just as shocked by Cade's attention as she'd been, Sloane knew he was avoiding her.

It was nearly midnight when she went in search of him. She found him in Beck's bedroom, lying on his back on the bed, one arm tucked under his head as he stared at the ceiling. The only light in the room came from the lamp on the bedside table, the glow slanting over his fully dressed form, jacket and all. Only his boots were strewn haphazardly on the floor at the foot of the bed as if he'd kicked them off.

He didn't move when Sloane closed the door behind her with a soft click or when she slid out of her flip-flops and crawled onto the bed beside him. She turned on her side to face him, drawing both palms together under her cheek. "You have to leave, don't you?"

"Yes."

"When?"

"Soon."

"Tomorrow?"

"It's already tomorrow."

"Cade."

He looked at her then, and she was sure he'd heard the pleading in her voice. "Yes."

Sloane blew out a breath and rolled onto her back. "Where are you going this time?"

"Bullet."

"Is it dangerous?"

"You know I can't talk about work."

"You *can*, you just won't."

"It's not that simple," he said.

"I have a master's degree in education. I think I'm smart enough to grasp complex concepts."

"That's not it."

"So I'm just not worth the trouble."

"Jesus." Cade rolled to his side and propped himself up on his forearm. "You can't honestly think that."

"What am I supposed to think?"

"I came to see you graduate. I'm here because of you."

"Are you?" she said.

"What's that supposed to mean?"

"It means that even when you're here, you're not really here."

"That's not true."

Sloane threw him a look. "So, you didn't just spend half the day on your phone and the other half talking to everyone but me?"

"We just spoke last week."

"Actually," Sloane said, sitting up, "that was last *month*. And, even when we do talk, it's about the weather or my classes. It's never about anything important."

"You want to talk about something important? Let's start by talking about why you broke up with Dan."

Sloane froze. "He told you?"

"I think the better question is, why didn't you?"

She hadn't wanted to admit to Cade what she'd barely been able to admit to herself. That, even though they'd been together for years, she still didn't see herself living out Dan's five-year plan. It had been hard, but Sloane was grateful they'd stayed friends. "It happened months ago."

"Does that make a difference?"

"I don't know. I just…"

"Didn't want to talk about it?"

Sloane frowned. "It's not the same thing."

"No?"

"My breakup wasn't life or death," she said, softening her tone. "You can talk to me. It's not like I don't know what you do for a living."

"I know."

"I'm not a little kid anymore."

"Trust me," Cade said in a low voice. "I know that, too."

The air in the room shifted, growing heavy as Sloane blinked, suddenly all too aware of every one of the two inches of space between them. She licked her lips and saw the barest shadow of Cade's lashes on his cheek as his gaze slid to her mouth.

"You do?" she asked.

"It's all I ever think about."

Right then, all she was thinking about was what it would be like to kiss Cade Foster. Because she really wanted to. At that moment, she wanted nothing more. And that *was* simple. It was so glaringly, ridiculously simple that she almost laughed. She *wanted* Cade. And, from the way he stared at her, with a longing she'd never seen from her brother's best friend, she was pretty sure he wanted her too.

He shook his head. "I shouldn't have said that."

"Why not?"

"Which of the one thousand reasons do you want to hear first?"

"You don't have to protect me."

"You don't know what you're talking about."

"Explain it to me. I only want to understand why—"

"You *can't*," he said. "Don't you see? You can't possibly understand because you don't live in our world. You live in a world with backyard barbecues and balloons and guys like Dan who can provide for you." He rose to his knees on the bed and sat back on his heels, facing her. "I can't talk about my job, but even if I could, I wouldn't. The things I've seen…" He stopped, his pained expression making Sloane's chest ache. "I won't let it touch you. If you want to understand something, understand that. You're too good, too *perfect* for all of it. You deserve so much more than… this life."

Cade stumbled on the last words, but she knew what he meant to say, what he'd almost said. He was wrong, though, so very wrong. "What if I don't want more?" She said, rising to meet him. "What if I only want—"

Cade reached for her. "Don't," he rasped, eyes wide with desperation as he cradled her face in his hands. "Don't say those words to me. If you do, I might never leave, and I have to go, Bullet. I *have* to."

She parted her lips to say them anyway, to tell him exactly what she deserved, but he stopped her with his mouth.

If she thought she knew what it would be like to kiss Cade Foster, she'd been mistaken. She couldn't have predicted that the scent of him, leather and oak mixed with the sweet, sinful taste of her graduation cake's strawberry buttercream frosting on his lips, would hit her harder than anything he'd said. The kiss was wild and frantic, new but not unfamiliar. It was demanding but not wrong. Instead, she felt the rightness of it scoring her soul as if they'd rehearsed this dance for years without giving a single performance.

Through the haze, Sloane was vaguely aware of sinking back on the bed, of pulling him down with her. Need clawed through her, and she arched into him, wanting more.

As if he could read her mind, Cade slid a hand down her ribs and squeezed her hip. "Sloane," he murmured into her hair, and for the second time that night, she froze.

Cade shifted, partially lifting himself off her, but she wrapped her arms around his neck and tugged him close. "Say it again."

"Say what, again?"

"My name." She had always been *Bullet* to him. But tonight, she didn't want to be the little sister of his best friend. Tonight, she wanted to be the woman Cade wanted.

"Sloane."

And this time, when he said her name, it wasn't with want or need but something much more unbelievable. Fear. The man who fought his way out of every altercation, who had broken every rule and now hunted dangerous criminals so he could bring them to justice, was afraid.

But she wasn't, and as she lowered her hand to cover Cade's on the comforter beside them, she vowed to show him just how unafraid she was.

Slowly, she lifted his hand and placed it back on her hip. Cade's temple ticked the way it always did when he thought hard about something. He tried to pull away, but Sloane held firm as she slid both their hands under the waistband of her sleep shorts.

She watched him as she did so, not wanting to miss a single second of his reaction. He was so still but riveted as she inched their hands lower, gliding them under her panties. Then she paused.

"Cade." He looked at her, his tortured gaze showcasing the war raging inside him. But now, lust mixed with the fear. There was so much lust and desire that the next words out of her mouth were the easiest she'd ever spoken. "Touch me."

A heartbeat. That was as long as she had to wait for the dam to break. Cade let out a strangled groan, a sound that roared in her ears as he descended on her, kissing and licking his way up her neck as his fingers found her slick, wet center. They circled her clit, slow at first and then fast, so fast that it lit her up from the inside.

"Oh God," Sloane gasped, arching her back off the bed. "Yes."

Cade silenced her with his mouth, his tongue matching the rhythm of his fingers as he took her higher. Was this happening?

She had never felt this way before. Not even with Dan had she felt passion like this, the kind that made her want to both claw out of her own skin and beg to stay in the exquisite torture forever.

When Cade released her mouth to kiss a spot behind her ear that made more pleasure zing through her, she forgot all about Dan. There was only Cade. There was only this man, this bed, and what he was doing to her in it.

He lifted his head and gazed down at her, at once open and vulnerable in the way she knew no photograph could ever capture. "Jesus, you're beautiful," he said, his fingers working faster. "You're so damned beautiful like this."

She breathed his name. A whisper. A plea.

"I know, Baby, I've got you. I've always got you."

That was all she needed to come apart, to scatter and shatter like glass beads falling from a tipped jar. He rubbed her through it, milking her with his hand, stifling her cries with his mouth, until her ears stopped ringing and she came back to herself, back to him. It was too much and also not enough, and as Cade hugged her to his chest, she thought there was a possibility it never would be.

He nuzzled her neck and tugged her closer, and she felt him, long and hard, against the back of her thigh.

Sloane squirmed in his arms. "I can—"

Cade stopped her from turning, holding her tighter still. "No."

"But, I'm on the pill. We can—"

"Sleep, Bullet."

In that moment, she didn't mind that he'd used her nickname instead of her real one. She didn't mind because she wanted to pretend. But, when dawn broke, and she woke up alone in a cold bed, she realized it was no use pretending that nothing had changed when everything had.

31

Sloane leaned back against the cool leather of the town car's seat and tried to calm her nerves. She'd be fine. She would get what she needed from Doyle, and she'd be out of there. It would be simple, easy.

The phone on her lap vibrated for the tenth time, reminding her that the situation she found herself in was anything but easy. Doyle's driver cast her a glance in his rearview mirror, but Sloane smiled sweetly and slid the phone back into her purse, placing it on the seat next to her.

She didn't have to look at the screen to know who it was. The calls and texts had started only fifteen minutes after she'd left the villa. Sloane hadn't looked at any of them. She'd seen the look in Cade's eyes the instant she'd slapped him and knew he regretted what he'd said, but that still didn't make it right. His words also didn't give her any confidence at all that he trusted her to do her job. Was that Cade's problem? Was he still mad that Albright had chosen her instead of him?

Every time she thought they'd moved on from petty grievances, he proved the opposite, something she should have expected. Nothing he did should surprise her, especially after he'd disappeared from her life without a second thought and when he still lied to her.

That reminder was way past due.

Sloane dropped her hand to her purse and traced the outline of the pocket knife sewn into the lining. She would use it if she had to. She recalled their conversation that first day when she told

Cade she'd do whatever it took to get the job done. Long before Cade inserted himself into her operation, she'd determined how far she would go to beat Doyle at his own game. What she did next wasn't up to him.

The town car slowed to a stop, pulling Sloane from her thoughts. As if Cade also knew she'd arrived, her phone stopped vibrating and went blessedly silent. That didn't matter, though; once she saw where they were, the screaming in her head instantly drowned out all background noise. The chauffeur swung the door open, and her heart leapt in her throat as he helped her out of the car.

They were at a deserted harbor, on a private dock, in a secluded bay. The traffic on this side of the strip was nonexistent, as were the crowds that normally milled around in the evening. There were no couples perusing for a dinner spot or families gathered to watch the impending sunset. There were no restaurants or shops of any kind, only a couple of well-maintained yachts docked or moored in the bay, the driver, Sloane, and…

Water.

Miles and miles of ocean that was so crystal clear that Sloane was sure if she got close enough, she would see her reflection on its surface. She wobbled on her stilettos.

"Mademoiselle?"

"Y-Yes?" The driver gestured to his hand still in hers, the fingers of which were turning white as she held them in a death grip. Quickly, she let go and swiped her clammy palms down her dress. "Sorry," she said in English because, in that moment, any French she'd learned evaded her.

Frowning, the driver bowed and swept an arm in the general direction of where she should go before turning on his heel and returning to the driver's seat. In seconds, he was gone, and Sloane was walking on shaky legs toward the water.

She swallowed hard, feeling like a fool for not pushing for more details about their date. Did they know Doyle had a yacht?

Was that in the brief? She couldn't remember. Hell, she couldn't even remember her own pseudonym right now. *Elena*, she repeated as she forced herself forward. *Elena Caldwell. Traveler, curator, lover of art.*

Lover of land.

Her breath caught as she stopped in front of Doyle's boat. It was one of a few docked in the harbor, but Sloane knew it was his. With its sleek lines, sharp edges, and clean, green trim, it looked almost like the man himself. The boat had the name *Colleen* painted in broad gold strokes along the stern, the script bold and iridescent in the fading sun. It wasn't the largest yacht but, even knowing nothing about boats, she had no doubt that this one was powerful.

A man in a white uniform and cap waited for her. "Ms. Caldwell?"

"Yes?"

"I'm Captain Moore. Mr. Dubois requests you join him on the upper deck."

He pointed above them, and Sloane looked up to find Doyle watching them from a balcony. Behind him, the setting sun glowed a deep red-orange against gray clouds, like a halo of fire behind Satan himself. It was then that Sloane realized it wouldn't have mattered if they'd had two hours or two weeks to prepare because the devil was always one step ahead.

All she could do now was try to keep up.

Doyle disappeared from view as the captain helped her onto the boat. Sloane held her breath, staring directly at his forehead rather than down at her impending doom. A shiver of unease swept through her as the boat rocked under her weight, and she swayed.

"Hey," Captain Moore said with concern. "Steady."

"I've got it," Sloane snapped and then cleared her throat. "How do I get to the upper deck?"

The captain gave her a wary look but pointed to the stairs. "I can escort you if you prefer."

"Thank you, but that won't be necessary."

The captain nodded once and then disappeared into the darkness of one of the lower decks. Sloane took a slow breath. She felt sick in a way that had nothing to do with her not yet having her sea legs. She'd never had them to begin with or expected to need them.

Closing her eyes, she fingered the charm bracelet that circled her wrist. It was another insurance policy, one she'd thought twice about wearing before finally giving in. Now, she was glad she had. Gig had gifted it to her after their first successful mission. She'd been hesitant to accept it at first, but then he'd pulled out a similar, more masculine version and attached it to his own wrist.

"It has a built-in tracking device. Just press the back of this charm," he'd said, pointing to the miniature lifeboat along the inside of her wrist, "and I'll know where you are."

Even though the bracelet had gotten her out of more than one dicey situation, she hoped she wouldn't need to use it tonight. A lifeboat. Sloane opened her eyes, a faint smile touching her lips at the irony of Gig's choice.

But Sloane had her own choice to make. She could leave right now, disembark, activate the device, and wait for Gig to rescue her. Or she could stay, keep her date with Doyle, and do what she was there to do.

Straightening her shoulders, Sloane strode to the stairs.

✳✳✳

The upper deck was an expansive dining and lounge space at the top of the stairs. To the left of the staircase, plush, snow-white sofas surrounded a black lacquered coffee table, its surface polished to a glossy sheen. A giant, dark flatscreen TV hung on the wall across from a marble dining table, lit from above by an elaborate fixture that spanned the table's entire length.

Beyond that, there was nothing but blue water framed by a semi-circle of seamless glass showcasing the setting sun. The view was both amazing and frightening. One step forward and she could easily plunge headfirst into the waves.

Jack Doyle stood in front of the glass in white linen pants and a collared shirt, sleeves rolled up to his elbows. "Good evening," he said, his hands resting on the back of the dining chair in front of him.

"Good evening," Sloane replied.

His gaze raked over her lightweight coral dress and nude sandals, lingering on her bare legs. "You look ravishing."

"Thank you," Sloane said, shoving away her unease as she glided toward him. She slid her purse under her arm before accepting the glass of champagne he offered, and gestured at the dining table's twelve place settings. "Are we expecting company?"

"You're my only company tonight," Doyle said, moving toward the open glass doors.

Instead of following him out to the balcony, Sloane casually spun on one heel to face the seating area. "Your yacht is stunning," she said into the room before taking a sip of her champagne, the fizz doing little to settle her stomach.

"There are some who have a different opinion."

She turned back to Doyle to find him watching her over the rim of his glass. "How do others see it?"

Doyle shrugged. "As ostentatious, extravagant, unnecessary."

"It's those things, too."

"And yet, you don't hold that against me."

"I never said that."

He grinned. "That's what I love about you, Elena. You're not quick to judge, but you're also not afraid to speak your mind. That's a dangerous combination in a woman."

"And yet you still invited me to dinner."

"I like a challenge."

"So do I," she said.

He lifted his glass to her from across the room, and they both sipped their drinks. Then he leaned an elbow casually over the back of a chair. "Is that why you're a curator? Because you like the challenge?"

Sloane studied him but saw nothing but mild interest. "I'm a curator because I appreciate art."

His brows drew together as if disappointed by her response. "You can appreciate something without making it your life's work."

"True, but very few careers result in the same satisfaction as uncovering something thought to be lost to time."

"Yes. There's a certain appeal to capturing the seemingly elusive. I can imagine that doesn't happen often," he said in a tone that was both polite and mocking.

"It happens more than you think."

He bowed his head in a placating gesture. "Forgive me. You must be very good at your job, or Celeste wouldn't have hired you. Come," he said, setting down his glass and rounding the table. He pulled out a chair and looked at her expectantly. "Sit. The chef will serve dinner shortly."

After a moment's hesitation, Sloane walked to the table and took her seat, flinching slightly when Doyle set both hands on her shoulders.

He bent and leaned close to her ear. "Have you ever been sailing, Elena?"

The skin along the back of her neck prickled, and she reached for a napkin. "Once or twice," she lied. "Though never in the South of France."

"We'll have to change that." He gave her shoulders one last squeeze before removing his hands and rounding the table again. As soon as he took his seat, the chef appeared with two servers, each carrying a large tray. They set one in front of her and Doyle before disappearing as quickly as they'd come. "I hope you don't mind, but I planned the menu for tonight."

Sloane glanced down at the plate of seared scallops over a bed of risotto. "It looks delicious," she said, waiting for him to take a bite first before forking a scallop and bringing it to her mouth. Flavors of lemon, butter, and thyme exploded on her tongue as she chewed and swallowed. If this was poison, it was the best she'd ever tasted. "My compliments to the chef."

"It's one of Francois' specialties."

"Has he been with you for a while?"

"I rarely keep employees for long."

"Why?"

Doyle shrugged. "There's less chance I will eventually become dissatisfied with their work."

"It sounds like you're expecting to be disappointed."

"I'm not a pessimist. Complacency leads to error. I prefer to reduce the likelihood that they will make a mistake. It's important only that my employees are competent and, of course, loyal."

"How do they like working for you?"

Doyle put down his fork and leaned back in his chair. "If I was concerned about what people thought of me, I wouldn't be where or who I am today."

"And who are you?" Sloane asked, reaching for her drink.

"Like I said this afternoon, I am a man who knows what he wants. I simply employ people who can help me get it."

"Then you give them a bonus and a reference and part ways?"

"Sometimes."

Sloane put down her own silverware and glass, suddenly tired of the round-robin. "What exactly do you do, Mr. Dubois?"

"Luc."

Cade's face flashed in her mind, and Sloane hesitated a moment before repeating. "Luc."

"I'm an entrepreneur," he said, his finger grazing over the stem of his glass. "Actually, our professions aren't that different."

"Because you deal in art?"

"Because I aid my clients in locating things that are impossible to find."

"I see," she said. "And then they pay you when you've found what they want?"

"In a manner of speaking."

"Well, you certainly don't do it for free," she said, gesturing to their surroundings.

Doyle's blue eyes glinted like the pointy end of an ice pick in the sunlight. "There are many forms of payment."

Sloane shuddered as she thought of the harm Doyle had likely inflicted on those who couldn't pay. "Celeste mentioned you're on the museum's board."

He inclined his head. "Yes."

"She also said you're one of its most generous benefactors."

"Was I the sole topic of conversation this week, or did you talk about the upcoming exhibit as well?"

Too much. She didn't have her device, but she still heard Cade's voice as clearly as if she had.

Needing to move, she pushed back her chair and rose from the table. "Gosh," she said, shaking her head. "I'm acting like a silly schoolgirl with a crush, aren't I?" She casually moved to one couch and leaned her backside against it as she bit her lip. "I apologize. It was rude of me to use Celeste to learn more about you. It's just…well…" Sloane dipped her chin and then glanced up at him through her lashes. "I just wanted to make a good impression."

"You have certainly made an impression."

Sloane breathed a sigh of relief when she saw the interest return to his eyes. "Did the two of you meet through your work at the museum?"

For a moment, she thought he would call her out again, but then he stood and rounded the table to the chair she'd just vacated.

He slid his hands into his pockets, regarding her. "Celeste and I have mutual interests."

It was hardly incriminating but still served as confirmation that they were working together in some capacity. Sloane filed it away, making a mental note to ask Gig what he'd discovered about their shared history. Now, she only had to find out who else he was in business with.

"She's very good at what she does," she said.

"I suppose, though I rarely get to see her in action."

"Well, you should. Any woman who can run a museum *and* an archive of that size at the same time must be some kind of superhero, right?"

She said it easily like she was talking to a girlfriend, expecting him to agree so they could laugh about the force that was Celeste Armand. But Doyle didn't laugh. Sloane had spent months viewing photographs and video footage of the man and could recognize his tells. He might appear casual and relaxed on the outside, but he was as far from calm as she was from Lakehaven.

"I assure you," Doyle said, his voice hard. "Celeste is very much flesh and blood."

Sloane shrugged to hide her wince at his choice of words. "And lucky, I suppose."

"Lucky?"

"To be surrounded by so many treasures."

Doyle broke eye contact with her for the first time all evening to glance at the wall over her head. "One man's treasure is often another man's curse." Before Sloane could ask what he meant, he returned his attention to her. "Since you've seen the storage facility, perhaps you can tell me which was your favorite?"

"Which piece?"

"Yes." Doyle pushed himself off the table and stalked toward her, stopping mere feet away. "It is where she keeps the artifacts for the exhibits, right?"

Sloane nodded. "I wanted to see them all so I could determine which to include."

"Of course," Doyle said, his smile morphing into a sneer. "And?"

"They are all quite breathtaking, but…"

Doyle stepped forward, his eyes bright, manic in the same way they'd been in the garden the night of the benefit. "But?"

Sloane licked her suddenly dry lips and leaned further into the back of the couch. Her gaze darted to her purse, still on the table where she'd left it. To hell with it. She'd gone too far to turn back now. "There was this one gem."

Doyle's eyes flashed. "Yes?"

"An emerald. One of a set that belonged to three sisters of the Emerald Isle."

"*You* believe in legends? How curious."

"You know the story?" Sloane said, unable to hide her surprise.

"I do, though a tale about two sisters destroyed by a third wielding magical powers she conjures from an inanimate object is hardly historical fact. Your time would be better spent searching for truth rather than fiction."

"What is history if not part legend? I'd be remiss in my work if I didn't at least consider each artifact's cultural significance. I'm sure you do the same when your clients ask for something."

Doyle laughed. It was deep, with an unmistakably sinister edge. "My dear, my clients rarely *ask* for anything, but when they do, little research is required. In fact, one might even describe their needs as basic." One hand left his pocket, and he slid a finger down her neck, landing the tip at the base of her throat. "Primal, even."

Move.

Sloane screamed the word so loudly in her head her ears rang with the sound. But she couldn't. Not now that she finally had Doyle right where she wanted him.

She opened her mouth, but Doyle gripped her jaw hard. "And there are few things in this life as satisfying as getting what you want."

His mouth slammed down on hers, jarring Sloane into action. She shrieked and tried to pull back, but Doyle locked one arm around her waist, crushing her against him as he continued his assault. He tasted like death. Not even his expensive cologne could hide it. It was everywhere; *he* was everywhere, like a shadow, an impenetrable black fog.

Oh God.

Doyle's hands slid down the small of her back to the hip he'd injured. She'd thought it had healed, but one squeeze had Sloane breaking free from the kiss and crying out in pain.

"You are a little hellcat, aren't you?"

She yanked her arms free and blindly reached for something, anything she could use as a weapon, but it was too late. She'd waited too long. Doyle took control of her flailing arms and pinned them to her back as Sloane tried to swallow her panic.

Breathe.

She had to breathe, to think. Panic wouldn't help her now, but her training would.

"I would have thought a game of cat and mouse would be beneath you, but, as always, you never fail to disappoint. Lucky for you," he said, pressing his lips to her ear. "I like to play."

Doyle tried to kiss her again, but this time, she was ready. The instant his tongue plunged into her mouth, she bit down hard. The acrid taste of blood flooded her mouth, and Doyle reared back with a snarl and a swear. Instead of releasing her, though, he leaned into her with all his weight. Sloane's growl of frustration morphed into a squeak as Doyle's hand closed over her throat.

"You're all the same," he hissed. "Alluring and intriguing in a way that's meant to entice even the poorest of souls. Tell me, Elena, how does it feel now? How does it feel to be held hostage, unable to enact your own particular brand of destruction on those around you? Is it devastating to know you failed? That you've just laid waste to everything you once cherished?"

Doyle stared through her, the deranged look in his eyes proving to Sloane that he didn't know what he was saying. His grip on her throat tightened, and she sputtered and gasped for breath, fighting to stay awake even as her mind collapsed in on itself. She was almost out of time. If she lost consciousness, it would be over. Doyle would win, and she would—

You don't want him to win, do you?

Her eyes flew open.

Do you?

The voice echoed loud and clear, a sound she hadn't heard in months but one she knew better than her own.

No!

She screamed it in her head, screamed it as though Beck could hear her. She felt the adrenaline surge upward as a strangled, garbled sound escaped her.

Don't let him see your tears.

And she wouldn't. Not now.

In basic training, she'd learned how the simplest object could become a weapon. Not just basic household items like scissors or knives but less obvious ones, too. A power cord, a stapler, even a book.

Today, it would be every woman's nemesis.

Doyle's grip loosened, his manic smile a testament to how much he enjoyed dragging out her pain. *Bastard,* she thought as she clawed and scratched at the hand that circled her throat. The effort was futile, she knew, but she used it to distract him as she shifted her leg between Doyle's leg and the couch. It would be better to knee him in the balls, but the angle wasn't right. She'd have to settle for a broken toe.

"You are quite beautiful. It will be such a shame to—"

Sloane lifted her leg and crushed the heel of her stiletto down on Doyle's foot. He cried out, and Sloane spun away from him as he finally released her. She launched herself across the room, falling onto a couch as she gasped for breath. Then, stumbling to her feet, she backed toward the entrance.

Footsteps sounded on the stairs, and Sloane whirled as Babyface and the two servers from earlier appeared. In seconds, Babyface assessed the situation, noticing her disheveled appearance and his boss in pain, and then moved to restrain her. She might have had a chance against the captain, but not him. Not only did Doyle's bodyguard have the face of a God, but he was also built like one.

He caught her easily by the shoulders and turned her to face Doyle, who was still bent at the waist and howling. "Monsieur Dubois?"

Sloane braced herself as Doyle straightened and turned to them, realizing in an instant she'd been wrong. The howls she'd heard weren't howls of pain at all but of full, raw, hysterical laughter.

And he didn't stop laughing. Not when Babyface's hands slid from her shoulders or when she fled down the stairs to the lower deck. She heard his laughter as she jumped off the boat that was, gratefully, still docked in the bay, and it rang in her ears as she did the only thing she could do.

Run.

32

Cade shoved open the front door of the villa so hard it slammed against the wall. Then he marched into the dining room. "Anything?"

Gig's eyes stayed glued to his laptop. "Nothing, but I narrowed the search radius."

Cade groaned in frustration. *He'd* narrowed the search radius. He'd blown through every bistro and club in town, any place he could think of where a man might take a woman on a date. Except Luc Dubois wasn't just any man. He was a persona, a fake, which was likely why Cade had found no sign of either of them. "It's like they just disappeared."

"They didn't."

He crossed to Gig, grabbed the front of his T-shirt, and hauled him out of his chair. "Then do your job and find them."

Although Cade's take-no-bullshit meter was up to scary levels, Gig didn't cower in fear. Instead, he glowered. "I'm going to give you that one because I know you're worried about her. I am too. But this," he said, gesturing between the two of them, "isn't helping."

He was right, but Cade still wanted to punch something. Reluctantly, he let Gig go. "I never should have let her leave."

Gig snorted. "You didn't have a choice after what you said."

"I wasn't thinking."

"Yeah, well, that's common for men in your condition." Cade was about to ask what condition he was talking about, but Gig continued. "She's going to be fine, you know. You don't give her enough credit. Sloane can take care of herself."

Of course, he'd think that. All Gig saw was a smart, capable super spy. He didn't know her like Cade did, nor did he understand the vulnerability she hid under all that bravado. Sloane was brave, but she was also fragile, especially now, and he'd made it worse. Sloane could take care of herself, yes, but it was Cade's job to protect her, and right now, he was failing miserably.

He dragged a hand through his hair, tugging at the ends before letting them go. "Keep looking. I don't care if you have to hack into every street camera between here and Monaco. Do it. Just get me a location."

Gig nodded and moved to sit back down just as his computer dinged. His eyes widened, and a grin spread over his face. "Thattagirl."

"What is it?" Cade said, moving to look over Gig's shoulder. "Did you find her?"

"She activated her tracking device."

"I thought you said she turned off her phone's locator?" Before Gig could reply, the phone in Cade's back pocket buzzed and then rang. He dove for it. "Bullet?"

"It's me," Jean-Paul said in his ear. "A friend of mine just called. She's on her way back from the harbor now."

"The…harbor?" Cade's chest tightened at the thought of Sloane stranded out on the water with that psychopath.

"Before you freak out, my guy said they never left port. She's okay, Cade. He didn't have eyes on her the whole time, and he said she's a little shaken up, but she's fine."

Fine.

Cade repeated the word over and over in his mind, trying to convince himself it was true. It wouldn't be true, though. Not until he confirmed it with his own eyes.

"She's on her way to you right now."

Cade nodded even though JP couldn't see him and walked to the still-open front door with the phone attached to his ear. He looked out over the immaculately manicured lawn as if he could conjure her out of nowhere.

Then he did.

There was a flash of color through the trees beyond the lawn, movement where it should have been still. Cade barely registered the phone slipping from his hand. He didn't see Gig retrieve it or hear him speak to Jean-Paul because he couldn't. The only thing he could do was watch Sloane break through the trees and bolt across the grass, a sliver of light in his dark, dark world.

When she was close, Cade opened his arms, and she jumped into them, the force propelling them both backward into the hall. She clung to him, locking her arms around his waist and flattening her cheek to his chest like she was hanging on for dear life.

Oh, God. Was she?

He'd barely formed the thought before his hands roamed her body. He brushed her shoulders, slid his palms down to her waist and back up again, making sure she was alright.

She whimpered when he touched the side that was previously injured and squeezed him tighter. "It's okay," she said into his chest.

It wasn't okay. Not even close.

"Let me see." Cade tried to pull her away, but she clung to him like a scared animal, seeking refuge. He touched the crown of her head and stroked her hair, soothing her the way he had when she woke from her nightmare. "Come on, honey. Please," he said, surprised to hear his own voice crack as he tried to swallow the log that had wedged itself in his throat. "I just need to see—"

Cade flung his arms wide as Sloane shoved him backward into the far wall. A picture frame next to his head crashed to the floor, and Sloane crashed into him.

The kiss was wild, frenzied, and raw. He could feel the emotion spill out of her as he stood there, his arms still splayed out against the wall as if in surrender. Maybe he was surrendering, just like he had that night in her bedroom. Just like he always seemed to do with this woman.

Cade pulled her into him, kissing her back, letting the sweet, sweet taste of her fill him like he was a balloon. She was there in his arms, safe, and…*his.*

Suddenly, Sloane jerked back, the move so abrupt that Cade released her, thinking he'd hurt her, except she wasn't looking at him at all. She was staring at the ground, shifting from foot to foot as she reached one arm awkwardly behind her and tugged at the zipper of her dress. Cade reached out to help, but she slapped his hand away and shoved the straps of her dress down instead, exposing her bra.

He'd barely glimpsed the white lace against tanned skin before she jumped into his arms again, instantly wrapping her legs around his waist. She kissed him again, and he spun them both so her back was against the wall and propped her up on his hips, sliding one hand up her bare thigh. He squeezed her ass, half-crazed with hunger, his dick straining so hard against his jeans that it throbbed. When she linked her arms around his neck and moaned as she started rocking against it, Cade almost lost his ever-loving mind.

Except there it was. That niggling sensation he always got when something wasn't right, like a bee buzzing too close to his ear or the silent stillness before a thunderstorm. He slapped his free hand to the wall next to her head, fighting against it, trying to quell the clawing in his gut and…breathe. But who cared about breathing when Sloane's sweet, sassy mouth was doing things to him he never thought possible? That couldn't, wouldn't, ever be wrong.

But it was. And he knew it.

33

"Wait."

But waiting meant thinking, and thinking about all the ways the night had gone horribly wrong was the last thing Sloane wanted to do. Instead, she wanted to live in *this* world and pretend the one she'd left didn't exist.

"Wait," Cade said again.

"No." She fed the refusal into his mouth, sucking at his bottom lip and holding it between her teeth. *This* was real. This was the moment that kept her from running so far and so fast that she disappeared.

"Yes," he rasped, finally separating their mouths. He tugged her arms loose and placed both her hands against his chest. His heart raced against her palm. A freight train about to barrel off a cliff. "We have to stop."

Sloane scrambled to disentangle herself from his body, planting her feet on the ground again before shoving him. Hard. He stumbled back but didn't fall, regaining his balance just in time to face her wrath. "Why? Because you said so? Because it's what *you* want?"

"You think I want this?"

In response, Sloane glared at the bulge in his pants.

Cade shook his head. "That's not what I meant."

"Then what's the problem?"

"What's the…" Cade rested his hands on his hips and tipped his head to the ceiling. His chest rose and fell as he squeezed his eyes shut. "What the hell happened in there?"

Sloane shrugged, like the fact that neglecting to get anything useful out of Doyle while still also making herself his victim didn't matter. Like the weight of her failure wasn't holding her captive like barbed wire did a fallen soldier.

"So, help me God, Bullet, if you don't tell me what happened, I'll—"

"You'll what? Force it out of me?"

"What?"

"You obviously don't want to screw it out of me."

"Don't," Cade said through clenched teeth.

"What do you want to do instead? Tie me to a chair until I talk? It's effective, and maybe even a little kinky, but not really my style."

Cade ran a hand down his face. "Jesus."

"Or maybe you want to run me a hot bath and get me all soft and malleable so you can ease me into compliance."

"You think I want your *compliance*?" He said the word like it was dirty and wanted to rid the taste from his mouth. "Is that what you think I'm trying to do? Bend you to my will like a goddamned puppet?" There was anger in his glare; his steel jaw clenched so hard the words had to fight their way out. But the deep furrow of his brow told a different story. She'd hurt him.

Shame flooded her insides, throwing her off-balance. She nodded her head yes, then shook it no, not entirely sure how she felt. Thoughts of her night, what she'd said, and what Doyle had done clashed with the here and now, and she bowed her head as the first of her tears fell.

Cade sighed and took her face in his hands, his expression softer now but still just as intense. "The only thing I want is for you to trust me. I know I don't deserve it, I know that, but damn it, I want you to, anyway." He stepped closer still, melding his body into hers. "Please," he said, wiping the tears from her skin with the pads of his thumbs. He frowned as more replaced them and then leaned over and kissed them from her cheeks instead.

"You can't hide from me, Bullet. There's nothing you can say or do that will ever make me give up on you."

Sloane dropped her forehead to his shoulder, all her adrenaline suddenly fading into exhaustion as she let him fold her into a tight embrace. They lingered there until she stopped crying and calmed until she grasped the message conveyed through his tender touch and hushed words.

You're safe with me.

Her eyes drifted closed as Cade lifted her into his arms.

Weightlessness. Silk. The rustle of sheets, and then, warmth.

Nothing but warmth.

34

It was the silence that woke him.

Cade opened his eyes and listened. Even with the bedroom curtains drawn, he knew it was the middle of the night. After so many sleepless nights for too many sleepless years, he could tell what time it was just by staring at the shadows on the wall.

2 a.m.

It was 2 a.m, and Bullet was with him.

He propped himself on a pillow and turned slowly in the semi-darkness. She was on her back, gripping the bedsheets so tight against her chest that Cade knew it had to hurt. He sucked in a breath as she turned her head to look at him, awake and alert but with an awful stricken look on her face that made his chest ache.

"I froze," she said, her voice cracked and raw. "He cornered me, and I didn't have my knife. It happened so fast. I just kept thinking, how can I…how do I…and then he moved and I…I just…"

"You fought back?"

Sloane nodded.

"That's good," Cade said, letting out a breath. "That's really good."

"Is it?"

"Yes."

"Even if I gave myself away? Even if it means the end of everything we've worked for?"

"*Yes*," Cade said. "The answer to that question will always be yes."

"I just couldn't, you know? When he touched me, I didn't want…I just couldn't make myself…"

A sob escaped her, and Cade placed a finger over her lips. "Shhh," he said, as he tried to swallow the emotion clogging his throat.

Sloane grabbed his finger, wrapped it in her fist, and lowered it to her chest. Cade felt her fractured breath on his skin and the erratic thump of her heart as her gaze bore into his. "I'm sorry," she pled. "I'm so sorry."

There were some moments in life that could break a person. Because Cade was an unlucky bastard, he'd lost count of how many of those particular moments he'd experienced. But even watching his best friend die didn't hurt as much as hearing Bullet's apology.

Cade rolled over her, covering her body with his. Her breath hitched as he did so, but she said nothing else. That was good because he didn't want to hear this brave, broken, devastatingly beautiful woman blame herself for something Doyle did. As far as Cade was concerned, Doyle was a lucky son-of-a-bitch tonight. If he'd violated her in some horrible, irrevocable way, there was nothing on Earth that would have stopped Cade from killing him. But right now wasn't about Doyle. It was about Bullet and doing everything he knew how to do to make her whole again.

Cade released the blankets from her iron grip and dipped a hand under the sheets. He slid his fingers down her body and along the edge of her hip until they touched the sheer white lace of her panties. He knew they were white because he'd undressed her before tucking her into bed, where he knew she'd be safe.

Safe from Doyle, but apparently, not from him.

Cade paused there at the juncture of her hip and thigh, his thumb slowly caressing her skin. He met her gaze and watched the emotions flit across her face. Surprise, uncertainty, desperation, longing. It was the last one he held onto as he waited for something only she could give.

Then a nod. A nod so slight, Cade could have imagined it if not for the way her muscles relaxed under his hand.

He shook his head. "Say it." He needed to hear the words, needed to know she trusted him enough to give her what he knew she needed.

"Yes," she said.

It was barely a whisper, but the sound rang louder than a siren in his head. Cade closed his eyes and let out a long breath, willing his heart rate to return to normal. Not that it mattered. Panic attack or not, only Bullet could stop him now.

He slid the slip of lace down her legs and tucked it into the sheets at the foot of the bed before doing the same with his boxers. He took off his T-shirt and carefully lifted the sheet that covered her, tenting it over them both and positioning himself so she had enough space to move if she changed her mind.

He really hoped she didn't change her mind.

Her eyes widened when she saw the chain of black ink that circled low along his collarbone, ending at his chest. He'd wanted it that way, something his clothes would hide, a reminder for him and him alone. But he hadn't planned on this. He hadn't considered how it would feel to have her trace the black plate tattooed on his heart, engraved with the name of the man that was in both of theirs.

Awe registered on her face as she pressed a palm to his skin, the touch of her hand warming him from the inside. Sloane opened her mouth. Closed it. When she opened it again, he kissed her. Cade kissed her long and slow and deep. He kissed her until he was sure she understood that the time for words had come and gone, until he felt her squirm, feverish beneath him.

He trailed his mouth down her neck to her collarbone, pressing his lips to the trail of bruises already forming along her throat. Momentarily distracted, he pulled away, reaching up to swipe her hair back from her neck so he could see them better. A mixture of fiery rage and guilt burned through him like wildfire, leaving nothing but destruction in its wake.

What had he done?

Not Doyle, but him. Cade might not have been the one to exact the damage, but he was the one who had caused her pain. He almost stopped then, almost rolled over, got out of bed, and left.

But Bullet must have sensed his hesitation because she lifted her hand to where his lingered along her neck and jaw and twined her fingers with his. She arched into him and rasped in his ear. "Please."

He couldn't deny her, wouldn't deny her anything ever again. One smooth thrust and he was inside her, her sweet heat enveloping him in liquid fire even though he hadn't prepared her. He should have. Hell, he should have prepared himself for the way her breath hitched and her beautiful, perfect mouth formed an O when he sunk deep. He should have prepared himself for flushed cheeks and heavy-lidded eyes and for the feel of her under him with no barriers between them.

But, for maybe the first time in his adult life, Cade was wholly unprepared. And still, he moved inside her. Slowly. So damn slow he had to grit his teeth to stop himself from coming after the third thrust. But he didn't stop or adjust his pace. Instead, he kept moving. Cade moved inside her until her thoughtful look turned to blind lust, and she wrapped her legs around his waist to match his rhythm. He moved until there was no pain or fear or grief left on her face or in his heart and until the voices in his own head ceased.

He'd wanted to fix her, but as the night faded into dawn, Cade thought it was entirely possible that she'd fixed him instead.

35

"Where are we going?" Sloane shouted over the roar of the wind.

"The beach! Where else would we go on this beautiful, perfect day?" Bianca said, touching her thumb and forefinger to her lips and sending them to the sky in a blessing.

Sloane merely nodded and turned her attention back to the road because someone had to. Bianca seemed less concerned with driving her Ferrari convertible than she was with enjoying the scenery. Maybe if she hadn't been driving the Indy 500, Sloane would have been able to see some of it. As it was, she caught only glimpses of the lush landscape as Bianca raced down the back roads that led them closer to the shore and further from the villa.

"Relax," Bianca yelled over the noise. "I'm sure you need the rest after last night."

When she wiggled her eyebrows, Sloane knew it wasn't needing time to recover from her night with Doyle that Bianca was referring to. "It's not what you think."

Bianca gave her an incredulous look that went on long enough that Sloane had to reach over, take the wheel, and steer them back to the middle of the road. "So, this is the game we're playing now?"

"What game?"

"The one where we pretend that Jean-Paul and I didn't just see you come out of Cade's room this morning naked?"

"I wasn't naked…exactly."

"Bedsheets are not clothes."

"I don't want to talk about it." Sloane was unwilling to debate the definition of scantily clad with a woman who wore a bathing suit cover-up made of less fabric than her bikini.

It was accurate enough. She hadn't even talked to Cade about their night. She'd woken late to find him lying next to her, staring at her while she slept. There had been a wrinkle between his brows, and she'd reached up to smooth it with her finger without thinking before either of them had spoken a word. She didn't need words. Not when her only thoughts were of feeling warm, safe, and sated, and being at peace for the first time in months.

Then came the pounding on the door and the look on Gig's face when he'd seen her come out of Cade's room. It was acceptance of the inevitable, marked by just enough pity to cause the deluge of doubts that now swirled like a perfect storm in Sloane's mind. What would she have said, anyway? Thanks, Cade, for the pity sex?

But no, even that felt wrong. Sloane shook her head and turned away from Bianca, who, thankfully, dropped the subject. She didn't know how she felt now in the light of day and with some distance between them. Should she feel glad that it had happened or embarrassed and disappointed in herself for letting it go so far? What about Cade? Was he at that very moment telling JP last night had been a mistake?

And how could she be thinking about any of this right now, given the very real possibility that she'd just blown their entire mission?

Sloane jerked sideways as Bianca took a hard left and steered them into the parking lot. They screeched to a stop, and Bianca gave her a brilliant smile. "Ready?" Without waiting for an answer, she jumped out of the car, retrieved two towels and a basket from the trunk, and started for the shore.

Sloane hurried to catch up, her flip-flops apparently not a match for Bianca's cherry red stilettos. "Shouldn't we be doing something other than sunbathing at a time like this?"

"Like what?"

"Like trying to find Doyle."

"He's gone again," Bianca said with a wave of her hand. JP and Bianca arrived that morning with news that Doyle's boat was missing from the harbor, leaving them at a standstill once again.

"Shouldn't we at least prepare for what comes next?"

"Okay." Bianca paused on the sand and glanced up and down the beach before nodding to herself. Satisfied, she dropped everything, laid out her towel, and plopped down onto it before squinting up at Sloane. "What's next?"

Sloane blinked. "I don't know."

"You really are new at this, aren't you?" she said with a laugh. "Come. Sit. When you don't know what to do, do nothing."

Sloane caught the towel Bianca threw at her and joined her on the sand, still in her tank top and shorts. "That doesn't sound like a good plan."

Bianca spread a palm over her abdomen and smiled at Sloane. "The best gifts in life aren't always planned."

"You're pregnant?" Sloane stared at the woman's mostly flat stomach. "Are you sure?"

Another laugh. "Very. You may not see her yet, but this tiny *bambina* is already making herself known."

"It's a girl?"

Bianca shrugged. "Who knows? All I know is I'm hungry, so I eat. Then, I get sick and do it all over again. He or she can't make up their mind."

A thought occurred to Sloane, and she blurted the next question without thinking. "Does he know?"

"I should hope so," Bianca said. "It's his."

"It's…" Sloane trailed off as her stomach rolled.

"*Dio mio, cara.* What are you thinking? I meant it's my *husband's*, not Cade's." Bianca scrunched her nose in disgust. "Cade is like my sibling, and he and Jean-Paul are brothers. Not by blood, but that doesn't matter when you've been through what they've been through. And, no, Cade doesn't know about the baby, but I suspect he will soon."

Sloane thought back to the first time she'd officially met JP and Bianca and the unmistakable tension she'd sensed between husband and wife. "JP doesn't want you involved in this, does he?"

"As much as he'd like to think so, my husband is not the boss of me. I am here because I want to be." Bianca reached over her towel and took Sloane's hand. "You are not alone."

Sloane didn't know if it was the stress of last evening or Bianca's support that caused her eyes to fill with tears. The woman was not only risking herself but the life of her child to help her, and Sloane had likely ruined everything. "I'm so sorry."

"For what? Surviving? You should never apologize for that."

"That's what Cade said."

"You should listen to him."

"It should have been him." Sloane turned her attention to the waves. Just last night, she'd been terrified to be so close to the water. It was funny how now, after everything that had happened, it didn't seem so intimidating. "Last night never would have happened if Cade met with Doyle instead of me," she said, voicing the thought that had been running on repeat in her mind all morning.

"Or Doyle could have attacked him instead of you. Cade has been at this for a long time, but even he makes mistakes. We all do."

"Somehow, I doubt that."

"It's true. And mistakes in this job carry weight. Especially for Cade. Beckett carried it too, but differently."

Sloane looked at Bianca. "How so?"

"Beck understood the danger of what we do. He was more rational and knew how to separate the work from his life. As much as any of us can," Bianca said with a faint smile. "But Cade puts so much on himself. He works like he's trying to prove something. I used to think it was just to prove that he could. Now, I know better."

"You don't mean me?" Sloane said in response to Bianca's pointed look.

"Why not you? Cade cares about you."

"If he cared about me, he would have picked up the phone once in the last year." The words came out harsher than she'd intended, and Sloane muttered an apology. It wasn't Bianca's fault that Sloane's feelings toward Cade vacillated from one to the other extreme faster than even she could process them.

"And last night?"

"Last night was…temporary insanity," Sloane said, sighing at Bianca's disapproving frown. Even though she'd been vulnerable last night, she had still been in complete control of her faculties when they'd done…what they'd done. But there was still one thing she couldn't ignore. "He's lying to me, Bianca. He lied to me then, and he's lying now. No matter what happens between us, I'm not sure I can forget that."

"No, but can you forgive him?"

The question hinted at more than just mild curiosity, and Sloane braced herself. "Bianca, what happened to my brother?"

"I don't know details."

"But, you know something?"

Bianca sighed, resigned. "Only that they were together when it happened."

Even though she'd known that already, Sloane's heart sank.

"I know how you must feel."

Sloane snorted. "I doubt that."

"We live in a world of lies. Every day, there is a new lie to tell, a new person to be. It can be difficult, under these circumstances, to find our way to the truth."

Sloane knew that, didn't she? She knew it was sometimes necessary to deceive for the greater good. Though, for the life of her, she couldn't imagine how Cade benefitted from keeping this truth from her. "That's not an excuse."

Bianca gave her a thoughtful look. "Can I ask you a question?"

"Okay."

"Why are you here?"

"Isn't it obvious?"

"If I've learned one thing from all these years doing what I do, it's that nothing is obvious."

Sloane didn't hesitate. "To put Doyle away. For good."

"Is that all?"

Did there have to be more? Sloane folded her knees up to her chest, circling her arms around her shins. There was a time when she'd thought she wanted a normal life. A life where she had a boyfriend like Dan and a steady job, where the only threat was accidentally burning her fingers on a hot dish of lasagna. Then Beck died, and it had all seemed so…trivial. "I guess I thought I should do something that made a difference. Like maybe, in some small way, I could honor Beck by doing something that mattered."

"And now?"

Sloane hesitated. "I still feel that way, but it's harder than I thought."

Cade had been right when he'd said she'd been an errand girl for the last several months. Sloane hadn't known what it would take or what she would have to give. But it wasn't just the job, either. Last night, she'd let Cade in. She'd given him a piece of herself that she wasn't sure she'd ever get back. That scared her.

She looked at Bianca. "Is it worth it?"

"Only you can answer that. But you have your reasons for doing what you do, as does Cade. I believe when he's ready, he will tell you what you want to know. You might even find that your purpose isn't so different from his."

Sloane wasn't sure she shared that belief, but she kept that thought to herself. "Why do you do this?" She asked, suddenly desperate to know how a woman who was so intelligent, intuitive, and vivacious could end up living a life marked by so much cruelty.

"It was exciting at first." Bianca crossed one tanned leg over the other and leaned back on her forearms. "My world was small in Sicily, and I couldn't wait to get out. I met Jean-Paul while he was on holiday, and when he left to go home, I went with him."

Sloane's eyes widened. "But that's crazy."

"It was also romantic. I was very young and in love." Bianca looked at her. "I still am."

Sloane nodded because that much was clear. Even the arguments she had witnessed between her and JP seemed more like lover's spats than openly hostile.

"I was also eager to learn, and Jean-Paul knew much more than I did."

"Because he's older?" Sloane asked, confused. There couldn't be more than a few years of age difference between the two of them.

"Not only that. We're in the family business."

That was news to Sloane. "That must have made it very difficult for JP to refuse a job."

"Refusing was never an option for Jean. He might have had issues with his family, but he was always dedicated to the cause. And I was dedicated to him."

"And now?" Sloane asked, repeating the question Bianca had asked her earlier.

Bianca grazed her fingers over her abdomen. "Now, I think if this child has to be born into a world where evil exists, at least she will know her mother is a woman who knows her own heart and mind. She will know that, despite everything, I never stopped fighting."

And neither would Sloane. She couldn't do anything about the past, but she could fight for herself and the mission. So, as Bianca pulled some snacks out of their basket and settled in to read a French fashion magazine, she devised a plan to do just that.

<h1 style="text-align:center">36</h1>

"Wow."

It was the only thing Cade could think to say as he stared out at the stunning view of the mountain peaks that extended past the ocean. It was also the first word either of them had spoken in the two hours it had taken to reach the summit.

"I know," JP said.

"How do you know about this place?"

"I found it years ago, as a child."

Cade frowned. "I thought you grew up in Paris."

"That's where we lived, but *Maman* and I spent our summers near here."

JP's expression was grim, and Cade knew him well enough to know it wasn't the mention of his mother that put that look on his friend's face. Despite being a shit father, John Laurent was a skilled operative who took down many dangerous criminals during his time with the agency, a fact he'd learned from Albright rather than Jean-Paul himself. But even without that information, and even if Cade hadn't been the poster boy for a crap childhood, he would have recognized the signs. If he'd thought paying for his own father's sins was bad, it was nothing compared to what it must have been like to live in John Laurent's shadow.

"Thank you for your help yesterday," Cade said.

JP quirked an eyebrow. "I'm not the one you should thank."

"Do I know him?"

"What you mean to ask, of course, is whether you need to worry about him."

Cade shrugged, not willing to admit that was exactly what he'd been thinking. They had enough on their plates without adding another player to the game.

Jean-Paul shook his head. "He's a friend, a captain hired to charter Doyle's yacht. He was just someone with good instincts who was in the right place at the right time."

"You have a lot of friends."

"We're lucky I had this one."

Cade didn't miss the reprimand in JP's tone and tried not to think about what could have happened if the captain hadn't been there. It was dangerous territory, and he clenched his fists at his sides, a silent standoff against the invasion of what-ifs. "Well, I owe you."

Jean-Paul huffed in response, and they stood there a while. And then, a while longer.

"I know what you're going to say," Cade said.

"I doubt that."

"It's complicated."

"Judging by what I saw this morning, I'd agree with you."

"I didn't plan on…to…" Cade trailed off and raked a hand through his sweat-soaked hair. "It was a mistake."

"Are you trying to convince me or yourself?"

Cade didn't have a clue because even he knew what he'd said was a lie. He stared out at the view, squinting as though he could actually see Sloane from where they were. Even at that elevation, he could feel her, his body buzzing with the sense that she was near. "I hate that she's doing this."

"What you hate is that it's not you instead."

"It should be me."

"Why?" JP asked.

"She's been through enough."

"You both have."

Cade shook his head. "Beck wouldn't want her anywhere near this."

"What would he want for you?"

"After last night? He'd probably want me to jump off this cliff."

"I'm serious."

"So am I. It's my responsibility to keep Sloane safe."

"Is that what you've been doing?"

Cade met Jean-Paul's stare. "Jesus, we had a fight, okay? She stormed out. I couldn't reach her."

"What was the fight about?"

Cade bowed his head, his stomach roiling at the thought of what he'd said to Sloane before she left. "None of your business."

"It became my business the instant you dragged me and my pregnant wife into this mess."

Cade blinked. "What did you just say?"

"I was going to tell you," JP said. "Bianca begged me not to."

"Holy shit, man."

JP sighed. "Yeah. Holy shit."

"Is that what all this is about? Because I told you, just say the word, and you're out."

"And then, what? We go home and paint the nursery while we wait to hear that Doyle killed you, too?"

"That won't happen."

"It will if you don't stop thinking with this instead of this," JP said, stabbing a finger at Cade's chest and then his temple.

Cade slapped his hand away. "That's not what I'm doing."

"You forget, I know you. You don't stop."

"Damn right, I don't."

"Not even when you tear at the skin so hard that it bleeds," JP continued. "And that makes you an excellent officer, but it also leaves you vulnerable in ways you can't imagine."

"You're wrong," Cade said through clenched teeth.

"You and I both know this job isn't like all the others. The game has changed. *She* changed it, and every minute you spend thinking otherwise is putting all of us at risk."

"I know what I'm doing."

"No, you don't."

"I'm doing my job."

JP shook his head. "You're finding every reason *not* to do it."

"Fuck you."

"What are you more afraid of, Cade? Failing her like you failed Beck, or what will happen if you don't?"

Cade didn't notice his hand leaving his side. He wasn't even aware that he'd raised his fist until it connected with Jean-Paul's jaw. Pain lanced through his arm at the contact as JP stumbled back, reeling from the blow. Cade braced himself for the return hit, but JP slid on the gravel, arms flailing as he lost his balance.

"JP!"

Cade dove, just barely grabbing JP's arm before the rest of him fell over the cliff. He clasped his hand around JP's forearm as his friend let go of the ledge, his body becoming dead weight in Cade's grip. "Hold on, dammit."

JP threw him a what-the-hell-else-am-I-supposed-to-do look that brought Cade some relief as he pulled him up, grunting with the effort. It was another minute before JP could lift one leg up over the ledge, and then, with one final yank from Cade, they were both back on the mountain.

They rolled to their backs, exhausted and breathing hard, the sky overhead still a deep, cloudless blue.

"Are you sure it's yours?" Cade asked once he'd caught his breath.

JP punched him in the shoulder with more force than he expected, given what had just happened.

"You're going to be a father."

"Yes," was all JP said, but Cade could hear the smile in his friend's voice.

"Congratulations."

"*Merci.*" JP paused. "Tell her."

Cade sighed. "I don't want to hurt her."

"No. You don't want *her* to hurt you."

And there it was. A truth harder than the rock digging into Cade's back. "Maybe."

"If you don't trust each other, you can't finish this, and you have to finish it, Cade. You won't be able to move on until you do."

Before now, Cade hadn't considered what moving on actually looked like. For months, the future had seemed like a giant black hole. Did he dare think about it now?

"You couldn't have led with that?" Cade said.

"I could have, but then I wouldn't have this to show for my effort," JP said, pointing to his right eye, which was already bruising.

"Bianca's going to kick my ass, isn't she?"

"Run and hide, *mon ami*. Run. And. Hide."

But Cade knew with absolute certainty that the time for doing both had passed.

37

Instead of going back to the villa, Sloane asked Bianca to take her to the apartment in town.

She needed time to think.

The plan came together the instant she stepped out of the shower, and by the time she'd thrown on a pair of sleep shorts and a tank, she was positive it was the right one. Now, she just had to convince Cade.

Shaking her hair loose from the towel on her head, she ran her fingers through her wet hair and stared at herself in the bathroom mirror. Her skin was tan and smooth, and the natural highlights in her hair were nearly platinum from her time spent in the sun. She'd cut it before starting training to make taking care of it easier, but it was only now that she decided she liked the change.

Did Cade like it, too?

She didn't want to go there, but her mind did anyway. She recalled his gentle, almost reverent touch the night before, followed by a surge of unrestrained passion. Yes, they were attracted to each other, but was that all it was? Did she want it to be more?

The sound of the back door opening startled Sloane, and she went downstairs to find Cade adjusting the hidden camera in the living room. The bottom step creaked under her weight, and Cade turned to her. He looked tired and disheveled in gray sweatpants and a damp white T-shirt streaked with dirt. Her heart skipped when she saw the angry scrapes up and down his right arm.

"The camera went out again," Cade said.

"Thanks." Silence stretched between them as they stood frozen on their respective sides of the living room. Finally, Sloane moved to the bathroom down the hall and retrieved a first-aid kit from the cabinet under the sink. "Sit," she ordered when she returned, nodding to the kitchen island.

Instead of arguing, Cade crossed the room and slid dutifully onto the stool beside her. Sloane opened the kit and then a packet of alcohol wipes before swiping a wipe over the worst of the scrapes on his arm. He flinched, and she smirked, keeping her attention on her task. "Baby."

He chuckled and squeezed his hand into a fist, the corded muscles growing taut under her fingers before relaxing again. "You wouldn't say that if you were in this chair instead of me."

"That would never happen."

"Why not?"

Sloane set aside the wipe and pulled a gauze square and a roll of tape from the kit. "Because I have more sense than to brawl with a wild animal on my day off."

"Still afraid of bears, Bullet?"

She paused her work and looked up at him. "I'm afraid of a lot of things."

Amusement faded from Cade's expression, replaced by a look of concern mixed with regret. She hated that look and what it implied more than anything.

"About last night," he started. "I—"

"This isn't working," Sloane said, cutting him off. "With Doyle, I mean."

Cade sighed. "I know."

She returned to her task, applying the gauze to the worst of his wounds and taping it in place before sitting back on her stool. "I want to change the game." She held her breath, bracing herself for his instant refusal.

"Explain," he said at last.

"Do you remember Mom's vegetable garden?"

"What does that have to do with—"

"Just humor me."

"Of course, I remember it. That garden fed the entire neighborhood every summer for years."

Sloane smiled. "Still does, actually. Well, with Stan's help, of course."

"Now, that, I can't imagine."

"I think he missed his calling," Sloane said, recalling the last time she'd seen Fisher in his floppy hat and cargo pants standing over a bed of leafy greens. "Think of all the trouble you could have avoided if he'd chosen a career in gardening instead of education."

"If he had, there's a good chance I'd be in jail right now, or… worse."

He looked away from her, and Sloane didn't need or want him to elaborate. The thought of anything happening to another person she cared about made her sick. "She almost gave up on it that first summer."

"Why?"

"Something was eating the fruits…or vegetables…of her labor. It burrowed under the fence to get to the plants. Mom was upset, so Beck ended up camping out on the front lawn for a few nights, hoping to catch it in the act." Sloane still remembered watching Beck stumble into the kitchen before school in a sour mood from his unsuccessful stakeouts.

"Did he?"

"No, but he eventually came up with a plan."

"I'm almost afraid to ask."

She returned Cade's smile, ignoring for the moment the slight ache in her chest at the memory of Beck's scheming. "He went to a craft store and bought a few fake plants made of wax—lettuce, peppers, even an eggplant."

"Don't tell me he planted them," Cade said.

"He did. Right next to an iron cage he picked up at the hardware store and after he rubbed some kind of scent all over them."

Cade's grin widened. "Did it work?"

"It took a while, but yes, it worked." She remembered Beck's loud whoop from the garden a few mornings later. Sloane ran into the backyard to find the offending groundhog trapped in the cage.

"Let me guess," Cade said, leaning back on his stool. "You made him drive it out to the lake?"

"The lake was two hours away," Sloane said, as though she hadn't begged Beck to do just that. Then she sighed. "He drove it to Ludlow Park instead."

Cade sent her a look that reminded her of the way Mrs. Levinson used to look at her cat whenever Cuddles crawled into her lap.

A flush crept up the back of her neck, and she cleared her throat. "The point is, it worked. The groundhog thought the plants were real and came looking for its dinner." Sloane placed both hands on the counter and met Cade's gaze. "Doyle will, too."

"You want to dangle the carrot," he said, making the connection she knew he would.

"It worked before."

Bringing up the night of the benefit when Cade had used her to get Doyle's attention was a risk but one Sloane knew she had to take. She held her breath, expecting an argument, but Cade stayed quiet, his attention on his lap.

Finally, he looked at her. "There's no guarantee he'll take the bait."

"Doyle wants that emerald. You should have seen the look on his face when I brought it up last night. It was almost… proprietary."

"It's personal for him, then?"

"I think so. Celeste gave me permission to select any pieces I wanted for the exhibit. After I realized Doyle didn't have access to the storage facility, I figured it was safer to keep the emerald hidden. At least until we knew who his buyer was."

"But now, you think otherwise," Cade said.

Sloane nodded. "Instead of using his buyer as leverage, let's use Doyle himself. We can replace the real emerald with a fake and put it out in the open, making it easy for him to steal. When we catch him in the act, Albright will have the leverage he needs to get him to talk."

"Maybe."

"Remember what I said about his clients not wanting to sacrifice themselves? The same will be true for Doyle. He'll sell out his clients before himself, and we'll be in a better position than we are right now."

Sloane took another deep breath and told Cade everything she hadn't the night before about her attempt to get Doyle to talk about the emerald and his subsequent attack. She told him how Babyface had restrained her and how Doyle had let her go, like a wicked game of cat and mouse. There was no other way. If Doyle now knew who she was, she wouldn't only be putting herself and Cade in danger but Gig and the Laurents too. If something happened to any of them because of her, Sloane wouldn't be able to live with herself.

Cade, whose complexion had paled by degrees as she spoke, sat stock-still, hands gripping his knees.

"Please say something," she urged when she couldn't wait any longer.

He refocused on her, the dazed look in his eyes slowly clearing. "It's risky."

"I know, but if he knows we're on to him, we can't afford to wait." She stood from the stool and stepped into the space between his legs. "I can do this, Cade. I know you think I can't, that I don't have enough experience, but I—"

"I think you can do anything, Bullet." His voice was gruff, but there was no mistaking the certainty in his tone.

"You do?"

Cade stood, his hard body brushing hers and sending tingles down her spine. He cupped her face with both hands and grazed her cheeks with his thumbs as he lifted her face to meet his. "Yes."

His mouth was warm against hers, gentle and coaxing, but with the same underlying energy she'd felt from him the night before. One of his hands left her face, and he wrapped an arm around her waist, pulling her flush against him. She went willingly, savoring the feel of him and the spiced salt of his lips and tongue as she opened her mouth to let him in.

Cade groaned, and the sound reverberated through her as his fingers flexed on her waist. Then she was grasping his shoulders tight as he gripped her hips and lifted her onto the counter. Sloane gasped at the feel of the cool granite on the backs of her thighs and arched into him, wanting more.

But that was the problem. The thought rose unbidden from deep down in a place she couldn't reach. She *did* want more, she realized, answering the question she'd asked herself earlier. So much more than he'd been willing to give. Had he meant what he said? She could almost believe it as his hands glided up her spine and into the still-damp hair at her nape. Could she trust him, even with so many secrets still between them?

Yes, she thought as Cade tugged gently on her hair to expose her neck. Sloane obliged, tipping her head back as his lips found the base of her throat. At least for now, she wanted this and him.

Heat flooded her as he nipped at her collarbone before licking his way up to the hollow behind her ear, his ragged breath hot on her skin. "Okay."

"Okay?" She asked, breathless. Had she asked a question?

Cade pulled away, and Sloane bit her tongue to stop the protest that threatened to escape. He dragged her hands from his shoulders and clutched them together at his chest, just as he had last night. His forehead lowered to hers, his chest rising and falling under her fist, erratic but still no match for the rhythm of her own racing heart. "We'll change the game."

Sloane lifted her chin. "Really?"

Cade nodded. "We'll do it your way."

"Why?" Sloane shook her head to clear the last of the fog from her mind. "I mean, what's the catch?"

"There's no catch."

Sloane tugged her hands loose from his grip. "Are you sure?"

"Yes." Cade reached around her shoulders and braced both hands on the counter, caging her in. "As your partner, I can respect that this is what you want, but I have my limits."

Hope bloomed in her chest. "Partner?"

"Yes," Cade said. "Ask me what they are."

"What?"

"My limits. Ask me."

Sloane blew out a breath. "What are your limits?"

"Anything and everything that involves you putting yourself directly in the line of fire." When she opened her mouth, he raised a hand. "I'm not suggesting that you can't make a last-minute call in the field when it's warranted. But if things get out of hand, you will not, under any circumstances, sacrifice yourself for the sake of this mission."

His voice cracked as he said the words, and he dipped his head low before looking back at her, his eyes red-rimmed and raw. Sloane's chest ached, not from the emotion she saw in his face, but because he was letting her see it. For the first time in a long time, Cade Foster wasn't hiding from her.

Sloane brought a hand to his face. He flinched slightly at her touch before easing into her palm, his eyes drifting closed for only a second before refocusing on her. "Well, that's good," she said when she had his attention again. "Because I don't intend to let that happen."

"You may not have a choice."

"There's always a choice."

Cade was about to speak, but she silenced him with a kiss, conveying her promise to be careful.

He responded, but only for a moment before pulling away again. "I…should go."

"You're leaving *now*?"

"You need your rest."

"Is that so?"

"A lot has happened."

"No shit," she snapped, his rejection stinging more than it should have.

"You should take a minute. We both just need to take a minute and—"

"Pretend that last night didn't happen?"

Cade frowned. "I didn't say that."

Sloane slid from the counter and started for the stairs. "You didn't have to."

It was her own fault, really. Only she was to blame for expecting that his agreeing to her plan meant anything more than what it did. She didn't want his excuses or, worse, an apology. Oh God, she wasn't sure she could handle it if he apologized for what happened between them last night.

Cade's fingers wrapped around her upper arm and he tugged her to him, her back to his front. "Wait."

"I don't want to hear what you have to say."

"Too bad," he said, applying firm but gentle pressure when she continued to struggle in his grip. "Stop," he finally growled, the demand leaving no room for argument.

"You're so bossy," she muttered, sighing in exasperation.

"And you're a pain in my ass and…other places."

Cade inched closer to her, and she knew, or rather felt, what he meant. "Oh," she said as his hard length grazed her from behind.

His mouth lowered to her ear. "I said I *should* go, not that I want to."

"Then why didn't you just say that?"

"Because if I did, I wasn't sure how long I could have resisted not taking you right here on the kitchen floor."

Relief flooded Sloane, and she relaxed against him. "So, you don't regret last night?"

He nuzzled the side of her neck. "No," he said at last. "It complicates the hell out of...everything, but no. I won't ever regret being with you."

Sloane turned in his arms. The look on his face, resigned but resolute, told her it was true. "Me neither." Cade was right. It was messy and complicated, but she couldn't regret it. "Will you stay?"

"Not tonight."

She stared at him, her mind whirring over all the reasons he would deny them something they both wanted. Then suddenly, she knew. "Oh my god," she said, her mouth dropping open. "Are you kidding me?"

"No, I'm not."

"You're worried that if you stay, I'll think you only agreed to the plan because I slept with you."

Cade swiped a hand through his hair. "I just think we both need to keep a clear head right now."

"And you're choosing this moment to be chivalrous?"

"My trust in you doesn't come with strings, Bullet."

Sloane had been on the verge of laughing until he'd said that, but his words and the seriousness with which he delivered them sobered her. "I know."

He bent and kissed her cheek, just a flutter of lips on skin before he pulled away. "I'll see you tomorrow."

Sloane sighed, knowing she likely wouldn't be able to change his mind. Of course, that didn't mean she couldn't try. "Okay," she said, turning her back to him as she strolled to the stairs. She reached for the hem of her tank top and tugged it over her head. "I guess I'll just have to—"

The walls rattled as the back door slammed shut.

38

Sloane stood at the entrance to the main hall of the museum and watched the flurry of activity happening around her. It had been a long three days. Four, if she counted the weekend, though she'd only come into work on Sunday to talk to Celeste. She'd received a few polite smiles and head nods from the museum employees working that day, but her presence had gone unnoticed.

As it did now, while her assistant took charge across the room, giving orders in a voice that was both sweet and assertive. Sophie would make an excellent teacher, Sloane thought, with no small amount of irony. Maybe even better than Sloane had been.

"She's talented, isn't she?"

Sloane jumped. "Celeste!"

"We have to stop meeting like this," Celeste said with a smile.

"I know, I'm sorry. I just…didn't see you." Even if Celeste had a habit of sneaking up on her, Sloane couldn't afford to be distracted.

Instead of calling her out on her lack of focus, Celeste returned her attention to the exhibit. "Apologies for my late arrival. There were a few things I needed to take care of."

"I understand," Sloane said. "And yes, Sophie has been a godsend. I'm not sure what I would do without her."

"And yet, you're still nervous."

Sloane looked at her, surprised. "Do I seem nervous?"

"A bit."

"I suppose I'm…cautiously optimistic."

Celeste's gaze sharpened. "Yes, I imagine so."

The same tingling sensation she seemed to get whenever she spoke with Celeste flared to life once again. "There's no need to worry," Sloane said, unsure whether she was trying to convince herself or her boss. "Everything's all set for the exhibit's grand opening tomorrow evening."

"Oh, I'm not worried," Celeste said, folding her hands in front of her. "These things have a way of coming together the way they're supposed to." She looked to the center of the space, and Sloane held her breath. "That's good placement," she said, nodding to the glass case that held the emerald. "Everyone will see it when they walk in."

"Y-Yes, exactly."

"Relax," Gig said in her ear. "She's too far away to notice anything. Besides, that gem is a work of art, no pun intended. You're welcome."

Sloane glanced at the nearest security camera above the entrance to the hall and rolled her eyes. He was right, of course. She should and did thank him after he found a replica of the original emerald, right down to its weight. He'd had just about a week after they mobilized their plan to find one, and as always, Gig came through.

But the problem wasn't the copy; it was the woman staring at it. Celeste showed no reaction on Sunday when Sloane asked her to retrieve the emerald from the storage facility so she could add it to the exhibit. She also didn't hesitate to give her approval for Sloane to work late on Monday night when Sloane had made the switch. Gig had found no evidence linking Celeste and Doyle, but Sloane had to consider that she might be falling into a trap.

"I assume you'll be present tomorrow night?" Celeste asked.

"Of course."

"All evening?"

"That's the plan."

"Good," Celeste said with a tight smile. "I just want to be sure someone will be here should our patrons have questions."

Sloane nodded, even though it would be Sophie to whom she would delegate that task. "Won't you be here, as well?"

It was the first time Celeste had hinted at not attending the event, and Sloane couldn't imagine why. The exhibit had been Celeste's top priority for weeks. Confusion mixed with alarm settled in her gut as Sloane waited for an answer.

"I—" Celeste started but then quieted as she caught sight of something over Sloane's shoulder.

"Sloane," Gig said in her ear, but she didn't need the warning. She knew what, or rather, who was behind her.

"Good afternoon, ladies."

Doyle's smooth voice slithered up her spine and wrapped around her neck like a snake choking its prey. Sloane stiffened.

"*Breathe.*"

The sound of Cade's voice instantly calmed her, the panic that had seized her giving way to fiery rage. She let it burn and then tamped it down to a simmer, using it as fuel to do what she had to do.

"Mr. Dubois," Celeste said. "We weren't expecting you."

"I know, but I thought I would check on your progress. I hope I'm not interrupting."

"Well, Elena and I were just—"

"Not at all, Luc," Sloane said, turning to face him. "Would you like a tour?"

"I'd love one."

"I'm happy to take you through the exhibit," Celeste offered.

"No need. I have complete faith in Ms. Caldwell's abilities."

When Celeste didn't immediately respond, Sloane glanced her way, her boss's expression one of cool indifference. "Very well. If you don't need me, I think I'll retire early for the evening."

"Good night," Sloane said, softening her tone, not sure why she felt the urge to reassure the woman.

When she was gone, Doyle looked at Sloane. "You've done an excellent job of transforming the museum."

"That sounded like a compliment."

"So?"

"Aren't you concerned it will make me complacent?"

Doyle stared at her. "I would be if you worked for me. But you don't work for me, do you, *Elena*?"

The way he emphasized her name, like it was a pair of shoes he was trying on for the first time, was all the confirmation Sloane needed. He knew. Maybe not everything, but at least that she wasn't who she claimed to be. It shouldn't have mattered. She'd been prepared for the possibility, but the acrid taste of failure still lingered on her tongue.

"I'm sure," Doyle continued, "that my compliment also seems out of character given recent events. I very much regret my behavior the last time we met. It was quite rude."

He mentioned it as if he were apologizing for interrupting her or not refilling her wine glass. It had been less than a week since their dinner date, but Sloane's hatred for him had only grown stronger. "Do you always attack your dates or just the ones you don't like?"

She ignored the muttered curse in her ear and focused on Doyle's sneer. The hairs on the back of her right arm rose as his suit jacket grazed her skin.

"On the contrary. I find you more interesting than I have anyone in a very long time."

"Unfortunately, I can't say the same."

"Such ugly lies from such a beautiful mouth."

Doyle lifted a hand so suddenly that she flinched and then froze. Would he dare touch her here, in front of an audience? Her eyes darted around the room to see if anyone had noticed, but nobody was paying any attention. She took a minuscule step back just as Doyle picked an invisible piece of lint from his sleeve.

Disgust and anger flared in her veins when he looked back at her, not bothering to hide his pleasure at seeing her squirm. She had to do better.

Get it together, Easton.

She checked the watch on her left wrist. "If you're not interested in a tour, Mr. Dubois, then you'll have to excuse me. There's still a lot to do."

"Ah, yes," Doyle said, nodding to the back of the room where a couple of additional security guards observed the action. "I assume they're here at your behest?"

"These are valuable pieces."

"Of course," he said. "We wouldn't want any of them to fall into the wrong hands."

"Exactly."

Sloane watched as Doyle's gaze traveled from case to case, already knowing where it would land. "It's such a shame when people don't take care to avoid taking something that doesn't belong to them. So much unpleasantness and, for what?"

"Some things are worth the risk."

His attention returned to her. "I thought grand gestures didn't turn you on."

"They don't. But do you know what does?" Sloane said, leaning forward. "Having a front-row seat when it all goes to hell."

His eyes flashed. "You like to watch."

"I like to fight."

"You certainly do." Revulsion turned her stomach as his gaze traveled the length of her. "But let's not forget the first rule of a good fight."

"Never underestimate your opponent," Sloane said.

He clucked his tongue. "And here I thought we were becoming friends."

"No, you didn't."

"You're right, and that's quite unfortunate."

"Why's that?"

"Because, Elena," Doyle said, his tone colder than the Arctic in January. "I'm a much better friend than I am an enemy."

39

Cade snuck glances at Sloane through his aviators as he drove the Aston with the top down back to the villa. She was too quiet, and she'd barely looked at him since he'd picked her up almost immediately after Doyle had left the museum. It wasn't her silence that worried him as much as the way she sat staring straight ahead, hands folded in her lap like a dutiful child attending Sunday services.

Bullet was a lot of things but obedient wasn't one of them.

"Are you hungry?"

"Whatever you want," she responded, still not looking at him.

Was it what Doyle had said? Yes, he knew she wasn't who she said she was, but provoking him had been the point. Maybe his words had affected her more than she'd thought they would. Cade would know if she'd just talk to him. He remembered how easily she'd yielded to him the other night. When she woke with a lazy smile that spread over lips red and swollen from his kisses, he didn't know what to say. He hadn't wanted to spoil the moment, but he knew he'd already sullied it just by being there.

It was why he'd restrained himself the following night at her apartment. She'd been ready, despite everything, to give herself to him again, but he couldn't let her do it. He had wanted her to trust him, but not if she'd regret it. Ironic, considering if she knew the truth, she'd likely never trust him again.

Sloane's voice carried to him over the wind.

"What?" He said.

"Stop!"

Sloane reached over and grabbed the wheel, and Cade swore as he pumped the brake, regaining control and awkwardly steering the car to the side of the road. "What the hell, Bullet?"

But she was already out of the car and running toward a thin tree line that blocked two towering sand dunes. He jumped out of the car and started after her, passing a decrepit wooden sign barely legible in the fading light.

Plage paradisiaque. Paradise Beach.

"Shit," he said aloud as he climbed the dunes faster.

Once, in an airport, he'd read a magazine article about a man surviving in the Sahara Desert without food or water for days. He'd been through hell—sun exposure, frigid nights, snakes, and sandstorms. But the worst of it had been when he'd collapsed on the sand the day before his rescue and saw a circle of palm trees shading a pool of water. He'd crawled toward it, trying to reach it, only to discover that it was a mirage.

Cade's training had taught him that a fatigued mind and a depleted body could convince anyone that something existed when it really didn't. Still, he'd never experienced what that man in the desert had. Not until the moment he reached the top of the sand dunes and saw Sloane standing at the water's edge, her blue slip dress in a tangled heap on the sand by her feet.

He stared at her long enough for the evening glow to fade to purple and black like the sky itself was recovering from a fight. He could relate, even though he felt like he was still fighting. As Sloane unclasped her bra and bent to slide the scrap of lace down from between her thighs, he felt like he was being pummeled repeatedly and without mercy. There was no defense against this, against watching her bravely wade into the water, her fingers softly caressing its surface, just like they had his body.

Cade knew nothing about art, but at that moment, he appreciated the hell out of it. He finally understood why artists starved for perfection and musicians struggled to write lyrics to the songs that played in their heads. He knew now how longing could drive a person crazy and how the tiniest sip could cause an unquenchable thirst.

Sloane sank lower, her chest hovering at the surface, and Cade imagined her nipples puckering in the cool water. Was the water temperature here different from the water near the public beaches? He tried to recall anything and everything he knew about water currents in that part of the world as he monitored Sloane for any sign that she might be cold. He stared so damn hard that her figure blurred, and he had to rub his eyes.

He quickly returned to the car and searched the trunk for something to keep her warm. Finding nothing, he lunged for the backseat and grabbed the suit jacket he'd forgotten he'd abandoned the night of the gala on the car floor. He pushed even harder on the way back, lungs and limbs burning hotter than they had during his hike with JP. He raced down to the water's edge and froze.

She wasn't there.

He glanced from the surface of the water to the beach and then back again. He spun in a circle and squinted into the fading light. Someone who had never stepped foot in the water wouldn't be able to swim, and he'd left her by herself in the goddamned *ocean*.

He splashed into the waves, panic clawing its way up his throat as he dove headfirst into the water. Was this where he'd last seen her? The water was as warm as bathwater, and he swore open-mouthed at his foolishness for going back for the jacket. It wasn't like it was a life vest. She needed a life vest. He surfaced coughing and planted his feet on the sea floor. At least it wasn't deep there. At least…

Cade looked to the left and was just about to dive again when he saw her. She rose, her head, neck, and bare shoulders coming into view as she surfaced several feet away. He'd judged her location wrong, he realized, as he watched her swipe water from her eyes and wade back in. But that didn't surprise him. He'd been so very wrong about so many things.

She paused at the shoreline, her gaze combing the empty beach and then meeting his where he still stood fully clothed and waist-deep in the ocean.

Step.

One.

Step.

Two.

Step.

Three.

The closer she got, the louder the voice in his head boomed until his counting blared thunderously in his ears. He'd never been this close to an attack without crashing, had never hovered on the brink the way he did now without succumbing to the inevitable. But, as she glided toward him, water dripping from her glistening skin, Cade felt the panic inside him recede until it was barely a ripple.

"Is that for me?"

Confused, Cade looked down to find the now-soaking jacket still tight in his grip. He lifted it out of the water and held it out to her, the most inadequate offering in the history of rites and rituals.

Her smile was the kind that started wars between nations, that drove men to the edge of reason, only to cause them to lay down their arms in surrender. It was the smile from his dreams and nightmares, the one she'd given him long before he craved it and long before he knew he was in love with her.

"Thank you," she said, putting on the jacket.

But it did no good. As Bullet took his hand and led him back to the beach, Cade understood that not even a life vest could save a man from drowning on dry land.

PART 3

And when the end loomed dark and mean,
I wouldn't try to make a scene,
because I would know just what to do,
to find my way back to you.

40

Cade woke in the middle of the night to an empty bed.

She'd come to him when they'd returned to the villa. It was late, but he'd been waiting. She slipped into his room and stood at the foot of his bed, an apparition in white silk that covered the most beautiful body he'd ever seen. He was lost even before she peeled the slip over her head and crawled onto the bed, before she straddled and leaned over him, staring at him through eyes brighter than the sky at dawn. He was lost until she found him, the way she always did.

He rolled onto his back, spreading his arms out wide. He could still feel her. She wasn't physically there, but she was under his skin, buried so deep that she'd become a vital part of him, like an organ he needed to survive. He knew that now. Just as he understood that accepting Albright's offer years ago hadn't been entirely about finding himself. It had also been about escaping the man he believed himself incapable of being. For her.

He'd been afraid, so he ran. He'd made it his life's work to be anyone other than himself, and he'd taken Beck with him.

Cade squeezed his eyes shut against the pain that throbbed in his temple. No, he wouldn't spiral back into the pit of guilt and shame that had plagued him since his best friend's death. He still had a job to do, one that had nothing to do with bringing Jack Doyle to justice. If he truly wanted to stop running, he had to stop lying and not just to himself.

He found her sitting on a lounge chair by the pool, staring at the water, a single bare leg dangling out from under the bedsheet she'd wrapped herself in. He paused at the gate, gut clenching as he took a mental picture of the way she looked, bathed in white light like the moon itself had chosen her—just like he should have.

She looked up when he opened the gate, the squeak of rusty metal jarring in the silence. Her eyes stayed on him as he crossed the patio, her gaze settling on the tattoo on his bare chest.

His skin heated as he recalled how she'd touched it last night as she rode him, her palm covering the tag that bore Beck's name. He'd wiped the tears from her cheeks and then closed his hands over hers, wanting to carry the burden that had always been his to bear. At least they'd had last night, not that it would make what came next any easier.

Nothing would.

He sat on the edge of the chair next to her and rested his elbows on his knees. "Couldn't sleep?"

"No."

"Did you go for a swim?"

Considering she was completely dry, it was a stupid question, but she answered anyway, a faint smile tugging at the corners of her mouth. "I can't swim."

"You can't swim *yet*."

"Maybe never."

"Never say never, Bullet."

She looked at him, her eyes wide but also sad. "Right."

"What you did tonight was brave. There aren't many people who can face their fears like that."

"It was a silly fear."

Cade shifted in the chair, angling his body toward her. "No, it wasn't. And making light of it won't change the significance of what you did."

"I didn't plan it. I saw the sign on the road, and I just thought…why not?"

Cade thought it was probably more than that, but he didn't push her. Instead, he asked her a different question. "What was it like?" He suddenly needed to know. If he was going to take his own dive off a cliff in the middle of the night, then he wanted to know what it felt like.

"At first, I felt nothing," she said, her attention settling on something over his shoulder. "The whole way down to the water, I don't think…well, I wasn't *thinking* at all. It was…"

"Instinct?" he offered.

Sloane tilted her head, considering. Cade's gaze slipped from her face to the curve of her neck as she did so, noticing the love bite he'd given her at the base of her throat.

"Maybe," she said, looking at him again. "I guess so. It wasn't until my toes touched the water that I felt some resistance."

"You did?" He hadn't noticed her hesitation, but then, he had been more than a little distracted.

"Well, not resistance, exactly. More like that feeling you get at the top of a rollercoaster ride right before you're about to take the plunge. You can see where you're going, but you don't know what's going to happen on the way down. And the only way to get through it is to…"

"Let go," he finished.

"Yes."

He slipped a hand around her neck and grazed the bite with the pad of his thumb, smoothing the skin. "I'm sorry."

"It's alright," she said, closing her hand over his. "I didn't mean to scare you."

"I know." He wanted to tattoo the way she looked at him on his skin, right next to Beck's tag. Instead, Cade dropped his hand. "There's something I need to tell you."

41

"What is it?" Sloane asked, even though she already knew.

Cade stood from his chair, his sweatpants falling even lower on his hips as he turned away from her, his back straighter than the edge of a blade.

Thoughts of him had woken her from sleep, and she'd been too distracted to think about getting dressed before coming outside. Those thoughts had led her here, to this very moment, one she'd been waiting for for a very long time.

Her pulse thrummed in her veins, her heart skipping as she tugged the sheet tighter to her chest.

God, she wished she'd put on clothes.

Cade put his hands on his hips and looked out beyond the pool. The yard was dark and silent, as though even the crickets sensed what was about to happen. Sloane held her breath and didn't let it out until she heard his voice.

"We were on a job in Miami," Cade began. "Albright had received some intel that arms dealer Cesar Juarez was making a move. It was only supposed to be surveillance. Juarez wasn't the target."

"Albright wanted to follow the guns to the source," she said.

Cade nodded. "That was the idea. Except we knew something was wrong the minute we entered the shipyard. There was too much activity. Juarez's men were being careless, moving too much too fast and out in the open. It was like—"

"They were expecting someone," Sloane finished.

"Yes, but there was no evidence of that. It was very early morning, like 4 a.m. For all we knew, Juarez was just trying to beat the dawn."

"So, you went in."

"I wanted to call Albright. I tried to convince Beck to wait, but that night, he didn't want to."

That night.

A breeze swept over the patio, and even though it was warm, Sloane shuddered as a chill swept up her spine. She folded her hands in her lap and squeezed, fingers digging into her knuckles as she listened.

"I don't know why," Cade said. "He didn't take chances on the job. He was always so careful, methodical. Hell, if it had been in the playbook not to take a shit without asking Albright first, he wouldn't have."

Careful. Methodical.

"It didn't make sense. He'd been off all day, but in that moment, he seemed so…sure that I just said, ok."

Off all day.

"We split up to cover more ground and so we could get close enough to ID the inventory. I boarded the ship they were using as transportation while Beck made the rounds on the dock. At some point, I went below deck. I told him before I did it, but my position must have messed with our devices because I don't think he heard me."

Sloane's stomach rolled, and she swayed as a bout of dizziness assailed her.

Cade looked back at the water, the pool's blue lights casting an eerie glow on his skin. "When I returned to the deck, all hell broke loose. Juarez's men shot at everything that moved. Beck and I were armed, but I didn't want to give away my position, so I took cover. I tried to contact him, but if he replied, I didn't hear it. It was too goddamned loud."

Cade swiped a hand through his hair and tugged at the strands. He looked like he wanted to crawl out of his own skin, and in that moment, Sloane knew he wasn't with her at all but back there on that ship.

"Eventually, I knew I had to move. I didn't know how many men had ambushed Juarez or who they were, but I knew they were coming for the guns. What I didn't realize was that while I'd been busy considering an exit route, a few of those men had already boarded the ship."

Sloane sat so still her muscles ached. It was an ambush. Her brother had been ambushed.

"I circumvented some men on the route I'd chosen, but more came at me. With most of Juarez's men either dead or gone, I knew I wouldn't have a chance of escaping unless I jumped from the boat. I was on the railing of one deck, about to do just that when I heard the sirens."

"Beck called for backup." The words tumbled from her mouth because, of course, he had.

Cade looked at her. "He must have changed his mind when he saw what was happening. All I know is that all the men on the boat scattered like ants when local law enforcement arrived. At least, that's what I thought."

His shoulders slumped, his expression twisting into something Sloane wanted to look away from but didn't.

"I knew Albright would have my ass if I spent hours in a police interrogation room. I planned to double back and meet Beck at the rendezvous point, just like we'd agreed. But…"

Understanding flooded Sloane's senses, the ringing in her ears growing almost deafening. "He came after you instead."

"Yes," Cade said, and that one word held so much grief and pain that this time Sloane looked away. "The guy came up behind me. I didn't see him until he'd already fired a round. I heard my name and then—"

"But weren't you wearing vests?" she asked.

"Yes, we were, but the bullet, it…grazed his neck," Cade said. "I got a shot off but—"

"It was too late." A sensation began in the pit of her stomach, the sizzling and gurgling of piping-hot steam.

"I'm so sorry," Cade said.

"That bullet was for you."

"Yes."

"He saved your life."

"Yes."

A strangled, hopeless moaning sounded in the silence, and it wasn't until she felt Cade's hands on her knees that she realized the sound had come from her. She felt his arms come around her, but she stood, almost tripping on the sheet as she scrambled away from him. When he took a step forward to steady her, she shoved him hard in the chest. "*You* killed him. You killed my brother."

She saw it then, the same misery she saw in the mirror every morning since Beck's death. It was all there in the way Cade looked at her, the sorrow, grief, and anguish spilling from him and onto the ground between them like blood from an open vein.

She felt it all, and still, she couldn't stop. "How could you?"

"I didn't…I couldn't…I tried t—"

"*Tried?* What you tried to do was save your own ass."

Cade paled. "No."

"You just told me you were going to jump ship and go to the rendezvous point."

"Because that was the plan."

"You mean the plan that should have ceased to exist the minute you realized something was wrong?"

"I didn't know it was. I just sensed it."

"Just like you *sensed* something was off with Beck?"

Cade shook his head. "We shouldn't have gone in."

"But you did," Sloane said, her voice cracking. "Beck trusted you. And now he's dead."

"I would take it all back if I could."

"But, you can't. Just like you can't take back your silence in the months since or your lies since we started this. My God," she exclaimed. "This whole time, you've been doing nothing but lying."

"Bullet, I—"

"Don't."

"Please." He reached into the space between them, grasping nothing but air. "Tell me what I can do to make this right."

"Nothing," she said, choking on a sob. Cade's image blurred as her eyes filled with tears. "Nothing you do will ever make it right."

42

Sloane tore through the villa and up the stairs to her bedroom. She hastily dressed in jeans, a black hoodie, and sneakers and hauled her travel bag out of the closet. With shaking hands, she pulled out the envelope addressed to her from the bottom of the bag and shoved it into her pocket, along with her phone, before storming back out of the room.

There was nothing else from this place she wanted to take with her. She just needed to go.

Now.

She raced back down the stairs and through the house.

That night.

Swiping the keys to the Aston from a nearby table, she opened the front door and slammed it behind her, heading for the driveway.

He didn't take chances on the job.

It didn't make sense.

Gravel crunched under her feet as she glanced over her shoulder to make sure Cade wasn't following her.

Careful. Methodical.

Sloane stopped, the car keys falling from her hand as she sunk to her knees beside the car.

Off all day.

I don't know why…

She doubled over, wrapping her arms around her body. No, Cade didn't know, but she did.

She rocked back and forth, trying to ward off the pain and grief that came anyway, along with hot, shameful tears. She'd blamed Cade when it hadn't been him at all. He wasn't the reason Beck was dead.

She was.

A fresh wave of guilt flooded her when she thought about how easy it had been to accuse him, so much easier than blaming herself. It might have been Doyle's man who pulled the trigger, but there was no doubt in Sloane's mind that she was the one responsible.

One phone call. Just one phone call was all it took to kill her brother.

A chime sounded in the silence, and she jumped at the accompanying vibration in her back pocket. Sloane wasn't superstitious. She believed in tangible things, not in signs that revealed themselves from somewhere out beyond the great divide. But, just like the night on Doyle's yacht when she'd heard Beck's voice in her head, a feeling swept through her, an electric charge that shot right to her toes.

With trembling hands, she reached for her phone, inhaling sharply when she saw the text notification from an unknown number on the screen. She tapped the message.

Come play with me, little mouse.

As she read the words, another text appeared, this one an image of a terrified-looking Gig, strapped to a chair with duct tape covering his mouth. Sloane gripped the phone tighter as a third message came through.

Don't wait too long.

She scrambled to her feet and stared hard at the screen, waiting for more messages that never came. How did Doyle find him? She hadn't seen Gig when she and Cade returned to the villa, but then, she hadn't really been looking for him either. More guilt threatened to consume her, but she shut it down. Now wasn't the time. She needed to figure out where Gig was.

It was possible he was on Doyle's yacht. She'd only seen one room on that boat, but there were others. How would she know which one he was in? She studied the image again. Gig was sitting in front of a white wall in a chair. No, not a chair, Sloane realized. A throne. She remembered Sophie moving that same throne to the museum's main hall for the exhibit. But, if he was at the museum, then…

Sloane's stomach dropped. "No, no, no, no, no."

Gig was a trained analyst, not a field agent. If Doyle tortured him for information about the emerald, then…oh God, *had* he? She didn't see any visible signs of injury, but that didn't mean Gig wasn't hurt.

Sloane bent and grabbed the keys from the ground. She made it two steps before she stopped and turned toward the backyard. She should tell Cade. Regardless of what had just happened, he would want to know. But *she* didn't want him with her. Not because of the truth he'd finally given her but because she wouldn't be able to live with herself if anything happened to him. She'd been the one to start this, and she alone had to end it. No one else would get hurt because of her.

No one.

43

Because his mother, father, and best friend were all gone, Cade thought he knew what it felt like to be left. But watching Sloane walk away from him proved he knew nothing at all.

He sank into a lounge chair and dropped his head in his hands. She was right. Beck's death was his fault. But that wasn't the only reason he was culpable. He'd also done the one thing he swore he'd never do. He'd not only failed his best friend, but he'd failed Sloane, too.

Devastated. That was the only way to describe the look on Sloane's face when he'd told her the truth. Devastated and enraged. Her anger had jumped out and bit him, brutal and violent. It would leave a scar deeper than any other. And he'd wanted to make it right? Nothing about any of this was right.

Nothing, except for how he felt about her.

But all that was over now. He could leave. Cade could go inside and pack a bag right now and disappear. It was what he should do and was no less than what Sloane deserved. A huge part of him was already halfway out the door, but the other part, the part that loved her, knew he wouldn't leave while Doyle was still out there. He would finish it for the both of them and then he'd take himself out of the picture.

For good.

The house was silent when he walked back inside and he let out a breath, glad Sloane had gone to bed. It would be easier to do what he needed to do without her. He headed down the hall to the room that housed all their security equipment and opened the door.

"Gig, I want you to—"

Cade stopped when he realized he was talking to an empty room. With the exhibit opening tomorrow night, he'd expected Gig to be camped out in front of the cameras.

He frowned and turned to the bedroom Gig had claimed across the hall. "Gig?"

The door eased open at his knock, the only lamp in the room casting pale light over piles of clothes and equipment strewn over the floor. No Gig.

Cade headed back across the hall and scanned the top of the desk. Unlike Gig's bedroom, the desk was clutter-free, and a quick search of the drawers told him that wherever he'd gone, he hadn't left a note.

Unease swept through him, and he turned to the cameras. One screen displayed nothing but snow, and he didn't have to check its location to know which one it was.

He swore and bent over the desk, fumbling with the keyboard. "Come on, come on."

He clicked rewind on the footage of the living room of the apartment in town. If he could just figure out when it had gone out, then maybe…

Several images suddenly came into focus, and then the screen flashed black. He'd gone too far. Cade fast-forwarded the feed until Gig's face filled the frame. The picture tipped to the right, then the left as he reset the camera. Then Gig turned, and in the space between the edge of the frame and his head, Cade saw a man in a black suit enter and shut the front door.

Jack Doyle's man.

Surprised, Gig jerked back into the camera, and a blizzard of black and white reappeared on the screen. Cade skipped ahead, hoping, by some miracle, the camera had fixed itself and there was something on the live feed. There wasn't.

Gig knew he wasn't supposed to leave the villa without Cade, and he'd chosen tonight, of all nights, to fix the goddamned camera himself? Why hadn't Gig come to him? Didn't he know they were home?

Cade's gut clenched. Yes, he knew. It was also highly likely that Gig knew how he and Sloane were spending the night. Rather than interrupt, he'd handled the situation himself.

Movement on one of the other screens, the one recording a view of the museum's lobby, caught Cade's attention. He froze when he saw the grainy image of someone else he recognized crossing the marble floor.

Bullet crouched low as she moved, weapon out and ready. *His* weapon. The one from the glove compartment of his…

"No!"

Fear sliced through him, and Cade scrolled through the rest of the cameras, pausing when he found what he was looking for. Doyle, his bodyguard, and Gig were in the main exhibit hall. Gig sat tied to a chair while Doyle and his bodyguard stood over him…waiting.

He looked back at the camera in the lobby, but Bullet was out of sight. He didn't know how she'd known where they were, but it didn't matter. There was no chance in hell she was going after Doyle alone.

Cade stalked back to his room and grabbed his phone off the nightstand.

Then he made the call.

44

The museum was dark and eerily quiet. Moonlight shone through the stained glass windows, guiding Sloane as she moved silently on the marble floor. Her hands shook as she flexed her palm around the barrel of Cade's Glock 19, aiming the weapon at the shadows. It was all she had, and she would use it if she had to.

Even if that means taking a life?

It had been Cade's way of asking her if she understood. Target practice had been part of her training, as had practice missions designed to simulate the real thing. She could differentiate between a shotgun, rifle, and pistol and knew how to handle them, but using them was about more than just mechanics. It was about being prepared for the responsibility that doing so yielded. She'd thought she understood, but she didn't.

Not until now.

As she passed the security desk at the rear of the lobby, her foot came into contact with something on the ground. She looked around her and then down, her eyes widening when she saw two legs poking out from underneath the desk.

Sophie?

Sloane dropped to her knees beside her assistant and quickly placed two fingers at the base of the girl's throat, breathing a sigh of relief when she felt a pulse.

Sophie stirred at Sloane's touch, her eyes fluttering open. "Elena? What—"

Sloane shushed her with a finger to her lips and shook her head. Sophie nodded, and they slowly stood just as the sound of a gunshot pierced the silence. Sophie opened her mouth, but Sloane slapped a hand over it to stop her scream. A sliver of light shone to her right, coming from the museum's main hall where they'd finished setting up for the exhibit earlier.

Sloane looked at Sophie, who clutched her forearm so hard Sloane's wrist ached. Though she was trying to be brave, her eyes were brimming with tears. *Go,* she mouthed, and Sophie hesitated, finally seeing the gun in Sloane's other hand. She shook her head wildly, but Sloane shoved her toward the door. *"Now,"* she hissed.

Sophie obeyed, stepping back. "I'll get help."

Sloane only nodded as Sophie rushed toward the door, knowing it wouldn't make a difference even if she did. She wouldn't wait. Gig needed her, and she wouldn't leave him alone.

Sloane followed the light to the main hall, a smooth, calm voice greeting her as she rounded the corner. "Hello, my dear. Please, join us."

Jack Doyle stood some distance away, his hands tucked neatly into his pockets. Even though it was the middle of the night, he wore the same pressed linen suit as he had earlier. Relaxed and confident, he looked like he was about to give a speech to potential museum donors instead of being party to a kidnapping.

Sloane tightened her grip on the Glock. "Where is he?"

Doyle stepped to the side, and there was Gig, still bound and gagged, but luckily not shot. Sloane's relief turned to concern when she noticed Babyface standing behind Gig, his weapon aimed at her friend's head.

When Gig saw her, he tugged on his restraints, shaking his head and moaning into the duct tape. He jerked his head in the direction she'd just come, urging her to leave, his fear for her jolting through her like a shock.

Sloane silently shook her head. *Not a chance, partner.*

"I worried you wouldn't make it," Doyle said. "Of course, that would have been most unfortunate for Marvin."

"Well, I'm here now, so you can let him go."

"On the contrary. Marvin has proven himself quite useful."

Doyle turned his back and moved to the closest podium, the one that Sloane could now see contained the emerald. Pulling a set of keys from his pocket, he unlocked the glass case and lifted the lid.

Sloane braced herself for the sound of a blaring alarm, but none came. Surprised, she glanced at Gig, the slump of his shoulders telling her he'd been the one to disable it.

"You know I can't let you leave with that," she said as she sent Gig a reassuring look. Even though they'd planned for the possibility of Doyle breaching their security, it didn't mean that Gig had expected to be the one to do it.

"What you mean by that, of course, is that your sense of duty won't allow it. Isn't that what all you government types pride yourselves on? Duty, responsibility, and loyalty, above all else?"

Sloane tensed. "You know."

"I didn't. Not at first. I suspected, of course, but you confirmed my suspicions the night you joined me on my yacht. No, not then," Doyle said, holding up a hand when she tried to speak. "It wasn't your rather aggressive response to our conversation that caused me to question your intentions."

She frowned at the edited description of his attack on her. "What, then?"

"Despite your assumptions about why I'm on the museum's board, I do actually appreciate fine art."

"Really?"

He nodded. "I enjoy being surrounded by beautiful things, especially when I'm traveling. The main salon on my yacht, where we had dinner, for instance, has an array of fine paintings on display. Art that only one with an accomplished eye could appreciate."

And Sloane didn't appreciate them. She hadn't even noticed the paintings were there.

"Don't be too hard on yourself, though. You fooled me until then. Of course, if you had noticed the paintings, we might not be in this situation right now. You are right, though. I can't leave with this emerald." He pulled an object out of his pocket and held it up to the light. "But I can leave with this one." Another emerald, the *real* emerald that she'd kept hidden in her office, glinted in the light.

Shit.

Doyle turned to a nearby case and retrieved a wooden box from its surface. He opened the lid and tipped it forward, revealing two emeralds side by side on a bed of white velvet.

Sloane sucked in a breath. "You do have them all."

"I do now." He added the one he held to the box and flipped the lid shut. "My client will be thrilled."

"There is no client. You never had a buyer," she said, finally voicing her theory aloud. She glanced at Gig, his groan once again muffled by the tape.

"You are enchanting," he said with a note of awe. "It's a pity you won't live to see the morning. I would have truly enjoyed breaking you."

"Fuck you."

Doyle's deep, raucous laugh echoed in the cavernous hall. He placed the box on top of one case and started toward her, weaving around the podiums like a slinking cat. "Did you know that in the old days, there were many who referred to emeralds as truth stones?"

Sloane shook her head and moved a half-step back, bumping into the podium behind her.

"They believed an emerald could cut through illusion, falsity, even lust, to get to the truth." Doyle advanced until he was standing barely five feet in front of her. "Shall we test that theory and play a little game?"

"No."

"Suit yourself."

From the corner of her eye, she saw Babyface approach Gig and raise the gun higher. "No!" She released one hand from the barrel of her weapon and held it up. "Ok, f-f-fine. I'll play."

"Excellent. We can both play. You tell me a truth, and then I'll tell you one. You start," he said, leveling her with a stare. "What do you want with me?"

It was a trick question because right now, what she wanted didn't matter. She just had to keep him talking. The longer she did, the longer Gig stayed alive and the more time she had to figure a way out of this.

"You'd have to ask my boss," she said. "I just do what I'm told."

"Somehow, I doubt that." Doyle merely lifted his chin, and Babyface moved to Gig's right, aiming for his temple. He cocked his gun, the click as loud as cymbals clashing in Sloane's head.

"He wants you to talk," she said, relief coursing through her when she saw Babyface's arm slacken.

"Ah, yes," Doyle said. "And I suppose he also thought he could get to me through my non-existent buyer, maybe get him to admit he hired me, and then use that as leverage to gain access to my client list?"

"Yes."

"And what makes you think I'd ever betray one of my clients, leverage or not?"

Sloane could see now that Albright had been wrong. *She'd* been wrong. Doyle would never give up his network, and from his scornful tone, she could tell that the insinuation offended him. In any other situation, she might have laughed at his misguided ethics, but right now, she didn't feel like laughing.

"A truth for a truth," she said. "My turn."

"You're right. Go ahead."

"Why do you want the emeralds?"

"They are quite valuable. I may not have a buyer right now, but I'm sure I can find one."

"You don't need the money."

"True. Besides, some things are priceless." Doyle stepped forward until the barrel of her gun rested on his chest. He lifted a finger to flick at a lock of her hair, and it took everything in her not to flinch. "You look like her, you know. The resemblance is so striking that the first time I saw you, I thought Colleen was back from the dead," he said, scanning her face. "Only the eyes are different. Hers were the color of snakeskin. Fitting."

Colleen?

Recognition stirred at the name, but Sloane couldn't remember where she'd heard it. Then it came to her. "That's the name of your yacht."

"Ah, so you noticed something, after all."

"She's the reason you want the emeralds? You just said she was dead."

"Eh, eh, eh," he said, wagging a finger at her. "You're cheating."

"You didn't answer my question."

"Yes, I did."

"Fine," she said through clenched teeth.

"What do you want with me?" Doyle asked.

"I just told you."

"No, you told me what your boss wanted. What do *you* want?"

Sloane swallowed hard. "What do you mean?"

"You've gone to great lengths to find me. And now you're here, with a gun pointed at my heart. Why not just use it?"

"Because you'll kill my friend if I do."

"Did you hear that, Mason?" Doyle said over his shoulder, though his eyes remained fixed on her. Babyface grunted, and then she saw him lower the gun to his side. "Well?"

Sloane poked Doyle in the chest with the gun. He backed up a step and raised both of his arms in surrender, though she saw no fear in his expression. Instead, his eyes flashed with excitement, clearly enjoying their game.

"You killed my brother."

She realized she'd shocked him when Doyle's mouth dropped open, his arms falling to his sides. He recovered quickly, though, his expression morphing into something sickeningly sweet. "There," he said, his voice as smooth as honey. "That wasn't so difficult, was it?"

But it was. It was so very difficult to stand in front of the man who had caused Beck's death and not put a bullet in his chest. He didn't even bother asking who her brother was because he didn't care.

Sloane glanced at Gig, who sent her a look filled with so much sorrow and understanding that she nearly cracked. She held back a sob, not willing to give Doyle the satisfaction.

"Who was Colleen?" she asked instead.

"My Juliet, of course. Though in this story, I lived. She didn't."

"You killed her?"

"Colleen didn't die by my hand, but I've spent my entire life wishing that bitch was alive so I could kill her all over again."

"What did she do?" It was her third question in a row, but Doyle seemed not to notice.

"It's what she failed to do that sealed her fate. Colleen was always very good at hedging her bets. I suppose her inability to commit wasn't a surprise, considering we were only eighteen years old when we met. I, however, suffered an affliction of a completely different kind."

"You loved her," Sloane said, unable to hide the shock from her voice.

"No, I was *in love* with her. You probably think a man like me, who does what I do, doesn't know the difference between loving someone and being in love, but I do. I know all too well."

His tone was grave now, melancholy, like he was more human than a monster. Sloane knew better. "What happened to her?"

"Karma happened. I might have been in love with Colleen, but she was in love with those," he said, gesturing to the box of emeralds. "So much so that it killed her. Or, perhaps, it was her betrayal that killed her. I prefer to think it was the latter."

"I don't understand."

"You've never wronged someone you love? Of course, you have," he said when she didn't respond. "It could even be the reason you're here right now. Perhaps it's not justice you seek but retribution for your sins?"

Sloane fought to keep her hands steady. "So, all of this is revenge?"

"In a manner of speaking. In those days, we worked together. We were two common criminals, interested only in petty theft and each other, or so I thought. Then, she discovered the emerald she'd been obsessing over for years was en route to Dublin, and she had to have it. She'd read the story, you see."

Sloane inched a centimeter to her right, trying to give herself better access to Babyface and keep an eye on Doyle at the same time. Doyle moved with her, and Sloane bit back a swear.

"Even though there were three, Colleen was convinced that emerald was Agata's," Doyle said. "She wanted it more than anything. Once she had it, I realized she wanted it even more than me. Of course, by then, it was too late for her."

"I thought you said you didn't kill her."

"I didn't. We succeeded in stopping the emerald's transport, but then I got…held up."

Sloane's eyes widened, the truth finally taking shape in her mind. "She left you."

"And I got my revenge," Doyle said. "I freed myself in time to see a guard shoot her, and the exact moment she realized her mistake. When the guard left to get help, I watched the life drain from Colleen's eyes. That was all I needed. All of this," he said, waving a hand, "I do because I can, and she can't."

"You're sick," Sloane spat.

"What I am is alive. Colleen is not. And soon, you won't be, either."

"You seem confident for a man with a gun pointed at his chest."

"Shoot me, and your friend dies. Drop it, and he lives. It's really quite simple."

Simple.

Sloane supposed for Doyle, it was. She knew what would happen to her if she dropped her weapon because she'd known this moment was coming. Everything she'd done since the night she'd fled Doyle's yacht had led her here. Maybe even earlier than that. From the time she'd discovered his location, Sloane had been full-steam ahead. Now Doyle had pulled the emergency brake, and she had no choice but to let go.

She looked at Gig, his emotions flickering over his face like an old movie reel. Frustration, anger, denial, desperation, despair. It would take time, but he would eventually forgive her.

Cade wouldn't.

Her heart squeezed as she thought about their earlier conversation. Cade wouldn't forgive her, but she'd already forgiven him. Sloane wished she could tell him, wished she could apologize, but all she could do was hope he knew how sorry she was.

The tightness in her chest eased as resolve flowed through her and then settled. Was this how Beck had felt right before he jumped in front of a bullet meant for Cade? Had there been any other choice? No, Sloane decided as she slowly lowered her weapon to the ground.

There was no other choice, then or now.

45

Cade stared at Sloane in disbelief as she surrendered. He'd been biding his time, waiting for an opportunity to defuse the situation that wouldn't cause a shootout. His weapon being in his hands would increase the odds of avoiding that, but he would just have to improvise.

Crouching low behind the wall of the exhibit's opposite entrance, he peered around the corner. Both Doyle and his bodyguard had their backs to him. Only Sloane could see him, but she focused on Doyle as she slowly rose from the ground, hands raised. Weapon or no weapon, there was no way he was going to let his beautiful, brave Bullet sacrifice herself.

Not today. Not ever.

Cade stood and walked into the main hall, raising his own arms into the air. Immediately, Doyle's bodyguard swung his weapon in Cade's direction. Mason seemed like a shoot-now-ask-questions-later kind of guy, but, to Cade's surprise, the guard didn't pull the trigger. He didn't even blink.

"Well, now," Doyle said, angling his body toward Cade. "Who do we have here?"

"Nobody," Sloane snapped before Cade could respond. "I've never seen this man before in my life."

"Because he's unarmed, I'm inclined to believe you."

"We both know you're not that stupid, don't we, Jack?" Doyle smiled, but Cade didn't return it. Instead, he looked at Sloane. "Are you okay?"

"Doesn't she look okay?" Doyle responded.

"For now. But I'm here to make sure she stays that way."

"How do you plan to do that?"

"By making a deal. Let them both go, and I'll let you leave with those," Cade said, gesturing to the box that held the emeralds.

"No!" Sloane said, capturing the attention of all three men. For the first time since he'd walked into the room, she met Cade's gaze. "That's not going to happen."

But it was. Nothing would stop him from saving her. He would save her from Jack Doyle, and herself, over and over again for all eternity if it meant he'd never lose her. Barely an hour ago, he'd told himself he would leave when all this was over, but that was a lie. He wasn't going anywhere. Even if she hated him forever for what he'd done, he wasn't leaving her ever again.

You and me, Baby. Always.

Sloane closed her eyes. It was quick, just a blink, but Cade could see she'd heard him even though he hadn't spoken a word.

The panic that had been burning a hole in his chest since he saw the footage of Sloane entering the museum suddenly fled, replaced by cool resolve. He turned his attention back to Doyle. "Do we have a deal?"

"It seems you and your partner suffer the same delusion. Tell me, is it self-preservation or ego that makes you think you can make such demands?"

"It's a question of priorities," Cade said. "Yours and mine. I'm offering you an opportunity. Take it."

"And what will stop me from killing you all when I do?"

"Me." Every head in the room swiveled to the entryway where Celeste Armand stood, arms raised, a revolver with a pearl handle tight in her grip.

Cade glanced immediately at Mason, who pointed his gun at Celeste and then lowered it back to Gig, unsure of his target. The Glock on the ground was still too far away for Cade to reach.

"Celeste," Doyle said, his once smooth tone taking on an edge of impatience. "Now's not the time."

"But it is," Celeste said. "In fact, this is long overdue."

She inched further into the room, her weapon aimed at Doyle's chest. Her rumpled suit and red-rimmed eyes concerned Cade, but it was the determined set of her jaw that really had his attention. He tried to catch Sloane's eye, but she warily watched Celeste as the woman moved to stand a few feet to her left.

"I don't think it would be wise for you to make a scene," Doyle said. "Especially now that we're in mixed company."

Celeste laughed, the sound verging on maniacal. "Do you really think I care what happens to me?"

"What about your precious legacy?"

"What legacy? Your dirty money has tainted this museum for years."

"It was my money that kept it afloat after Max—"

"Don't you dare speak his name," Celeste hissed. "Not after what you did."

"I helped him."

"You *ruined* him. You waited until we were nearly destitute, and then you swooped in and took everything for your own selfish gain, including his life."

Cade bit back a swear as Sloane slowly turned toward Doyle, who didn't even wince at the accusation. "Your husband died from complications resulting from a stroke."

Celeste shook her head. "He died from the stress *you* caused."

"Let's not forget who came to whom. Max asked me for a favor, and I delivered."

"He had no choice!"

"And why was that?" Unfazed by the gun pointed at his chest, Doyle took a step closer to Celeste. "If we're going to tell bedtime stories, let's not make them fairy tales."

"Maxime was a good man," Celeste said.

"A good man that gambled away his business, the museum's proceeds, and his life savings. Should I have turned him down when he asked me to intervene on his behalf? Should I have refused to buy back his assets?"

"He didn't know it was a loan."

"I am a businessman, Celeste, not a philanthropist. Though, in hindsight, I probably should have assumed a man as sick as your husband never could have paid me back."

Celeste's hands shook. "He made a mistake."

"A mistake I rectified, just like I said I would, so that neither your reputation nor the museum would suffer."

Cade let out a breath as the pieces fell into place. Celeste wasn't working with Doyle, but they had made a deal. She had made a deal with the devil to preserve her husband's legacy.

Celeste looked at Sloane. "I didn't know. I swear, I didn't know who he was or what he'd done until later. But by then..."

It was too late. Two more lives destroyed. Two more victims of Jack Doyle's greed.

Cade looked at Sloane, her expression matching the anger that roiled low in his gut. Could he really let Doyle walk away? Yes, Cade admitted. As excruciating as that would be, he would do it if it meant keeping Sloane alive.

"All I did was to ensure the survival of a significant historical landmark. That's hardly a crime."

Celeste turned back to Doyle, and Cade felt it. The calm before the storm, the shift in the air that always accompanied all hell breaking loose.

Celeste's expression transformed from guilt and regret to pure hatred. "What about your other crimes? Who will answer for those?"

"No court would ever hire you as a judge."

"Perhaps not," Celeste said with a small smile. "But justice will still be mine."

It happened fast. One shot, then another. Cade dove toward the gun at Sloane's feet just as she swept it out from under him.

He hit the ground hard as a third shot echoed in the room, a bullet fired from his Glock right into the center of Mason's chest.

Cade barely had time to register that Celeste and Doyle were also down before law enforcement streamed into the space, armed with gear. Sloane was on her knees, gun still aimed at the now fallen bodyguard.

One officer yanked Cade's arm back behind his head as another moved to restrain Sloane. "Don't touch her!"

The officer didn't listen and instead spun her to face Cade as he took her gun and secured her hands behind her back. She didn't resist. In fact, she didn't move at all as the metal cuffs closed around her wrist. "Are you hurt?" Cade asked, scanning her body, his eyes darting over every square inch of her as she stared unblinking at a spot over his head. "Look at me, goddamn it!" Cade tried to get free, growling in frustration as the officer shoved him to his stomach on the ground.

"Stay," he said, and Cade let out a string of curses as the officer planted a knee between his shoulder blades.

"Let them go," said a voice above them.

The pressure on his back disappeared, and Cade sprang to his feet. He glared at the officer, who wisely moved to the other side of the room before addressing the man beside him. "You're late."

JP smirked. "It looks like I'm right on time to clean up your mess."

"It's not mine." Cade spun in a circle, his heart racing when he didn't see Sloane. He scoured the room, letting out a sigh when he saw her on her knees on the floor beside Celeste.

He stepped forward, but JP blocked his path. "She's okay."

"She just shot a man."

"Let her be."

"Go to hell," he growled.

JP sighed. "Tell me what happened."

"I—*oomph*." The breath left Cade's lungs as a body slammed into him, throwing him off balance.

A pair of scraggly arms wrapped around his middle, pinning his own arms to his sides. "Oh man, did you see that? That shit was intense. I freaked out. I mean, I was already freaking out. They kidnapped me! And then Sloane showed up, and Doyle told that tragic love story about his old girlfriend and the emeralds. I almost felt sorry for him, but, I mean, not really because of the whole cold-blooded killer thing."

"Gig," Cade said.

"And then you showed up, and then Celeste, and I was like, what the hell? Did you see that coming? Because I totally didn't see that coming. And then…"

"Gig."

"…she *shot* him! Celeste shot Doyle, and I was thinking I didn't think she had it in her, but she did. I swear I thought I was dead. But then Sloane grabbed the gun from the ground and took out the bodyguard. Just one shot! I didn't know she could do that. Well, I mean, I guess I did, but target practice isn't the same as the real thing. You really have to have some balls to—"

"Marvin!"

Gig cut off his tirade and lifted his head, which was just inches from Cade's chin. "Yeah?"

"If you don't let me go, only one of us is going to be without balls."

Gig blinked and glanced down at their joined bodies. "Right," he said, slowly removing his arms from around Cade's waist. "Sorry."

Cade looked at JP, who stood watching them with one eyebrow raised. "Good enough?"

JP shook his head as his cell phone rang. He reached for it, holding up a finger in a silent gesture for Cade to wait. Cade groaned and glanced over at Sloane, who still sat vigil next to Celeste's body. Chaos was happening around her, and still, she sat, head bent low, covering Celeste's hands where they rested on her stomach. Concern for her flooded him until he could barely breathe.

"Are you really okay?" Gig asked.

Cade tore his gaze away from Sloane. "Yeah. You?"

"Yeah, thanks to Sloane. She saved my life."

"Mine too." He'd wanted to protect her, but it was clear Bullet didn't need saving. Maybe she didn't need him at all.

A hand clamped down on his shoulder, and Cade turned as JP shoved his phone at Cade's chest. "He wants to talk to you."

Cade didn't have to ask who the caller was, just as he knew he couldn't avoid the conversation. He wouldn't get a reprieve until it was done, and Sloane was in no shape to do it. This, at least, was something he could do for her.

So, he relayed the night's events to Albright as he had a hundred times before and tried not to think about all the ways it could have gone wrong. He tried not to think about the way Sloane had looked right through him seconds earlier or how she must feel now, in the aftermath. He would ask her himself. It wasn't until after he hung up that he realized he wouldn't get the chance.

She was gone.

46

When Sloane dragged herself into *Bookends* twenty-four hours later, and Agnes waved her forward, bypassing the usual security protocols, she knew two things. One, she looked worse than she thought, and two, her appearance should probably be the least of her concerns.

She silently followed Agnes to the back of the store, which was a ghost town, even though it was nearly midday. That was deliberate, she knew, but today it was also unnerving, the wide, empty aisles making her feel like a prisoner on death row. She just hoped what she had in her possession was enough to stay her execution.

Agnes didn't bother knocking as she smoothly slid the office door open and stepped inside. "Sebastian? You have a visitor."

Sloane winced at the familiar greeting, but when Albright glanced up from his desk, he didn't look the least bit perturbed. "Sloane," he said, the slight rise of one eyebrow the only sign she'd surprised him. "Come in."

He didn't know she'd left France, she realized, and that he'd let her in the door meant he also didn't know she'd gone after Doyle alone. Her guilty heart squeezed. After everything she'd done, Cade still protected her.

"Can we talk?" she asked.

"Of course."

"I'll just give you two a minute," Agnes said as she backed out of the room.

"Thanks, Aggie."

Aggie?

When she was gone, Albright gestured for her to sit, but Sloane shook her head. It would be better to accomplish what she had to do standing.

He leaned back in his chair. "Are you okay?"

"I'm uninjured."

"That wasn't what I meant."

Sloane tried not to fidget under Albright's scrutiny. "Yes, I'm okay."

"It's expected that agents debrief post-mission at the closest in-country agency."

"I know."

"But you're not in Paris."

"No."

"Why not?"

Sloane glanced at her feet, her chest tightening again when she thought of the mess she'd left for Cade. He wouldn't be happy, but he'd handle it, and this was more important. "I wanted to apologize."

"Oh?" Albright said. "For what?"

"For my part in what happened at the charity benefit a couple of weeks ago. I never should have put the team in that position."

"They were there to protect you."

Sloane bowed her head. "I know, and I'm sorry. Things changed after that, though. With Cade, I mean."

"I see."

Albright said nothing more, and Sloane was grateful he didn't ask her to elaborate. How could she explain when she was still processing it all herself?

"I also wanted to deliver this in person." She retrieved a flash drive from the back pocket of her jeans and dropped it on the desk between them.

"What's that?"

"Research."

"Yours?"

Sloane shook her head. "Celeste gave it to me before she… died," she said, the word scraping up the back of her throat. "It's a list of all Jack Doyle's contacts, business partners, and clients from the last decade."

"Have you confirmed its contents?"

"No," she said honestly. She didn't have a computer with her on the plane, and even if she did, Sloane wouldn't have had to verify anything because she believed Celeste. Despite her pain, she had spent the last few moments of her life telling Sloane what she'd done as she shoved the drive into her shaking hands.

Promise me, Celeste had said. *Promise me you'll use it.*

It was the easiest promise Sloane had ever made.

"You were fond of her," Albright said.

"Yes."

"And you blame yourself for her death."

Sloane tried to swallow past the lump in her throat. Of course, he knew. She didn't know how, but he'd just uttered aloud the truth that had plagued her since she left the museum. "It was my fault."

"From what Cade told me, Celeste and Doyle had history."

"Yes, but if I had done a better job of convincing Doyle that I was Elena, he wouldn't have seen through me. He wouldn't have kidnapped Gig, and Celeste would never have been caught in the crossfire."

"Do you really believe that?"

"Don't you?"

Albright stood and rounded the desk, taking a seat instead in the chair next to her. "Did I ever tell you about the day I met Cade?"

Sloane blinked at the change of subject. "No."

Albright gestured to the chair next to him, and this time, she sat down. "We met on the train while he was on his way back from the city, and I was on my way to Boston to visit my sister."

"You have a sister?" Sloane asked, surprised. Albright had never shared anything personal with her before.

"Two sisters, actually. Twins. Younger than me and both pains in my ass since the day they were born." Sloane thought of Beck saying the same about her on multiple occasions and smiled. "Anyway, I was standing in one of the train cars reading the paper when a man walked by and lifted a wallet from a woman's open purse while her nose was in a book."

"Really?"

Albright nodded. "I thought I was the only one who saw it, but I wasn't. When the train pulled into the next station, Cade moved down the aisle to stand next to the thief. I thought he was going to get off the train too, but when the doors opened, the thief stepped out onto the platform alone." Albright laughed and shook his head. "I still remember the look on his face when he patted his pocket and realized what happened."

"Cade stole the wallet back?"

"He did. When the doors closed again, he returned the woman's wallet, and I gave him a job."

"Just like that?"

Albright scoffed. "Hardly. It took him weeks to accept my offer."

"But you knew he would come around."

"Eventually, yes."

"How?"

"Cade could have kept the wallet. Hell, he probably could have used the money, but he did the right thing. Even then, he understood the value of what we're fighting for, and that's something you can't teach. I saw the same thing in you when we met."

Sloane shook her head. "I was a mess when we met."

"Maybe, but you were also determined. And if I thought for one second all you wanted was vengeance, I never would have hired you."

Sloane knew what he meant. She'd wanted more than anything for Doyle to pay for what he'd done, but it was justice, not vengeance, that had kept her going these last long months. "I guess, I just thought…I mean, I thought I'd feel…"

"Relieved?"

Sloane nodded, and Albright sighed. "The thing about this work is that it's not just a job. You walk with it all day, take it to dinner, and fall asleep next to it every night. It's the shadow over your shoulder when you brush your teeth in the morning and the voice in your head that just won't quit." He leaned over and placed his hand atop hers on the arm of the chair. "You can't run or hide from it because it's who you are. The only reassurance any of us can hope to have comes with acceptance. If you can make peace with the past, accept what is and who you are, you can move forward."

Could she do that? Was she capable of letting go of what was for the sake of what could be?

Sloane sighed. "Now I know why Beck called you Obi." Albright's blank stare forced a garbled laugh from her throat. "Like, Obi-Wan Kenobi? The—"

"Yes, yes. I'm aware."

"Did you just roll your eyes?"

"No," Albright said, sounding affronted.

"You did!"

He grunted and stood abruptly. "Now you sound like my wife."

"Your…" Sloane trailed off, her mouth dropping open as she glanced at the closed office door.

When she looked at Albright again, his expression was serious once more. "Beckett was an excellent agent, but he was an even better man. I am honored to have known him."

Sloane smiled through the ache in her chest. "He would have said the same about you."

"Do you still want to know what I believe?" he asked.

She merely nodded, no longer trusting herself to speak.

"I believe that your actions on this mission saved the lives of two of your partners. If you're going to tell yourself a story, that's the one to tell."

Maybe, Sloane thought as she left Albright's office, it was time to rewrite hers.

47

Hey Brother,

If you're reading this, it means I kicked the bucket. And before you yell at me for using a euphemism at a time like this, remember, I'm dead. It's bad to talk ill of the dead.

How'd I go? Dude, if I died from something stupid like jaywalking or choking on a chicken bone, please do me a favor and lie to Mom and Sloane. After all these years working for Uncle Sam, I think I deserve that much.

I know we said we'd write these letters years ago. Because Albright is Albright and ironically can't lie to save his life, he's probably already told you this letter is overdue. Even if you're reading this 50 years from now, he probably left you a letter of his own, explaining it took me seven years to write one.

I couldn't write this then because I wasn't ready. I'm still not ready. Who's ever ready to write "upon my death" letters to the most important people in his life? But call it intuition or voodoo or some other ghost-story-campfire shit, but I feel like something big is coming. Whether or not I'm here to see it, I need to get some things off my chest.

You are and always will be my brother. I knew it the day I shared my lunch with you under the bleachers when we were nine, and I know it today. And because we're brothers, I know that regardless of the circumstances of my death, you're going to blame yourself. Don't do it because it wasn't your fault. I know because I was there, and it was my choice. I can only hope I died showing up for you the way you've always shown up for me.

We've been through a lot. We've seen more than anyone should, and we still keep going. I know it's because we're doing the right thing. At least, that's what I tell myself. But doing the right thing doesn't always feel *right, you know? Sometimes it just makes you tired. Do you ever feel that way?*

Sloane's tired. I know because she told me. Well, she yelled it at me, anyway. And now we're on our way to Miami for another job, and I can't get her words out of my head. I worry about her. Well, I worry about Mom, too, but mostly Sloane.

I know you do, too, because I know how you feel about her. You never told me, but you didn't have to. You're my best friend in the world, and she's my sister. Nobody knows either of you better than me.

Everything she does will be a knockdown, drag-out war, but that's our Sloane. She's a fighter. It's when she doesn't fight that you have to worry. I would tell you not to give up, but you were always better than me at waiting her out. She'll need you when I'm gone. It has to be you. It can only *be you. Be her safe place, and she'll come around. She always does for someone she loves.*

I know right now you're probably wondering how I got to be so wise, but I don't have to try. It's a gift, and so is your life.

Don't waste it.

And don't live with regrets because I don't. I regret nothing.

Also, try not to think about my sorry ass every time something happens. You won't need to anyway because I'll be watching. I'll haunt you forever, you lucky fuck.

Love you, man,
Beck

***

Tap, tap, tap.

Cade jumped and looked up from the letter in his hand to the man standing just outside his Mustang. He waved hesitantly, and Cade lowered the driver's side window.

"Fisher," Cade said in greeting because it still seemed wrong to call the former principal by his first name. And, since he wasn't Cade's principal anymore, that only left one option.

As if he knew what Cade was thinking, Fisher smirked. "Cade."

"Is everything alright?"

"Oh, sure," Fisher said, rocking back on his heels. "Faye and I were just wondering how long you were planning to stay out here."

He glanced over the roof of the car, and Cade followed his gaze through the passenger side window to find the front door of the Easton house wide open. Faye stood in the doorway, back straight and arms crossed over her chest. Even from the car, he could see her pursed lips and forehead creased with concern.

He whirled back to Fisher. "Shit, I'm sorry." He hadn't been thinking. "Sloane is fine. She's okay. She jus—"

Fisher held up a hand. "We know. She was here earlier."

"You saw her?" Fisher nodded, and Cade let out a breath. "Good." At least it would be easy to find her before he killed her. "That's good."

"She looks like that because she's worried you're going to leave. Are you?"

Cade looked back at the house. Faye was on the front porch now, her fingers wrapped around one pillar as she watched them. The hope in her eyes pierced Cade's heart, and he slowly shook his head.

Fisher opened the car door. "It's time, son."

It was past time, but as Cade got out of the car and trailed Fisher to the house, he hoped it wasn't too late. When they reached the porch, Fisher climbed the stairs ahead of him, stopping to place a kiss on his wife's cheek before slipping inside. Cade had taken Beck's letter with him, the letter he'd found in a pile of mail at the post office box he kept in town, a box he hadn't checked in over a year.

But Faye didn't even glance at the letter he held. She did nothing at all but stare back at him, the brown eyes that reminded him so much of Sloane's flooding with unshed tears.

"Hi," he said.

Hi? He'd missed the funeral of Faye's only son and the man who had saved his life. Then he'd completely cut off all communication with her, and now he was making the woman who had been more of a mother to him than his own cry.

Before he could say anything else, though, two powerful arms wrapped around his middle so tight he feared for his organs. The hug was stronger than he'd expected, and he told her so, only to be put in his place by a muffled voice against his chest.

"Don't you dare ruin this for me, Cade Foster, or it will be years before you so much as lay eyes on another one of my baked goods."

Because Cade was an asshole, but not a *stupid* asshole, he shut his mouth and let the hug happen, embracing the feeling that rose to the surface above all others.

Home.

48

Dear Sloane,

I'm sorry.

Mom always used to say that no matter what we did, we could always fix it as long as we apologized. Even though you're reading this because I'm dead and I can't fix that, I know you'll forgive me. I know this because I'm irresistible, and you've never been able to stay mad at me for long.

How can I make jokes at a time like this? Because, even in death, I'm still me and you're still you and we're still us. Me being buried six feet under doesn't change that. Nothing will ever change that.

And so, I'll say it again. I'm sorry. I know I let you down. You expected me to come home and be the brother you knew, and I couldn't do that. I know this life has been tough on you and Mom, and I never wanted to cause either of you any pain, but I know this will. I can only hope that one day you will understand what this work means to me and why I do it. It means a hell of a lot. That's why I won't quit, why I can't, even if you ask me to.

But that doesn't mean I love you any less. It means I trust you to be the brave, intelligent, and resourceful woman I know and push through. Hell, there are days I think you'd be better at doing what I do than me, which is something I'm only comfortable admitting on this page. That probably makes me a coward, but at least I won't be around to see you beat me on an obstacle course.

You could probably beat Cade, too, but I wouldn't mention that if I were you. You know how competitive he is, and it would only end in a fight. If you do, and it does, forgive him. He needs to know that you'll forgive him for anything and that you won't leave when things get rough. Forgive him even when he pisses you off or does something stupid in the name of protecting you because he will. Cade always protects his family, even if he's scared to death of failing us. You and I both know that's impossible, but he won't know it. Not until you show him.

So, make it right. Forgive him the way you've always forgiven me and the way I hope you will forgive yourself. Because I already have.

I'm running out of time. Our ride is here, and we have to go. Is it bad that I wish we weren't going? Today, just this once, I want to pretend the bad guys don't exist.

Never doubt yourself or let someone else make you feel small. Love hard, and never, ever pass on a moment to stand in the sunshine. Life's too short to live in the dark.

Give 'em hell, Sis, and know that wherever I am—heaven, hell, or reincarnated as Mrs. Levinson's cat—I'm proud of you, and I love you. Then, now, and always.

Love,

Beck

***

Sloane crinkled the letter in her grip, squinting at the words until they blurred. She wanted to begin again. She wanted to go back, start over, and be a better sister when Beck needed her most.

But she couldn't. Beck was gone, and she was here, and he was right. She couldn't fix it. At least, not the way she wanted to.

She looked up and out across the sand and to the lake beyond. Summer had already come and gone in their hometown, and the beach was empty. School had started last week, and kids had traded in their swimsuits for sports uniforms, their parents likely already tired from the change in routine.

That had almost been her life. If things were different, she'd probably be in her classroom right now, clearing her desk before heading to the gym or out to dinner with her mom and Stan, or maybe Dan.

She closed her eyes, trying to picture it, but all she saw was the way the lake looked the last time she, Beck, and Cade had all been camping together. She saw the three of them roasting marshmallows in the twilight, laughing and dreaming together.

The way it was supposed to be.

Guilt, anger, and helplessness rose inside her like a swarm of killer bees ready to attack. She opened her mouth and unleashed them, their stings causing an inexorable wildfire to spread through her chest.

She screamed for Celeste and Gig and Sophie, for every person Jack Doyle had ever hurt or killed, and for the man *she'd* killed. She thought of her mother, who had lost a husband and a son, and of Stan, who had stood by them for years. Mostly, she screamed for Beck, who had forgiven her even though she didn't deserve it.

She didn't stop, not until her voice was hoarse and there was no air left in her lungs. Not until familiar arms wrapped around her waist and tugged her into a hard chest.

"Shhh," Cade soothed. "It's okay. You're okay." Sloane sagged against him, letting her head loll back against his chest as he swayed them from side to side. "It's over," he whispered into her hair.

But it wasn't really over. Not yet.

"I'm sorry, Bullet. If I could go back and change it all, I would."

"How?" Sloane said, breaking free of his hold. She spun to face him as the flames in her chest reignited. "By sacrificing yourself instead?"

"Yes."

Sloane laughed, wincing slightly at the soreness in her throat. "You're such an idiot."

"Excuse me?"

"How would that make anything better?"

"You wouldn't have lost your brother, and Faye wouldn't have lost a son."

"But we all would have lost *you*." Cade stared at her blankly, and Sloane shook her head. After all this time, how was it possible that he still didn't get it? But hadn't Beck said as much in his letter? If she wanted Cade to understand, she'd just have to make him. "It wasn't your fault."

"What?"

"I know what I said in France, but it wasn't true. You didn't kill Beck," Sloane said, lifting her chin. "I did."

Cade's brow furrowed. "That's ridiculous. You weren't even there."

"I didn't have to be."

"What do you mean?"

"Did you ever ask yourself why Beck was so distracted that night?"

"Of course," Cade said. "You don't think I've replayed that night in my mind every day since it happened?"

"I have, too. Every hour since you told me."

"And you've somehow convinced yourself that it's your fault?"

"Because it is!" Sloane shoved a hand through her hair. God, this was difficult. It was harder than she thought it would be.

She turned her back to Cade and stared out over the empty stretch of beach, the only thing in her life that had ever really stayed the same. She wanted to disappear, just curl up into a ball in the sand and let it bury her. But she didn't want to hide anymore. She wanted to fight, even if it meant she would lose.

"Explain," he said.

Sloane let out a breath. "I talked to Beck the day he died."

"You…did?"

"I didn't put it together until you told me what happened at the villa."

Cade said nothing, but she could still feel his silent urging for her to continue.

"I called him that day because I missed him and wanted to hear his voice. You'd disappeared on me, and neither of you had called or emailed in more than a month. I couldn't take it anymore. I didn't really expect him to answer, but he did."

Sloane closed her eyes, finally letting herself remember. "I was glad at first, you know? I thought we'd talk about mundane things like teaching, Mom and Stan, maybe the weather. He always asked me questions when I called because I couldn't ask him anything. But that day, he just sounded so…tired. It worried me, and I lost it."

"What did you say?" Cade asked, his voice quiet but encouraging.

Sloane opened her eyes again and looked down at her feet. "I accused him of abandoning us. I said, if he really cared about me or Mom, he would quit and come home. When he said he *did* care, I called him a liar and brought up every important event he'd missed in the years he'd been gone, including my graduation. I blamed him for everything, even my pissy mood, and do you know what he did?"

"What?"

"Nothing." She turned to face him, and the tears that had been absent during her screaming episode streamed down her cheeks. "I went on and on, and he just stayed on the line and let me attack him without once defending himself. And when I was done, he said he was sorry. He *apologized*. For all of it. Even the things he couldn't control. And do you know what I did?"

"What?" Cade repeated, taking a step toward her.

"I hung up on him. I told him to stuff his apology, and I hung up the phone."

Cade sighed. "Bullet."

She shook her head wildly and swiped at her cheeks. "That's why he was so distracted that night. It was such a stupid, silly fight, and it killed him." Her knees buckled under the weight of her confession, and she stumbled. "I killed my brother."

Cade caught her and pulled her into him. She stared at his chest, afraid of what she'd see if she looked him in the eye. But when Cade lifted her chin with his finger, it wasn't pity she saw in his gaze, but sympathy. Sympathy, understanding, and the same heart-wrenching agony that mirrored her own.

"It wasn't your fault," he said.

"It feels like it is."

"I know."

"You can blame me like I did you. I deserve it."

"Is that what he said?" Cade asked, nodding at the folded piece of paper she'd dropped on the beach. "That you deserve it?"

Sloane shook her head. "I couldn't read it before today, but even if I had, I'm not sure it would have changed anything."

She didn't realize it was the truth until she said it. Even if she'd opened the letter when she received it two weeks after his death and knew he'd forgiven her, she doubted she would have been ready to forgive herself.

"I'm sorry for lying to you," Cade said. "I should have told you what happened, but I—"

She dropped a finger to his lips. "I forgive you. It wasn't your fault, either."

"It feels like it is," he said, repeating her words.

"That's because it still hurts."

"It does. So much."

Sloane swallowed the lump in her throat and nodded. "It's been a year." One year ago today, and the pain was still so raw. Would it ever get better?

"I know."

"He loved you, Cade. He would have died over and over again if it meant saving you."

"I would have done the same for him. Any time. Any day."

She smiled. "I know, and so did he."

"And I would do anything for you, too." Cade's hands moved up her body until he cupped her face with both hands. "Tell me you know that."

"I do."

He dropped his forehead to hers. "You scared me."

Guilt flooded her, and she grasped his wrists. "I'm sorry for walking out on you at the villa, for the things I said and going after Doyle alone. I thought you hated me, and I didn't want to hurt you any more than I already had. And then you came to the museum, and I—"

"I will always come for you," he said, lifting his head to meet her gaze. "*Always*. And it's not because of some job or because you're Beck's sister. It's because I can't breathe without you. I didn't breathe from the night I left you sleeping in Beck's bed until the day I won our wrestling match in the villa's backyard."

Sloane half-laughed, half-sobbed. "You wish."

"I love you, Sloane Bullet Easton. I've loved you my whole damn life. Who knows what tomorrow will bring or where we go from here, but I know that will never change."

Her heart, which had felt hollow for so long, was suddenly so full it overflowed. She didn't know how to stop the flood and wouldn't have, even if she could. Yes, it would get better, she realized. They would make it better.

This was life. This was living in the sunshine. And she was going to enjoy every minute.

"Did Beck tell you to say that?" she asked.

Cade looked at her with confusion as she unclasped his wrist and slid a hand into the breast pocket of his jacket. Her fingers closed around the slip of paper she'd seen there earlier, and she pulled it out and held it up between them.

He smiled. "No."

"What did he say, then?"

She tried to open the folded note, but Cade plucked it from her hands. "He said you love me."

Sloane lifted an eyebrow. "Oh, really?"

"Yup."

"And what do *you* think?"

"I think you better say it quick, or else I'm going to tell Faye you're the reason we're late for Sunday dinner."

Relief swept through her at his mention of Faye, so glad he'd finally come home. "If you do, I'll tell her the total cost of all the bills she racked up, letting you fix the van for years."

"No, you won't."

"What makes you so sure?"

Cade grinned. "Because you love me."

She leaned into him, her lips hovering just above his as she whispered, "I do love you."

"Just remember who said it first."

Sloane groaned. "Shut up and kiss me."

And then Cade proved he was, in fact, capable of taking orders from her, after all.

Epilogue

15 Months Later

The man had been told to dress discreetly, but his jeans and coat fit him about as well as Bruce Banner's did right before someone pissed him off. The snow on the ground reflected off his mirrored shades, and Cade gestured for him to remove them. He needed to see the man's eyes to make sure he knew why he was there, and to make sure it was his choice to be.

If Banner Junior's automatic adherence to Cade's unspoken order didn't give him away, then his military haircut would have. He wasn't Air Force. Maybe Marines? No, Cade thought as he observed the determined set of the visitor's jaw and his steely gaze. If Junior went batshit right now and lost his shirt, it wouldn't be *Semper Fi* tattooed on his chest. It would be a green, four-legged creature that never ventured far from the water.

Cade grinned. "Password?"

He barely had a moment to enjoy the mix of confusion and annoyance on Junior's face before two hands shoved him back into the heavy door. "Ignore him," Sloane said, appearing in the doorway. "He woke up on the wrong side of the bed this morning." If that was true, it was only because she was gone when he opened his eyes, something Cade kept to himself when Bullet sent him a look that could melt balls. "I'm Sloane, and this is Cade. Are you Ryan?" Junior nodded. "We were expecting you. Come in and meet the rest of the team. We'll start in a few."

Junior nodded again and stepped inside, eyeing Cade as he crossed the threshold. He smirked and sauntered away, taking his sweet time as he headed down the hall to the gym. The arrogant asshole didn't know he was about to be schooled.

Cade closed the door and was about to start after Ryan when Sloane's hand closed around his wrist. "You need to stop torturing the new recruits," she chided. "If you keep pushing them, JP is going to—"

"Give me an award for being so good at my job? I know. Don't worry, though, I won't take all the credit."

Sloane rolled her eyes. "You're lucky he likes you."

"*He's* lucky we volunteered to do this. Have you seen that crew in there?" Cade said. "It'll be a miracle if they make it past the first week."

"You mean the three ex-Seals, two guys from Special Forces, and the former FBI agent?"

"You're right," Cade said, considering her question. "The agent won't last a day."

"Well, it's our job to make sure they do," Sloane said, moving into him. "Play nice."

Cade gripped her hips and tugged her closer. "Oh, I can be very nice." She laughed and squirmed in his arms but didn't pull away. He still got a little thrill every time she didn't.

"We have to work," she said.

Cade spun them so that her back was to the door instead of his and kissed his way up her neck. "I am working."

"No, you're distracting me."

"I'm conditioning you."

"Oh, really?" Sloane said.

"Mmmhmm."

"And what condition will you leave me in?"

Cade looked up from his ministrations and caught the wicked gleam in her eye. "The kind that will leave you wanting more."

Sloane bit her lip, her golden eyes clouding with lust.

He bent low, more than ready to taste her, but stopped at the sound of a throat clearing behind him. "Go away," Cade said, staring hard at Sloane's lips.

"We've got five new recruits waiting," Gig said.

"Six," Sloane said. "Ryan just got here."

"Right." There was a pause and then the unmistakable sound of clicking keys. "Jean-Paul just called and said he needs evaluations by next week and a fully functional team by the end of the month."

"No," Cade growled, reluctantly releasing Sloane. He whirled and glared at Gig. "That's not enough time."

Gig sighed. "Crime waits for no man. He's giving you the pick of the litter and said it's your choice. You can veto anyone who doesn't cut it."

"I can do that, anyway."

In fact, it was the one and only stipulation of their agreement. Not that he'd needed it to accept the job. After everything went down with Doyle, both he and Sloane knew it was time for a change. Cade thought she'd want to get out altogether, but, as usual, Bullet surprised him. Soon after their mission in France, the agency promoted JP to handler, and Sloane pitched her idea for an offsite training facility for new recruits. JP approved the idea, and here they were. Turned out Sloane was meant to be a teacher after all.

Cade would be lying if he said that making the switch from the field to in-house work wasn't a change, but it wasn't up for debate. He would be wherever Sloane was.

Today, tomorrow, forever.

"JP thought you'd say that, which is why he reminded me that you both promised to spend the holidays with them."

"Of course, we'll be there! I'm not passing up an opportunity to see my goddaughter. And don't look at me like that," Sloane said when he made a face. "You know Mia has you wrapped around her little finger."

Cade pretended to be annoyed, unwilling to admit that the pint-sized, dark-haired princess turned him into the Pillsbury Dough Boy just like JP would never admit that he'd taken the promotion to keep his family safe.

"And?" Cade asked expectantly.

Gig sighed. "And five minutes later, Bianca called to ask if we'd ever considered opening a training facility in Paris."

Cade smiled and held out his hand. Sloane groaned and reached into her pocket, retrieving a five-dollar bill, and slapped into his palm. She mumbled something under her breath.

"I heard that," he said, wiggling his fingers. She added another two dollars to their imaginary swear jar, and he stuffed the loot into his back pocket. "Don't feel too bad. I doubt JP will let her go back to work, even if she wants to."

Sloane sent him a sly smile. "Care to make a wager on that?"

"No," Gig said, shaking his head. "No more bets."

"Why not?" She said.

"Because the last one you made resulted in me acting as a recruit's personal punching bag."

"Your country thanks you for your sacrifice," Cade said.

"Well, at least someone does."

Cade glanced at Sloane. "Why did we hire him again?"

Gig snapped his laptop shut and tucked it under his arm. "Because I get shit done. And because nobody else can deal with you when you're on your period."

Before Cade could say anything, Sloane sidled past him to stand in front of Gig. "Any other updates?"

"Yes. The utilities are all paid up for the month, and the new equipment arrives on Monday. The enhanced security system will be ready on Tuesday. I'll check the software for bugs as soon as it's installed."

Gig sent Cade a knowing look, and he knew Gig would check that software one hundred times if it meant avoiding a repeat performance of last year's kidnapping. Dealing with the aftermath hadn't been easy on him, but he'd come through it better than Cade expected. He also committed to ensuring the safety of the recruits and their operation, which had earned Cade's respect, even if he was still annoying as hell.

"Good," Sloane said. "Thank you. You can go."

"Go?" He glanced at his watch. "It's not even 5:00."

"Jessica will kill me if you're late for your anniversary dinner."

Gig slapped a hand to his forehead. "I totally forgot."

"If I were you, I'd leave that part out when you see her," Cade said.

He said it, even though it was likely Jessica Giggler would forgive her husband for anything. Gig's proposal and quick marriage to his girlfriend just four months after they returned from France hadn't surprised Cade. He understood the impact of a near-death experience better than anyone, as he did the desire to keep the people you loved close. Gig and Jessica had left D.C. and settled in Lakehaven, joining them as both contractors and guests at Faye's dinner table.

"Right," Gig said. "Also, this came in today's mail."

He pulled a postcard from his back pocket and handed it to Cade. On the front was a photograph of two lounge chairs on a beach, a rainbow-colored umbrella, and *Cabo San Lucas* printed in red in the clouds above the water. There was no message on the back of the card when Cade flipped it over, just a return address belonging to the store where it was purchased. It didn't matter. He knew who it was from.

"Albright?" Sloane said, peering over his shoulder.

Cade nodded. "I guess he and Agnes are enjoying their retirement."

"Weird," all three of them said in unison.

"Alright, guys, I'm out," Gig said over his shoulder as he made his way to the side entrance that led to the parking lot. "See you tomorrow."

When he was gone, Sloane stepped in front of Cade and wrapped her arms around his middle. "Ten bucks says he won't make it to work tomorrow."

Cade pulled her into him. "I only have seven on me, but you're welcome to it."

"Afraid you'll lose?"

"That's impossible."

"Why?" A smile played at the corner of her gorgeous mouth as she reached into his back pocket, feeling around for the cash she'd given him earlier. Instead of money, she pulled out something else and held it between them.

"Because I've already won," he said, taking the emerald-cut diamond on a platinum band and slipping it on her ring finger.

She looked down at her hand and then back up at him with wide, teary eyes and a smile that pierced his heart. There was no pain, though. This time, and with this woman, Cade Foster was bulletproof.

"You sound pretty sure of yourself," she said, playing with him. She slipped her arms around his neck, and he chuckled when she glimpsed the ring on her hand over his shoulder.

"Is there a reason I shouldn't be?"

"No. I'll marry you."

"Thank you," Cade said, amused.

"On one condition."

"Are you turning my proposal into a negotiation, Bullet?"

"That depends."

"On what?"

"On whether you have the balls to negotiate."

Cade smirked. "I think you know the answer to that. And, if you don't," he said, pulling her against his hard length, "I'd be happy to show you."

Her cheeks tinged pink, making him think about all the other parts of her body that he wanted to make flush that exact color. "Do you want to hear my condition or not?"

"Alright," he said, playing along. "What's your condition?"

She looked at him, her serious expression fading into one of pure delight. "That I be the only one allowed to give our children nicknames."

And Cade agreed because he wouldn't have it any other way.

ACKNOWLEDGMENTS

It is with heartfelt gratitude that I thank my champions on this journey.

To my early readers, and forever cheerleaders Ashley, Faith, Veronica, Ris, Eileen, Jade, and Lil – whose support, encouragement, and willingness to celebrate all the things, no matter how small, continues to fill my cup. Thank you.

To Bette – my friend, there is nobody I would rather share coffee and talk writing with than you. If I'm any kind of writer, it's because you showed me the way.

Special thanks to the skilled, talented people I work with everyday who have made my professional life so full and who serve me daily with inspiration of a different kind.

To all those that have supported me in other ways – the fine authors and writers of CTRWA, Jim Alkon, and Beth Werner for the recommendations that started me down this path, and my critique group of determined women who will no doubt be writing their own acknowledgements very soon. I appreciate you.

To Cathy Teets and the Headline Books team – thank you for your work in publishing this novel and for taking a chance on me.

I'm blessed to be a part of an amazing extended family of strong women and men who love and support me every day. To Joe and Mimi, Josephine, Frankie, Barbara, Rosemarie, Frank, Karin, and Joe. Thank you for supporting my crazy, pie-in-the-sky dreams. This success is a result of your constant and unwavering faith in me.

Joey – thank you for being my partner-in-crime as kids and letting me take all the credit for being the storyteller in the family, even though we both know your imagination is far better than mine.

Dad – thank you for always, always being there. And for calling me after you finished Chapter Three to tell me which character you wanted to play in the movie. I love you.

Stephen – thank you for watching every new spy thriller I add to our Netflix list without complaint. You are my real-life adventure.

Every morning when I sit down to write, there's one voice that rings louder than the cacophony of character voices in my head. Mom – thank you for your constant and unconditional love, and all the ways you encourage me to be the best, most courageous version of myself. This novel is as much yours as it is mine. I'm forever grateful to be your daughter.

To all those not named here who have read a paragraph, a page, or a chapter of anything I've ever written – I'm thankful, humbled, and beholden to you.